DADDY IN DISGUISE

CRESCENT COVE BOOK 7

TARYN QUINN

Books are not transferable.

They cannot be sold, shared or given away as it is an infringement on the copyright of this work.

This book is a work of fiction. The names, characters, places, and incidents are products of the writer's imagination or have been used fictitiously and are not to be construed as real. Any resemblance to persons, living or dead, actual events, locales or organizations is entirely coincidental.

ISBN: 978-1-940346-61-8
Daddy in Disguise
© 2019 Taryn Quinn
Photograph by Lindee Robinson Photography
Models: Sam Parker & Shannon Lorraine

Cover by LateNite Designs

All Rights Are Reserved.
No part of this book may be used or reproduced in any manner whatsoever without written permission, except in the case of brief quotations embodied in critical articles and reviews.

First print edition: January 2020

DEAR READER...

While most of our books are completely standalone, there's always going to be a little bit of teasing and mystery for future books set in Crescent Cove. We promise we didn't forget about answering ALL the questions about side characters in a book. Sometimes those answers won't come for a book or two...sometimes three!

Oh, and we make up fictional places that end up having the same names as actual places. These are our fictional interpretations only. Please grant us leeway if our creative vision isn't true to reality.

For the dads who step up.
And the women who love another woman's child unconditionally.

ONE

Sometimes the universe just did not see fit to provide what you wanted. In this case, I wanted to be alone.

"Are you sure you don't want me to stay and help clean up?"

"Go." If I had to watch my frighteningly pregnant friend—and original employee—teeter around the café any more tonight, I was going to have a damn nervous breakdown. "Moose has texted me no less than three times looking for you."

Veronica Masterson, café baker extraordinaire and wife of Murphy aka Moose, sighed. "He's always worried."

"Considering you barely fit behind the wheel of your huge-ass SUV, it's not shocking." Because, of course, Vee had to overachieve in all ways, including babies. One wasn't enough. Which, hey, I got it. Baby fever was at an all-time high in Crescent Cove. But man, twins right after having a baby?

Yeah. No thank you very much times a billion.

"Give Bray a big smacking kiss for me." Okay, yes, I was soft on her little boy. I couldn't help it. Every time he saw me, he suction-cupped himself to me like an octopus. And he was just as leggy as one, thanks to his huge dad.

"I will. Murphy said he was conning him into another bedtime read."

"*Llama, Llama*?"

"Is there any other book these days?"

I hid a smile. I rather liked that one myself—enough to give it to most of the kids in the ever-expanding baby-crazy group of women who kept taking over my café, Brewed Awakening.

I steered her toward the door. "It was a light evening. Cleanup will be a snap."

"But Clara already left. She had that test—"

"Vee, I'm a big girl. I've been closing this place for well over two years now." And as sweet as my server was, I was a helluva lot faster than Clara anyway.

"Almost three, actually."

My heart did a little twist in my chest. "Yes, three." I wasn't exactly sure where the whole of the summer went, but my anniversary was coming up again. Which just happened to coincide with Halloween, my favorite time of year.

"I don't want to leave you here alone."

"What exactly is going to happen in the Cove?"

"You don't know. Serial killers love to use small towns because it's least expected."

I sighed as I nudged her toward the door. "You gotta stop listening to those podcasts."

Vee gave me some side-eye. "You love horror movies, and yet you won't look at the realistic parts of the world."

"I don't need to. Shit is hard enough. Besides, I like the pretend kind of murder and mayhem where I know the killer is going to get his comeuppance." That wasn't exactly true. At least in the good kinds of horror movies, the bad guy had to come back at the end.

However, my favorite worrywart had to be on her way. And thankfully, she wasn't into watching scary flicks, so she was none the wiser.

"Is Gideon next door at least?" Vee hung her cross-body purse over her head and swung it around to the back since, surprise, it didn't fit in the front.

I jumped back a step before I got smacked with some sort of the baby paraphernalia that was forever spilling out of that thing. "I'm not sure. I'm not his keeper."

Okay, so that sounded a little bitchy. I was definitely *not* his keeper. Even if I kept sneaking over there to see what was what. However, it wasn't because of the man.

Not exactly.

Nope, it was because he and his crew were working on my newest acquisition, The Haunt. A restaurant that combined my two favorite things, food and horror movie memorabilia. I'd managed to procure a good mix of employees from the café who wanted to do something different as well as bring in some fresh blood—pun intended.

Not only did I have an anniversary deal to figure out for Brewed Awakening, this year, I was adding another whole business to that annual event. And my nerves were at an all-time high. At this point, I didn't even know if the restaurant was going to be ready.

Mostly because my favorite carpenter-slash-contractor wouldn't give me a straight answer about what was going on next door. In fact, he kept barring me from going over there. Oh, he gave me really good explanations as to why I couldn't. Insurance and safety and blah, blah, blah.

But I was going crazy. I needed to freaking know how far off schedule he was. Surely, he wouldn't keep putting me off unless that was the case. Guys needed that ego stroke. He'd want to show it off.

Then again, Gideon never quite reacted how I expected. I knew from experience his work was beyond compare. He'd remodeled the café exactly how I wanted it with a few detours I hadn't known I needed. I trusted him. At least when it came to the things in his tool belt.

Under the belt? Well, that was debatable.

I mean, how many times had we almost kissed in two years? A damn fuckton, that was how many. And he never sealed the deal. So, either he wasn't that into me or…

I didn't have the mental bandwidth to figure out the or.

Vee turned around just as I towed her through the door. "I'll just sit down in the corner. I won't make a sound."

"Creampuff, you don't know the definition of not making a sound."

She huffed out a breath, blowing a blond curl out of her softly rounded face. "Text me when you're done."

"I never leave, remember? My apartment is literally upstairs. I'll be fine. I'll even lock the door right after you."

Her huge blue eyes were about three minutes from full-blown tears. Preggo hormones must be wreaking havoc today. I so could not deal with that. I pushed the door open and unclipped her keys from the bag of death. "Take these," I handed them to her, "and go home to your husband."

"But—"

"Goodnight. Go cuddle your men." I closed the door and dug out my own keys and jangled them in the window. "Go."

She finally turned toward her car. Her dejected eyes almost made me waver. Almost. Finally, she waved, and I saw just how tired she was when she sighed and got in her car.

I snicked the lock and even typed my code into the security panel. I was from Chicago. Security was automatic for me, regardless of the ultra-safe small town I'd ended up in. I'd needed a change after…well, just after everything.

I'd literally thrown a dart at the state of New York and ended up moving my entire life to Crescent Cove. That was after I'd played a drunken game of pin the tail on my future. A bastardized version of the childhood game with a map of the United States instead of a cartoon donkey.

The map had been pinned to the ectoplasm green wall in my old house. A color I would never have chosen but had happily painted to make Malcolm happy. Hey, he was a kid. Made sense. But me? I might as well have been one too.

Back then, I'd been young, eager, and stupid. Back then, I'd thought I was building toward a future.

Then I'd learned the truth and there had been much Jack Daniels. I'd needed a fresh start.

While I was drunk, I found New York.

When I sobered up and stopped crying about shit that would never change, I got angry. And that was when I'd gone into research mode. I sold my house and my coffee truck for a sizable figure and started over.

And here I was, taking another gamble with my savings. This time, my emotions were in check. This time, I'd created a business plan and had taken steps to correctly position myself for success. Not the blind luck I'd backed into with the café. I'd grown quickly and invested wisely, but it was still insane to open a restaurant. I was gambling on the small town's upward climb. More people were moving in and Crescent Cove was ever expanding with its epic baby boom.

Maybe I should have gone with baby-centric themes instead of the life-sized animatronic Michael Myers I'd sunk an absurd amount of money in. Whatever. It was too late now.

I was banking on my style.

It had worked for Brewed Awakening. The coffee shop was full of pieces straight from horror movie culture. Rylee had been right about pushing forward with the movie idea with viewing parties and specialized popcorn and treats. Money was pouring into the bank. Enough that I'd added a banquet room to The Haunt for gatherings and bigger viewing parties.

There just wasn't much to do for people in this town. They were starving for fun.

And I was going to give it to them. If John Gideon and his crew actually ever finished the damn restaurant.

Maybe I'd just take a little peek. It was my place, after all.

I scrubbed my palm down my jeans as I made my way to the connecting doors. A huge eyesore in the form of a piece of plywood had been taped over the double doors. Not only was it taped, but Gideon's crew had added a few nailed pieces of wood to keep me out.

I pried my fingers under one of the planks until the nail wiggled enough for me to pull it free. The nail at the top of the two-by-four allowed me to swing it down to rest against the wall. I winced at the scratch I made in the toffee-colored paint. That was what touch-up paint was for, right?

Now there was just enough room for me to duck behind the huge sheet of plywood.

I'd sneaked in last night, but I'd been waylaid by Lucky, one of Gideon's employees. He was the one who'd tacked up the extra wood.

Like a few pieces of soft pine were going to stop me.

I slipped inside and the scent of stain with a sawdust chaser nearly knocked me over. Drop-cloths were draped over everything, leaving ghost-like figures that could be booths or tables or monsters. With my place, it really was a crapshoot which you'd find.

I'd won an auction for a replica of the 80's movie version of *Swamp Thing* last month. It had been delivered to much fanfare during the week. I wondered which lump was the former Dr. Holland.

I made it to what should be the main dining area and the low murmur of voices had me scrambling back behind a—*son of a bitch*. I clipped my pinkie toe on the carved foot of a booth. Goddammit. I spun around in circles and resisted the urge to howl.

The only things not draped were the sawhorses Gideon was forever using to cut stacks of lumber. I gripped the top of it and touched my forehead to it as the stars and black spots receded.

Fuck.

When the pain lessened, dialogue from *Halloween* dented the quiet of the night. The telltale piano and spine-tingling strings were broken up by the lame love scene. I knew this movie by heart.

I hobbled my way to the back of the dining area to the bar. A ridiculously large laptop was sitting on the half-covered bar top. The low light from the screen flickered in the near dark.

A LED lamp threw the band of carved wood along the front in stark relief. The closer I got, the louder the movie became. Then I noticed the tick of shavings hitting the floor around a very familiar pair of Timberlands.

John Gideon. It couldn't be Lucky or Frank. Nope, it had to be the man himself. And it had been a damn long day. That was the only reason I let myself do a nice long perusal of all six-feet-three inches of him.

Sure.

That's the reason. Tell yourself another lie.

He had his yellow safety glasses on as he used the world's smallest chisel to carve into the corner of my bar. His dark hair was slicked back, but the ends were curling up. He tried so hard to keep a smooth, well-groomed look but his hair just wouldn't be tamed.

I didn't mind. I liked it a little wild.

I always mourned his hair when he actually remembered to go to the lone hairdresser in the Cove. The town barber had retired to Florida. Many men had learned the fine art of hair products this past year. John Gideon included, damn him.

I frowned as more shavings came pinging over his shoulder.

What was he doing?

I dared to creep a little closer. It seemed like a lot more delicate work than just a regular corner finishing. I was well-versed in Gideon's woodworking capabilities. Brewed Awakening was full of his innovative shelves and benches.

He didn't take the time to do intricate work very often. Every once in a while, I caught him doing something special, but he was often rushing to do five different jobs in and around town. The citizens of the Cove kept him very busy.

"Well, come on. Take a look then. Damn woman, always ruining any surprises."

I jumped. "Shit, Gideon."

He glanced over his shoulder. "I told you to keep out of here until we were further along."

I put my hands on my hips. Now I didn't want to look, dammit.

Liar. You want to see it so bad that you can taste it.

"It's my place. I should be able to come in and take a look around."

He swiped at his forehead with his forearm, leaving behind a trail of sawdust. My lips twitched. And okay, I couldn't stop myself from trying to see what he was blocking. Too bad his rather delicious ass was throwing a shadow over it.

I did love a man who had a little junk in his trunk. So many didn't. Not that I had a huge amount of knowledge there, but I'd done enough soul-searching—read, stupid hookups—in my twenties. As thirty approached, I'd become a little more discerning.

Evidently, a lot more. Cobwebs had been growing in my lingerie drawer since I moved to the Cove.

"You trusted me to take on this job, so trust me to finish it."

I crossed my arms over my traitorous tits. The deep timbre of his voice always activated my stupid nipples. It was like they were damn divining rods to our very favorite water source. "It's not a matter of trust."

"Isn't it though?"

"We open in six weeks, Gideon. I need to train people in here, get the bar set up. I've had the liquor license forever and the booze is sitting in my backroom gathering dust."

Mostly because I'd heard horror stories about the liquor license process in New York. Late night forums and Googling were my life. I didn't know how to sleep. Caffeine was my friend for more than one reason.

"And if you'd stop sneaking back here every hour and distracting my guys, we'd be further a-fucking-long." He raked his fingers through his hair and the sawdust doubled.

"If you'd bring me up to speed, then I wouldn't have to fucking sneak back here." I knew I was shouting, and I didn't even care. Frustration and stress had been eating at me for weeks—months—now. Not to mention the tension caused by my ever-growing personal sexual desert.

He stalked by me and whipped off one of the coverings behind me. A darkly stained booth came into shadowy view. He slapped his hand against a panel and a low hanging pendant light flicked on. The booths were obviously not in the right spot yet. His shoulder brushed the stained glass hood and it swayed, throwing light all over the room.

Deep red paint with a super subtle darker stripe coated the walls. The dizzy beam of light threw the corner into relief. There was something akin to blood splatter along the walls. It was a trick of the light with some sort of clear paint to create the effect, but it was breath-stealing. A poster of Dracula leaned against the rich, midnight stain of the bead-board that covered the lower half of the wall. Kickplates were half installed as well as jet black vents piled against the freshly painted trim.

My gaze bounced around the room. The booths matched the stain of the bead-board. It was a simple style, but the high, arched back had a relief carving of a raven. He whipped off another sheet to show the same booth style, this one with a bat mid-flight.

I spun around to get a look at each one he revealed. Some were achingly chilling, some were funny—all captured everything I didn't even know I wanted.

As always.

I reached out a shaking hand to touch the bat. The light was still dancing since Gideon was stalking around the room, flicking dropcloths to the floor. Sawdust and other sundry construction dust floated in the pale shafts of light. I was trying to bring it all into focus, and my heart was racing like I'd run down Main Street. It was too much to take in without proper light, but it was even better than I could have ever imagined.

Finally, I turned to him. His hazel eyes were angry and wild. They were bloodshot with fatigue and something else. The thing that always arced between us like electricity from the climax of a vintage monster movie. Dr. Frankenstein and his creation had nothing on us.

It was terrifying and electrifying.

My fight or flight response kicked into gear. Part of me wanted to run, and the other half of me wanted to stay. To demand he finally fucking man up and touch me.

My heart raced, and I dragged in deep breaths. Black dots danced around my periphery. I didn't know if it was the adrenaline or the shadows being thrown from the little Tiffany pendant light.

As I stepped closer, my pulse tripped at the madness flickering in his eyes. Every muscle bulged in his forearms, shoulders, and all those little ones in between that climbed up his arms. The ones I didn't know the names for but made my mouth water every time he lifted something heavy.

Jesus, he was fucking hot.

He opened his arms, his ever-present white T-shirt stretching tight across his broad chest. A stub of a pencil was tucked behind his ear, peeking out from the flipped-up ends of his hair.

His chest heaved as he stared me down. "Well? Are you happy now?"

I took another step closer, my heart slamming so hard against the walls of my chest I couldn't hear anything else in the room. Even the chilling soundtrack from the climax of *Halloween* couldn't dent the heaviness vibrating between us.

I grabbed his shirt and dragged him down to me. His mouth crashed onto mine and there was barely a breath of shock before his arms went around me and crushed me to him.

He tasted like my coffee—the special blend of chicory and dark chocolate I'd created just for him. That I brewed for no one else. That maybe, just maybe, I drank when the nights got too lonely. It burned my tongue as he invaded my mouth. His kiss was just as quietly overwhelming as the man himself.

No gentle first kiss between us. Nope. There was only lust unlocked.

And I was fucking here for it in every goddamn way.

Here in the place that I'd been dreaming about since I purchased the dilapidated building last year. Coffee was what I knew. What flowed in my veins, but I wanted more. I always wanted more. I was forever stretching past the boundaries set on me.

Even here in this sometimes stifling town, I wanted to demand more. Make my space more than just a pit stop in someone's day. Why I pushed myself to create drinks for strangers. To unlock their hearts and make them feel special for a second.

No one knew that but me.

But maybe this man knew a little bit of what I felt. I could see it in the details he'd brought to this project. Maybe it wasn't just a job.

Hope fluttered in my chest as I savored the long, slow, and dizzying way he kissed me. Like I was the best part of his day.

Then my phone buzzed against his thigh. Insistently.

"Do you have a vibrator in your pocket, Mace?" he asked against my mouth. "I'd figure you'd be less surly if you had a pocket rocket."

I dug my fingers into his stupidly firm pecs. "Shut up. Ignore it and go back to kissing me like you mean it."

He laughed into my mouth and cupped my face, but the stupid phone started up again. I was prepared to ignore it. Brewed Awakening was fucking closed.

"Do you need to get that?"

"Nope," I mumbled against his mouth and pulled my phone out to silence it.

He grinned and looked down. "Shit. Is that the time?"

"Got somewhere to be?" I took a step back. The phone went silent again.

Gideon shoved his hands into his hair. "Shit." He dug into his pocket then frowned and went back to the bar. He did something on his phone, and suddenly, it started buzzing and ringing as well.

My little bit of happiness and hope popped like a soap bubble at the way his face went from smiling and sexy to serious.

"Hello? Karen? Is everything all right?" He turned away from me.

Actually, he may as well have planted one of his big boots into my now too tight chest. Something was very wrong. Who the freaking fuck was Karen?

He listened for a second, his big shoulders sagging as he tunneled his fingers through his hair. He shifted around and those worried eyes caught mine.

Dear God, not again.

This could not be happening to me again.

TWO

Gideon

Fuck, fuck, fuck.

No wonder I'd had so much time to work in peace. Only my phone being turned off by some fluke would allow me that respite.

I'd caught one of Karen's texts as it whizzed by mentioning Dani's sprained ankle. What the hell?

Goddamn dad guilt was about to choke me. And Macy was waiting for an explanation.

This was exactly what I had *not* wanted to happen.

Swallowing hard, I pointed at her. "Give me a couple, then we'll talk."

Macy crossed her arms and stared at me with fire in her eyes. A different kind than I'd seen pre-kiss. As a wise man, I knew that meant my ears were about to be blistered.

We'd danced around each other for so long that my brain was still trying to understand how we'd even found ourselves in this position. We spent the bulk of our time arguing and exchanging hot looks. A few times, I'd wondered if the heat between us would ever boil over or just fizzle out entirely. If she would find someone and I'd be left with a whole lot of tension in her direction and not much else.

Not all sparks were meant to burn into something significant. Often enough, they just extinguished themselves.

Tonight, all of that had changed. Well, kind of. A kiss was a start. A beginning. Not a stopping point to fight, unless you were us.

Even right now, looking at her with her wild, fraying braid and her narrowed eyes, I wanted to drag her onto that bar.

But we couldn't, because my daughter needed me. Besides that, I was now the guy who'd lied about having a kid. That was the slot Macy would slide me into. I just couldn't worry about it right now.

I had bigger priorities at the moment.

Half-expecting Macy to bolt—though this actually being *her* place helped my cause—I lifted my phone from where I'd pressed it against my shoulder. "Go ahead, Karen, sorry."

Karen spoke in a frantic rush. She told me about taking Dani to the ER and how she'd called me so many times, as the flurry of text notifications that had scrolled across my screen testified to.

Someday I'd stop feeling guilty. Maybe.

"How is she doing now?" As I asked the question, I was already gathering tools.

I didn't have to do a ton of cleaning up since this was an ongoing work site, but I didn't leave my equipment just laying around. Crescent Cove was exceedingly safe, but there was no need to tempt thieves who wanted to make a quick buck. Not to mention that this wasn't my only job at the moment, although it was the most important.

And not simply because I'd just kissed the proprietress.

Fucking finally.

Hope you enjoyed it. You know it won't be happening again.

It probably shouldn't have happened, period. I wasn't stupid enough to mix business with pleasure.

Except I had. Again. As if I didn't remember how well that had worked out with Jessica.

There was a slew of noises on the other end of the phone, and I could tell Karen was talking to someone, likely my daughter.

"Karen? Let me talk to Dani, please."

Behind me, the heavy thud of Macy's footsteps told me she was either pacing or assembling weapons to use against me. Both ideas were valid. I kept picking up my tools, the leash I had on my impatience shortening by the minute.

"Karen? I need to talk to my daughter."

Some part of me got a sick thrill out of saying that, despite how I knew it would goad Macy. I shouldn't be driving the nail home any deeper, but Christ, it pissed me off that it had to be such a thing between us. I hadn't lied, because I was not usually actively thinking about Dani during the limited time I spent with Macy. Usually, our few moments together were too full of barbs and jabs for me to ruminate on what I was "keeping" from her.

Even if I really fucking hadn't been holding back anything.

It just hadn't come up. My daughter spent a good chunk of the summer with her mother, and I worked a lot. I wasn't trying to hide anything, no matter how Macy would likely spin it.

"Dad?"

"Yeah, squirt, what happened?"

"I was riding my bike, and I hit a groove in the sidewalk. I went flying over the handlebars. Toby said it was so sick, but it hurt real bad."

I exhaled. I had some choice words for Toby Brentwood. He was just a kid, so of course he would say something shitty like that, but I didn't need him influencing Dani. Thank God she had a good head on her shoulders.

"How are you feeling now?"

"Better. They wrapped it up and gave me the good drugs. I have a crutch!"

"Good drugs? Where are you hearing this stuff?" I shook my head as I closed the top on my toolbox. "Never mind, I don't want to know. You shouldn't be excited to have a crutch. Didn't you say you wanted to play in Little League this year?"

"I still can, can't I? It's just a stupid sprain. I didn't even have to have the crutch, but it was so sick."

I hefted my toolbox and set it on the stool in front of the still in-progress bar. Now I'd never work on that intricate bat carving without thinking about Macy dragging my mouth down to hers. I flicked my tongue over the corner of my lips just to catch a hint of the sweet and spicy flavor she'd left behind. Like cinnamon and apples. Fire and ice. Macy in a nutshell.

First and probably last time I'd ever get to enjoy such treatment from her.

"Little League tryouts are next week, so we'll see how it goes." I highly doubted she'd be ready to run around a softball field a week after a sprain, but I'd seen stranger things in my nearly thirty-five years.

"If I can't play softball, I'll need another after school activity for my resumé."

"Say what?" She said resumé like the word resume, no accent, but still. The kid was eight. Where was she getting this crap?

"I want to go to college," she said primly, as if I was just her clueless middle-aged father. Maybe I *was* clueless. I was batting about zero with the female contingent tonight. "I need to think ahead."

"Whatever you say, kiddo."

"It hurts when I have to climb. Can I sleep downstairs tonight? We can build a pillow fort and watch movies. Like there's that new one *The Borg*. You know, the oozy swamp thing." When I didn't respond right away, she tacked on the always effective kill shot. "Please, Daddy?"

"It's already late."

"So? I don't have school. And I'm hurting." She sniffled a little, and my stomach twisted. Worst of all, I couldn't entirely say she was exaggerating, and that made the pang even worse. "We haven't done a movie night in forever."

I couldn't argue there. "Okay, one movie. Then you can sleep on the couch. Let me talk to Karen now, honey."

My daughter passed the phone to Karen, and she let me know they were heading home. I promised to meet them at our house in a short while, then hung up to face Macy.

Who was still glaring at me.

"So, judging from that, you have a daughter."

I nodded.

"Other children as well?"

"Just Danielle."

"And Danielle's mother? Let me guess. You're on a break."

I let out a harsh laugh. "Yeah, for years, and that break began with our divorce papers. She lives on the other side of the country, which is the best thing for both of us."

Macy frowned. "You're divorced."

Her need for me to repeat it said a lot more than she probably realized. My tone gentled. "Yes, for five plus years now. We separated when kiddo was small."

"You don't even have a legitimate nickname for your daughter?"

I scratched my scruffy jaw, hoping the extra time would bring some sorely lacking clarity. Women were basically a whole different species. "Excuse me?"

"Squirt, kiddo, honey. Nothing that implies actual thought. Jesus." She shook her head and marched toward the rear exit. She skirted all the construction debris like a pro, her movements sharp and sexy as fuck.

"You're just leaving like that?"

When she didn't answer, I assumed that yes, she intended to split without even another parting shot. Then she whirled back and propped her hands on her hips. "Why would I stay? You're leaving. I've checked on the job and—"

"And kissed the hell out of me, in case you forgot."

Her lips pursed. "You didn't seem to mind."

"I certainly did not." I stalked toward her and fought every impulse that dictated I solve this by kissing her thoroughly enough that she would know no other woman even existed in my brain. But that wasn't the way, even if we'd just worked out our frustrations in exactly that manner. "I remember every detail, as I will when I can't sleep tonight."

"Listening for your daughter's cries in the night?"

"She's eight, not eighteen months. She sprained her ankle tonight, by the way. Thanks for not asking."

Macy's face softened. "Is she okay?"

"Yeah, other than some pain. Which she'll probably call sick tomorrow and confuse the hell out of me. What happened to kids calling stuff cool like when we were younger?"

The corner of Macy's mouth lifted, and for a second, I thought I might get an actual smile out of her. Then her expression turned as remote as a mask. "You're a little older than me."

"Not that much. And yes, I have a kid, which I didn't advertise on my T-shirt."

"No, you sure didn't. You also didn't mention it tonight, before we…" She forced out the word as if it burned her tongue. "Kissed."

"Yes, we kissed, and it was incredible." I stepped closer to her and her pupils widened. But she didn't hiss like an angry feline to ward me off, so I figured I was doing okay. "I wasn't thinking about my daughter in that moment. I wasn't thinking about anything except tasting your lips and seeing if they'd be tart or sweet."

She cocked her head, challenge written in every line of her gorgeous body. "So, what's the verdict?"

"Both. You're always both, which is why I keep coming back. I know you have layers beneath your crusty exterior, and I'm just ornery enough to be curious about what they are." Another step. "See, I'm observant enough to know that the more levels to a person, the deeper the reason why."

"I'm not some book for you to analyze. I just don't like bullshit. My life is simple and straightforward and that's the only kind of people I allow into it. What I have no time for? Lies. Head games. And—"

"Kids," I finished before she could kill anything from happening between us again. If that hadn't happened already. "I don't know what your issue is with them, and frankly, I don't care. I love my daughter, and she's a fucking awesome kid who deserves more than to be tolerated. The worst of it is? I think you guys would actually get along really well."

Macy seemed to be on the verge of saying something, then she shook her head and waited me out. So, I might as well put it all on the table.

"Dani wanted to build a pillow fort tonight and watch that crazy movie *The Borg*. Right up your alley, huh? More yours than mine. But I wouldn't dream of inflicting her on you." I pushed past her and walked toward the back door. "Goodnight, Macy." I slammed the door shut behind me.

Only when I was already to my truck did I realize I'd left behind my tools and my laptop. I was pretty sure that wasn't the only thing I'd left behind in there either.

She had a piece of my heart or my head or somewhere directly south. Maybe all three. I hadn't begun to figure out exactly what Macy Devereaux's hold on me was.

Now I probably never would.

THREE

Gideon

When I got home, Dani was asleep on the couch.

"She got too wound up, I think," Karen said apologetically, as if it was her fault my daughter had checked out.

I walked over to where Dani was sprawled on the sofa. She'd moved her left leg out from under the knitted throw our neighbor had made for her, and it was propped on a footstool that was slightly higher than the cushions. Her foot had some bruising beneath the Ace bandage, but her ankle didn't appear hugely swollen or misshapen. I'd imagined all sorts of things on the drive back from The Haunt.

Only a third of them were about Macy and how quickly she'd forget this night had even occurred.

"How did she sprain her ankle riding her bike and not her wrist?"

Karen shrugged. "Freak thing. That kid Toby said she rolled it when she went to stand up after flying through the air."

I shut my eyes for a few seconds before opening them again. I did not want to think about my daughter flying anywhere, thank you.

"What were those good drugs she was talking about? She's a kid, for Pete's sake." I'd managed not to swear, although it had been a close thing.

"Ibuprofen. She thought it was a big deal, but yeah, that's all they gave her and all they recommended for pain. And when she's awake, icing for thirty minutes every four hours for three days, depending on how badly she's swelling." Karen pulled out a sheet from her purse. "Here's some mild exercises she can do until the follow-up with the doctor. You'll want to call yours tomorrow." Nervously, she cleared her throat and fussed with her hair. "Sir."

I set aside the sheet of exercises. I'd look at those when I wasn't cross-eyed from fatigue. "What did I tell you about calling me sir?"

"Not to do it." She let out a little giggle and ducked her head. "I can't help it, sir."

Karen was a college student at nearby Syracuse University. She was shy and sweet and had been Dani's babysitter for over a year now. When I couldn't be home with Dani, I trusted Karen implicitly. If I hadn't, she wouldn't have been anywhere near my daughter, especially alone.

"Well, cut it out already. Thanks for all your help this evening. I'm sorry my phone was off. I don't know how it happened, but I'll be more mindful next time."

Except if I hadn't accidentally turned it off, the moment with Macy probably never would have happened. I would've rushed off to be with Dani, and Macy wouldn't know I had the audacity to be a father.

God forbid.

"No problem. I knew you were working. It was scary for both of us, but she barely cried. She's a real trooper, si—John." Karen flushed. "Anyway, I'll be here by eight tomorrow so you can get to work."

"Oh, I was going to go in later tomorrow, since you stayed later tonight than anticipated." Which I should've realized when I was working at The Haunt. I'd only had a couple of free hours, but I'd gotten so wrapped up in that goddamn bat carving that I'd lost all track of time.

"You can do that?" Karen stared up at me, her eyes almost comically wide.

"Well, I'm the boss." I didn't intend to puff up my chest, but I'd had to work my way up to the head of my own very successful business, so hell yeah, I was proud. "I usually prefer to get a jump on the day and

I'm an early bird by nature, but I'm sure you have homework or whatever—"

"Oh, no, I did that while I was waiting at the hospital. So, if you need me early, I'll be here early. Whatever you need, sir—John." She swallowed her giggle, but I still caught the tail end of it.

Was she extra solicitous tonight or was I just imagining things? God knows I was exhausted and could be seeing just about anything at this point. "Well, if it won't inconvenience you too much, then yes, earlier is better. The Haunt is taking up a lot of my time and the more hours I can devote to it, the better."

Not that I was in a hurry to get back to Macy. The bright side was she typically only swung through a couple of times a day at most. I also picked up my morning coffee on the way to the restaurant, but there were other places to get coffee that came with fewer icy looks and thin smiles.

Like my own kitchen.

I wasn't going to avoid her, exactly. But it was probably prudent for us to steer clear until the dust settled. Literally and metaphorically.

"Then I'll be here at eight. My class tomorrow was cancelled anyway, so I can stay straight through to afternoon if you need me."

"Didn't classes just start?"

"Yeah, but the professor had a…thing." Karen tucked her hair behind her ear and cut a glance at Dani. "She seems peaceful, so if you're all set, I'll just be going. Unless you need me for anything?"

"No, you were a huge help tonight. I really appreciate it, Karen. It takes a big load off me to know Dani is in good hands while I'm working."

"Not a baby," Dani mumbled, shifting restlessly.

"Of course you aren't, squi—" I stopped, thinking of Macy, and frowned.

Maybe she was right. I needed a more particular nickname for Dani. Something that referred only to her. My eyes narrowed on her fine strawberry-blond hair, pale skin, and freckles, so like her mother.

But her eyes were pure green, all me. Those eyes were frightfully direct. They never shied away from anything.

Unlike me. I'd turned my back on a lot just recently. Such as dealing with Macy every time things between us got a little too uncomfortable. Now that would be amplified by fifty.

"Of course you aren't, Red."

Dani's eyes popped all the way open while Karen coughed discreetly into her fist.

"Red?" Dani asked. "Like a dog? Also, my hair is actually basically blond."

"Your hair is not blond. Your mother's hair is red, and so is yours."

"Not anymore." Dani stuck out her chin. "Her hair is platinum blond, just like Marilyn's."

"Marilyn who?"

Dani made an annoyed noise. "Night, Karen. I think you're right, what you said." They both looked at me then away. What the heck?

"Oh, I don't know. Maybe not. I say all kinds of things when I'm revved up." Karen waved her hands. "Don't mind me."

Forget minding her, I was still trying to keep up.

"Thank you for staying with me, Kar."

"You don't have to thank me for that. We'll have fun tomorrow. Get some sleep, G-wiggle."

Dani grinned. "I will. Say hi to Professor Hottie."

My frown grew. So, Red was out, but G-wiggle was in? What did that even mean? And Professor Hottie? Had my daughter turned eighteen when I wasn't looking?

Blushing, Karen waved and headed across the living room.

I followed her outside at a much more measured pace. "What is this Professor Hottie stuff?"

"Oh, nothing. I just showed her a picture from my Soc class and told her some of the other girls had a name for the professor."

"I'm not sure that's appropriate for her." Then again, as an eight-year-old in today's society, Dani probably knew more about certain things than I did.

How truly horrifying.

"You're probably right. I was just showing her stuff on my phone to distract her while she was in pain. It seemed like the best option at the time." Karen hitched up her purse higher on her shoulder, and it suddenly occurred to me I hadn't even paid her yet.

"Shit." I dug out my wallet and grabbed three twenties, more than I usually paid her for a night. This one had been longer and more difficult than usual, so she deserved the hazard pay. "Here you go. Sorry. Completely forgot."

"No problem. This is extra?"

"You earned it. Thank you so much for being so good to Dani. And to me."

She blinked up at me then gave me a quick hug before hurrying down the stairs.

"What does G-wiggle mean?" died in my throat as her car started up in the driveway. I tucked away my wallet before giving her retreating vehicle a halfhearted wave.

Clearly, I would need to be more creative. I could do that.

I came back inside to find Dani snoring. Smiling, I adjusted the throw over her and grabbed another off the back of the sofa to bed down in the recliner nearby. Looked like I'd be sticking close tonight.

The idea of having a cold beer first was entirely too appealing, so I skipped it. There had been a time I'd appreciated the time after the workday ended more than the satisfaction of a job well done. Unwinding with a cold one at the local watering hole had stopped being a factor in my life once I'd wrapped my car around a tree—a small one, but it had hurt plenty—the same weekend Jessica told me she was expecting. After that, my world changed immeasurably.

I couldn't remember the last time I'd had more than two beers after work, and I liked not knowing. That pit was far too easy to fall into, so I'd just keep an eye on it from the sidelines.

Another thing I'd keep my eye on was Dani. Which meant the idea of sleep was basically a joke.

She shook off my attempts to help her to the bathroom a few times, insisting she could manage just fine. Which she did, thank God. I didn't think either of us needed to cross that bridge. She told me to go to my own bed, that she was big enough to take care of herself. My response was to pull the blanket over my head, both to make her laugh and to end the conversation.

She soon fell asleep after that, and amazingly, I did too.

The next time I opened my eyes, the room was gray with impending dawn. Dani was huddled on the couch, her throw wrapped around her nun-style so that just her face peeked out. She was typing furiously on her phone, her face illuminated from the screen. I hadn't even wanted her to have one of them—well, other than for safety reasons—but her mother had given Dani her old phone earlier this summer.

That was how most of our parental arguments went. I expressed concern, and Jessica did whatever the hell she felt like.

I threw off the blanket I'd kicked off about sixteen times overnight and stood, making Dani jerk up guiltily and stare at me owl-eyed.

"What are you doing over there?"

"What? Me? Nothing. Absolutely nothing." She tucked her phone under her hip and feigned a big yawn. "Boy, I feel so much better. How do you feel? That chair is lumpy, so probably your back's out?"

I rubbed it experimentally. "It's fine. I'm not eighty. My back doesn't just go out from sitting in a chair." Although now that she mentioned it, I could use a good stretch and a hot shower. "Sorry the movie night thing didn't happen. We can do it tonight if you want."

She was still darting glances at her phone, thinking she was being casual. I really wanted a look at it, but I wasn't going to violate her privacy.

Even if I really wanted to.

I could trust her to have good judgment. I hoped. Plus, there were parental blocks on there, assuming she and her hacker friends hadn't found ways around them. Maybe it was time to have another conversation about digital boundaries and safe spaces.

"We can rent *The Borg*?"

"Yeah. As long as there's no, you know, nude stuff."

She rolled her eyes. "It's a horror movie. Of course there's nude stuff, but it lasts like, a second. I know what boobs are, Dad."

"That's a relief," I muttered.

There was a good chance I'd be the one hiding my eyes during said nude stuff, not Dani. We hadn't even hit her teenage years yet. How exactly was I going to navigate all of these landmines?

It was probably different when you had a wife. A partner. Women somehow fundamentally understood how to deal with kids without scarring them before they reached adulthood.

"What does your mother do about movies?"

"Star in them."

I blew out a breath. Then again, Dani's family was not traditional by any means. "I mean, with you, squi—G-wiggle."

Dani made a face. "You can't call me that. It has special meaning."

"What special meaning?"

She tossed aside her throw and reached for the crutch leaning against the arm of the couch. "I'm hungry. I'll get breakfast."

"I was going to get breakfast."

"You should sit down. You look tired, Dad, and you're not as young as you used to be."

I sat, mostly from shock. Exactly how bad did I look after a night in that chair? "I need breakfast too."

"I'll make it. You need help around here. It would be different if you had a wife. Karen even said."

My head was reeling. "Karen even said what? And why do I need a wife?"

"To make you breakfast," she said as if it all made perfect sense. "And for you know, like companionship when you're old."

She was going to send me to the bathroom to check for wrinkles whether or not I wanted to. So, I was a little more salt than pepper at the temples lately. I certainly wasn't at the point of worrying about having a partner in my declining years.

"What exactly did Karen say? Exactly," I enunciated.

"She said how you work a lot, and it's hard to be a single parent. Her dad was too, and she said he changed when he started dating again. Until then, he was really mean."

"Mmm-hmm." I wasn't going to wonder if I was "really mean." I wasn't the world's friendliest guy, but I was far from an ogre.

No matter what Dani and Karen thought. Although that rather stung. I'd believed Karen and I were friends. Well, as much as you could be with a girl almost young enough to be your daughter.

"Have you thought about it?"

"Breakfast?" I rose again, unwilling to be deterred. "Yeah, I'm starving. Let me handle that end of things."

"Not that," Dani said impatiently before she screwed up her mouth. "Maybe pancakes? The apple kind?"

"Sure. Why not? I just got some apples from Mrs. Turner. First of the season."

"Mrs. Turner is married."

"That she is. And why are you obsessed with married people and me dating all of a sudden?" I cocked my head. "Is your mother seeing someone?"

Cagily, Dani looked away and leaned down to fiddle with her wrapped ankle. Yep, I had my answer.

Jessica was dating, and poor old Dad was not. He was probably going to turn gray and end up alone. I wouldn't have put it past my ex to even plant that in my daughter's head. One of her sly little jokes that so was not one.

I sat beside her on the sofa. "Just because your mom is dating doesn't mean it's the right time for me. I want to make sure anyone I bring home is going to love you just as much as I do."

"So, it's my fault you're alone," she said in a small voice, and my heart squeezed until dots hovered at the edges of my vision. "If you didn't have me, you'd be dating and happy."

"I am happy. What makes you think otherwise? Besides, I kind of like you, you know." I wrapped my arm around her shoulders and tugged her closer, making sure not to jar her leg. "I wouldn't want to live my life without you in it."

"Can we eat soon? I'm hungry."

I had to laugh. A sweet father-daughter moment interrupted by Dani's growling stomach.

"Sure. Go get ready, and I'll put the pancakes on. You might have to handle them for a few minutes while I get changed. Karen will be here in not too long."

Not that I'd glanced at the time on my phone yet, but I was pretty adept at guessing the time judging by the slant of the light. Already sunshine was creeping into the corners of the room.

Guess discussing my nonexistent love life took up more time than I'd realized.

"Okay." Dani muscled her way off to her room with her crutch without my help.

Stubborn, prideful, kindhearted girl that she was.

I let out a long sigh and pushed myself to my feet. That hot shower I wanted would probably take place in approximately three minutes between pancake flips while Dani manned the stove.

"See, if I had a wife, it would all be different," I said as I assembled ingredients in the kitchen.

Yeah, right. I'd had one of those once, and I'd still done the bulk of the cooking and getting up with Danielle when she was a baby. I'd never fully forgiven myself for missing her birth due to a job that had kept me away from Jessica's shoot, so I'd made sure to take care of everything else I possibly could. About the only thing Jessica had taken the point position on was nursing and that was because I lacked the right equipment. And thank Jesus for that.

Shuddering, I set to work chopping apples.

When Dani finally came out, the pancakes were nearly done. As were my chances of showering off the night before Karen showed up and giggled me into submission.

"Here you go." I set down the spatula. "You can handle this from here, right?"

Dani nodded and took her position at the stove like an old pro. "Got it, Dad."

I hauled off my T-shirt from behind my head, whatever I was about to say disappearing from my lips as I realized my daughter was taking a picture of me. What the hell?

"To show Mom," she said quickly, sending it off with a whoosh that made my eyes narrow.

"Your mom has seen my torso and we're divorced, in case you've forgotten."

I surely hadn't.

"Yeah, but she thinks you're getting sloppy. That's why you can't get any dates." Dani bit her lip and did something else on her phone before tucking it in the pocket of her sweats.

"Let me see your phone. I want to see that photo. Now." I was going to delete it. Possibly set it on fire.

Getting sloppy? Like hell.

"Ow, ow, ow! Burn," Dani said almost smugly, sticking out her hand for my inspection. The corner of her thumb was red. Not red enough for me not to drop her hand to grab her phone, only to be confronted by her lock screen.

Sometimes I really disliked her mother, and she didn't even have to be present for me to feel that way.

"What is your passcode?"

"It's my thumbprint and ouchie." She actually said *ouchie* as she waved her thumb in the air.

Naturally, Jessica had given her the iPhone 6 and not a newer model with facial recognition. Although I knew damn well that the passcode worked as well as a thumbprint.

"Danielle Alicia Gideon, you better—"

"Okay, okay, it's for a site. I had to send it. So they can size you. For Christmas!" She kept adding on phrases as if she was building the story as she went.

I was beginning to become very afraid where exactly my photo was on the internet.

In retrospect, I should have questioned her further. I should have demanded her passcode so I could find that picture and destroy it.

My abs were nothing to be ashamed of, but times weren't quite tough enough that I needed to use them to make a living—yet.

But I was very tired. And I just wanted a hot shower. In peace.

Those three minutes surrounded by tiles, pressurized water, and silence were drawing me like a siren's call.

That was why I muttered, "Keep an eye on those pancakes," and sprinted for freedom.

I stretched the shower into five minutes and emerged feeling semi-human. I brushed my teeth three times to extend my escape—a blissful time when I didn't have to consider my ex's motivations or my daughter's machinations—and came back downstairs in my standard work uniform of jeans, a white T-shirt, and Timberlands.

Ready for work, I was.

However, I was *not* ready to see Karen and Dani sitting at the table eating pancakes and passing her phone back and forth as if it was a nuclear reactor.

As soon as they saw me, they stopped laughing and playing keep away and soberly dug into their breakfasts.

"Food's all done," Dani said cheerfully. "It's delicious. Thanks, Dad."

Noticing she'd already made me a plate—or Karen had—I grumbled out a *thanks* and sat opposite them at the table. Almost immediately, my phone began to vibrate on the counter where I'd left it. My stomach was rumbling, so I ignored it in favor of scarfing down the pancakes. They were really good.

See, who needed a wife? I was quite capable in the kitchen.

Quite capable in all facets of my life, minus parenting. But I was beginning to think some body-swapping had occurred with the aliens while Dani had been visiting her mother in California.

It was as good an explanation as any other.

The phone vibrations started again. After that, they pretty much didn't stop.

Dani and Karen looked at each other, their mouths full of food, their expressions equally nervous.

My heartbeat went into triple-time. She hadn't emailed her mother. Hadn't uploaded a picture to some clothing site for measurement purposes.

Dear God, what had she done?

Rather than ask her, I decided to see for myself. I wiped my suddenly damp palms on my jeans and stood, determined to stoically meet my fate.

Then I picked up my cell and saw the hundreds of notifications tagging me on Instagram.

It took only one of them—*I'll help Gideon Get It Done, just give me a time and place*—for me to tuck my phone in my pocket.

Nope. Forget meeting my fate. Whatever my daughter had seen fit to do to her wonderful, loving, *devoted* father, I was not going to find out right now.

I was going to work.

FOUR

MACY

"Macy, we need another holiday blend."

Clara's sharp voice actually made me pause on my way through the door from the kitchen. A line of people snaked through the dining room. Instead of looking disgruntled by the wait, most were more focused on looking around.

And the ratio of women to men was alarming.

Phones were out, but that wasn't the weird thing. Everyone had their damn phones attached to their hands these days. But people were sharing their screens and craning their necks as if there had been some celebrity sighting. One of the rockers from a few towns over had to be visiting again.

Then again Ian Kagan's fanbase usually skewed a bit younger.

"A fall blend too." Jodi's voice sounded just as harassed. Very unlike my employees.

"On it." I turned around and grabbed my extra-large coffee carafe from the bottom shelf. I hadn't had to pull it out since the rainy Fourth of July this summer. On autopilot, I set the coffee grinder for an extra-large batch and refilled water reservoirs. I glanced at the corner of the counter where Gideon's thermos was still standing.

Nope. I wasn't going to think about Gideon right now.

Even if he had never, ever missed a coffee pickup since the first time he'd tasted my damn coffee.

Then again, he'd been lying to me for over two years. Why should anything surprise me now? Not to mention the fact that no one in freaking town had ever mentioned that he had a kid either.

"Macy, how's that coffee coming?"

What the hell was freaking going on? Were we living in OppositeLandia that Clara would be barking at me for coffee instead of the other way around?

I slammed the top on the first carafe and set it on the pouring station. Clara was building an espresso and had another Americana in progress. Brewed Awakening had singlehandedly turned people in the Cove into coffee snobs. Not that I was proud or anything.

I grabbed the last carafe and then jumped in to help.

"Hello, Mrs. Berkley, nice to see you."

The older woman raised a nervous hand to her simple cross peeking from her demure collar. "I know it's busy, but do you think you could…"

I grinned at her. "Donna special coming up."

Donna Berkley blushed. "I hate to make you do anything extra with it being so busy."

I waved her off and went to the espresso machine. Donna loved the idea of a fancy drink, but she was far too anxious to really enjoy a good caffeine-loaded latte. That and she was one of my eternals. Between the daily Box of Brews that she picked up for the school and the bakery items she purchased every Friday, the third-grade teacher was one of my favorite kinds of customers.

I quickly tamped down a quarter espresso bean batch and set aside the remainder to use with another order. A "Donna" was more cocoa powder and cinnamon with frothy almond milk.

She didn't really know what was in it. None of my customers were privy to their specialty drinks. I liked it that way. It kept a little mystique where the café was concerned.

I spotted two of my other regulars in line right behind her and started up their regular orders. It was busy enough that they'd get what I gave them and not fucking complain.

Clara and Jodi both had orders going, and we worked around each other in a choreography that only a coffee house would understand. However, this dance was usually done by now, which normally gave us some time to get ready for the even heavier lunch rush.

Not that I didn't love all the extra customers—and money—but at ten in the morning? Yeah, that didn't compute.

I glanced over at the far side of the counter to find Tish giving me some serious side-eye and an expression loaded with *what-the-fuckery*.

This was usually the time Tish and I snarked over coffee and a fritter. She tried to figure out what her secret ingredient was, I wouldn't give her a single clue, and we'd trade insults for ten minutes. It was the goddamn highlight of my morning.

Not to mention her guesses had definitely made my list for other secret blends.

I quickly made Tish's drink and snaked a fritter out of the case. I dropped it on top of her to-go cup. "I'll catch you tomorrow, Cayenne."

Tish Burns—auto body princess and metal mistress—jogged closer. "Girl, you rock." She shoved the pastry into her mouth and waved.

"Ladies, what's going on? Got a little backed up?"

Tish shot a look over her shoulder and we both rolled our eyes at Lucky Roberts's booming voice from the door. He was a massive tree of a guy with more hair than sense. For some reason, Gideon kept him on his payroll. Lucky seemed to flap his damn lips and flip his hair more than he worked, but I wasn't his boss.

Thank fuck.

The sea of women turned at his deep baritone. Some gave him a longer perusal—he was objectively attractive if you were into that sort of thing—but most were disappointed. The murmuring increased as Lucky waded into the fray. He pulled a pencil from behind his ear and dug out a little notebook from his back pocket. He licked the tip of the pencil and gave the nearest female his most charming grin. "Can I take your order?"

I rolled my eyes. That pencil action wasn't nearly as hot when Lucky did it.

Ugh. I had to get one particular problematic male out of my head. Especially if Lucky's over the top charm somehow reminded me of Gideon. You know, the guy who rarely flirted. Not to mention that Gideon was on my shit list. I didn't have time to think about him or the eye-crossing kiss he'd planted on me.

Okay, I'd started it, but I'd been caught up in the moment. Oh, and I'd still been a clueless idiot.

I didn't like that feeling. There was no reason he should have kept that very important detail to himself. A freaking kid.

It wasn't even so much the kid. It was that he'd slap me in the freaking face with a huge lie. Him of all people.

"Dammit," I muttered as a blast of steam got me on the side of my hand. Now I wasn't paying attention to what I was doing—again.

I looked up and groaned. Jodi's heart eyes for that big idiot Lucky were going to cause another pileup in the café. Jesus.

"Gonna need another holiday blend, Jodi."

"Huh?" She blinked her huge blue eyes at me. "Right. Right." She twirled and hustled to the grinder.

In no time, we'd taken care of another ten people between us, but the line never seemed to budge. In fact, it seemed as if it was getting bigger. Was I actually going to max out capacity?

Good God, please don't have a spot check from the damn fire marshal.

Fuck.

"What the hell is going on?"

Clara poured another two mugs. "Didn't you see the community page?"

The last time the community Facebook page had been mentioned in the café, I'd had to live through Veronica's blundering want ad for a baby daddy. Sweet Jesus. "Do I ever?"

Clara rolled her eyes. "That's true. Girl, you didn't look?"

I sighed. It was hard to imagine, but I didn't live for the gossip mill in Crescent Cove. "Obviously not. Is that rockstar dude in town or something?"

"No, better."

"Better?"

"Well, at least I thought it was better. And who freaking knew Gideon was hiding those washboard abs under his T-shirts?"

The incomprehension made me literally deaf for a moment. The whole café seemed like it was sucked into a vacuum. Why would Clara know what he looked like without a shirt? Hell, *I* didn't even know, and he'd had his damn tongue in my mouth. But beyond that, why the hell was it on Facebook?

"I'm sorry?"

Clara shook her head. "Well, beyond the whole *not* dad bod he's rocking, did you even know he was a dad? I mean, wow."

I snapped the espresso handle a little harder than was completely necessary. Enough that the grinds flew all over.

Clara's eyes went wide, and she reached for the bucket we kept under the espresso maker. "Sorry, Macy. Forgot you guys have—"

"We don't have anything. Look all you want. I don't freaking care. What I care about is why the line is never getting any shorter." I knew my voice held far too much venom for the situation, but I didn't care.

Clara didn't even miss a beat. Everyone was used to my snarling, and I wouldn't be changing anytime soon. "Right, well, his daughter posted a picture and tagged Gideon's Instagram business page. Kinda went insane from there. Firstly, hi, we didn't even know he was a dad, and secondly, damn, son."

"You're hanging out with Rylee too much."

Clara grinned. "More like gotta keep up with you." She finished a latte with a leaf flourish and brought the drink to the counter.

"I don't talk like Rylee," I muttered.

"Who doesn't talk like me?" Rylee came up behind me, tying on an apron.

"You were off today."

"Obviously, all employees were called in to deal with this insanity. You should have called me. Luckily, I was alerted to the mayhem."

I sighed. "Yeah, well, I just walked into this."

"Did you know Gideon's picture now has like sixteen thousand likes?"

"What?" What the hell kind of action was he hiding under his shirt?

Nope. I didn't care. Liar McLiarpants could keep his nice chest. Even if I'd felt just how firm and wondrous it was last night.

God, I had to be hard up if I was even still thinking about it.

Now who's the Liar McLiarpants?

Now that Rylee was helping out, the line started moving a little. People were not leaving, however. In fact, they kept peering around and checking their phones.

I knew an impressive chest could make women go ga-ga, but it wasn't as if he was Chris Hemsworth, for God's sake.

I headed to the kitchen to liberate my extra-large coffeemaker. I hadn't had to pull that sucker out since my last anniversary when we'd run a free medium coffee special as a thank you to patrons.

On the way by, I heard voices.

"Did you see those sweet pictures with his daughter? I came over from Syracuse. There's no way I'm not going to put my hat in the ring for this guy."

"What?"

I must have said it out loud because the very professional-looking woman looked up. "I suppose you think you have a chance?"

"Look, sister. I'm not looking for a chance. I have more than enough problems than to hook myself up to a single dad."

Okay, that might've been a little harsh. What was my problem?

"That's fine. More for me."

"What about me?" Her blond friend shoved a corner of one of Vee's peanut butter chocolate chip cookies into her mouth.

"We'll find out if he likes redheads or blonds now, won't we?"

"You are all crazy." I shook my head and pushed through the swinging door to the back.

I busied myself with making a supersized batch of coffee. There wasn't even six-thousand people in Crescent Cove, let alone sixteen-thousand.

"Don't do it," I told myself as I slammed the basket of coffee grounds into its slot.

Ivy Beck pushed her way into the kitchen, her eyes wild as she cradled her very pregnant belly. "Do I have backup ice cream in here?"

Saved by the pregnancy bell. More cold water to cool my damn jets about John Gideon. "Are you having a run?" I held up my hand. "I'll get it, Pregzilla."

Ivy pushed her ever present braids over her shoulder. "Have you seen it out there?"

I unlocked the big walk-in freezer and swung open the ancient door. But it was cold as fuck. I should probably sit my ass down in there a few minutes, so I didn't do something stupid like going looking for Gideon and demanding some answers about this insanity. "I've been kinda busy," I said from the bowels of the freezer. "How many do you need?"

"All of it."

I turned at her voice in the doorway. "Excuse me?"

Ivy blew flyaway strands that had come out of her braids out of her face. "I'm serious. The line around your café goes all the way down to that new clothing store, Vintage December."

I hauled out two tubs of chocolate truffle and debated unearthing my personal stash of caramel swirl. Nope. I had a feeling I'd need that one. I shoved it under a pail of cookie dough.

No one needed to know about that one but me.

I grabbed the spare vanilla I used for coffee shakes to ease my guilty conscience and loaded it all on my bastardized hand truck with a basket attached for just this kind of thing. "So, what does that mean? Are we talking—"

"Like it's a freaking One Direction concert."

"What? Oh my God."

"I sold out of all my ice cream. The diner has an hour wait for a stool at the counter. Women are planting themselves on the grass near the gazebo with freaking long-range lenses and binoculars."

"No, they aren't."

"Pinkie swear."

"Will you sit down or something?" I pushed her out of the doorway of the freezer and pulled over my rolling chair I used to do paperwork at my hidden corner desk.

She sat gratefully. "Do you have any of that special Gatorade?"

I spun and went to my restaurant grade fridge. I'd kept a six-pack of low sugar grape Gatorade for her since she passed out on us in the height of summer. Damn tin can of an ice cream truck was a sauna. Of course now it was chillier than my apartment, thanks to August, her big brother, and Rory Ferguson, her fiancé. They'd jerry-rigged a super conductor of an air conditioning unit for the truck so she could withstand even the craziest of pregnancy hot flashes.

I twisted off the top and handed the bottle to her. "At least the entire town is making out on this shitshow."

"Kinleigh convinced my brother to help her bring racks of clothing and her trunks out to do a sidewalk sale. It's like a festival out there."

"Festival of women on the hunt for single dads."

She laughed. "Pretty much. Add in all the Instagram stories that everyone is sharing and tagging your café and it's getting ridiculous out there."

I only knew what an Instagram story was because of Clara. She'd convinced me to get an Instagram account for the café and she managed it. She always had a damn camera in my face.

"The last I heard two of the local news vans were taking up residence just past the park."

"Good God."

"Macy?" Clara peeked her head into the kitchen. "Councilwoman Whitaker is here."

"Crap."

Ivy finished her drink and handed me the bottle. "I'll head her off. Give you a second to breathe."

Was I really going to let a heavily pregnant woman run interference for me?

Ivy straightened her apron and grabbed the handle of the hand truck, dragging ice cream behind her. Then I caught a glimpse of the crowd of people in the coffee shop.

Yep. I sure was.

I plopped my ass down at Ivy's chirpy and friendly voice. "Have you tried my newest ice cream, Irene? Why don't you come out to my truck?"

"I really need to speak with Macy."

"She's elbows deep in coffee grounds. She'll be out in a few." The door swung shut and I rolled forward to rest my forehead on my knees. First, to stretch out my back which was screaming. And secondly, to prevent *me* from actually screaming.

I was not going to look on Facebook. I had three-thousand things to do and about fifty customers waiting for drinks. It would be a banner sales day, thanks to that idiot man who evidently couldn't keep a shirt on.

I stared at the floor for three minutes before I caved.

"Dammit."

I pulled out my phone and opened to Facebook. I didn't even have to dig for the damn post. It was at the top of the page and had been reshared a staggering seven-thousand times.

I tapped on the picture to open it all the way. Were people that—

"Jesus."

It was John Gideon, all right. It was obviously a candid shot and from that vantage point, the photographer was either a shorter woman, or maybe a kid.

In the first shot, he was stripping off his T-shirt in that stupidly sexy way men had. The reach back and drag it off kind of move that had been murdering women for a millennium. It showed off all his ripples of muscle and a surprisingly cut bit of sin lines just below his belt. Why was that little bit of flesh always the most delicious thing on a built man?

I wasn't exactly the kind of woman who drooled after men, but I was still a flesh and blood woman. And while cobwebs were threatening to take over my girl dance space, there weren't enough to combat *that* photo.

Or the second picture where he was arching a brow at the photographer, which somehow was even hotter. His look of dubiousness was far more attractive than a cocky smile.

All that was hiding under his standard white T-shirt? That seemed cruel.

I clicked the photo closed. The cruelest part was that he was a freaking liar who didn't think having a daughter was a tidbit of information he should have disclosed before we played tonsil hockey. Or hey, maybe anytime over the last two years that we'd been flirting.

Maybe I was more of a fool than I'd thought. *Again.*

FIVE

Gideon

I WAS A GUY WHO ATE, SLEPT, WORKED, TOOK CARE OF HIS KID, AND crashed on the couch with coffee and *SportsCenter* and considered it the good life. I rarely dated, mostly by choice. It wasn't that I was bitter after my divorce so much as wary. My judgment could be questionable, especially when lust was added to the mix, so it was better if I just scratched the need when absolutely necessary and stayed single file the rest of the time.

The idea of using a dating app to meet someone horrified me. People lied and exaggerated and played games when you got to know them face to face. To start it all off online seemed like asking for trouble.

Clearly, the universe was now having a fine laugh at my expense.

I drove up behind The Haunt just before five am on Thursday. Karen had come over super early because she had afternoon classes, so I'd promised to return shortly after lunchtime. Assuming I could get back out. The only reason I could actually get in now was because many of the horny vampiresses were sleeping.

Or resting up for their next onslaught. Whatever.

Actually making it into the building without being verbally accosted seemed like a damn miracle. Maybe today would be a better day. Surely, they would get tired of stalking a man who didn't want their advances soon enough.

I just didn't understand what their purpose was. There was nothing that unique about me. Was the fact that I had a job and cared for my daughter that remarkable?

"Yes," Murphy Masterson aka Moose said as he replaced some floorboards near the wide picture windows in front of the restaurant.

We'd put up blackout curtains to cut down on the foot traffic outside, which meant we were using approximately fifteen spotlights around the place to give the effect of daylight. We had a finish carpenter helping us out, as well as a member of Macy's small hand-picked design team overseeing things, and simulating natural light was a must.

Ideally, we'd be able to let the real sunshine in, but God forbid someone catch me mopping my sweaty brow with the hem of my T-shirt. I didn't want to keep an ambulance on call.

I leaned against my ladder and guzzled water before rolling the bottle against my neck. "Okay, I'll bite. Why? If women were so hot for the blue-collar types, you wouldn't have turned to online dating and Lucky wouldn't be haunting the bars on a nightly basis."

"I have no need to haunt anything, son. Just walking down the street is an opportunity for me to star in my very own pornographic romantic comedy."

I just kept drinking my water.

"You're forgetting the most important ingredient." Moose pivoted to face me, his shirt dotted with sweat. Yet another pheromone-inducing event for the women outside. Thankfully, they weren't able to see in. "When I started online dating—although that was not quite like you're suggesting, since I knew Vee already—I didn't have a kid. That's the accessory they all want."

"All women want children?" I snorted. "Not hardly. In fact, I can think of one who thinks having a child is worse than being chased by Michael Myers."

"Macy," they both said in unison. Even a couple of the other guys chimed in from their different spots around the room.

"No, I didn't mean all women want kids, although it seems as if the population of Crescent Cove is a bit more child-friendly than your average small town. But women want good providers. Not even because they can't provide for themselves, because look around. They sure can. It's just the bedrock of a good human being, someone who does his duty." Moose reached for his level. "Similar thing to why many women find military men so attractive. Vee explained it all to me one day."

"Did she explain why if that's the case, it takes a post to make them all come swarming? I've lived just outside the Cove for years, and I've worked within the town and shopped here quite often. Yet all of a sudden, they're fighting each other to get a piece of me?"

Moose dusted off his hands. "Well, the spirit of competition motivates a lot of people. Now you're a prize to be won. Getting a date with you is a victory that will set them above their fellow contestants."

I barely stifled a groan. "Contestants? Is this a game show?"

"If it is, Macy is not playing. Yet she's the one you want, isn't she?" Lucky nudged Joe at his side. "They talk about hard nuts to crack. Dude, that chick is a nut surrounded by titanium with a platinum chastity belt. Your abs are impressive, but I don't think they're quite enough to make her swoon. Sorry. Mine, on the other hand…" He pulled up his own sweaty navy shirt and eyed his eight-pack. "Yeah, I feel like I need a kid, stat. That line out there would be three deep across if I could come up with one."

"Try eBay," one of the guys in back suggested.

"Hey, Moose, you seem to have extras in the child department lately. When those twins come out, how about you sell me one? Just for a weekend. So…like rent. I'll give it back, promise. It's not like I want one for real." Lucky shuddered.

"Hate to break it to you, but you can't just hold a kid and think it counts as parenting. It's a long-term commitment. Women are not stupid. You using a child as a prop will fool no one."

Lucky covered his ears. "Listen, dude, I don't like to hear the word *commitment* from women, so I definitely don't want to hear you say it to me in regard to children."

"Trust me, no one wants to hear it from you either." Dahlia, Macy's design expert, strode up to the built-in shelving unit Lucky was constructing on the far wall. The idea was for it to hold all manner of seasonal dishes and spooky memorabilia. "This unit needs to be twice the size. Consult your schematics."

She strode off, jet black fall of hair swinging. Lucky tried to roll his tongue back in his mouth and failed.

"Everything with Lucky is small. That's why his mouth is so big."

Lucky flipped a random middle finger over his shoulder at whichever member of the crew had waded into the fray this time. "I have schematics?"

Rolling my eyes, I strode to the bar and grabbed the paper in question. "Yeah, you do, and you better get to expanding that built-in. When it comes to Macy and witchy shit, think more, not less."

As if her name had conjured her, a commotion sounded at the pass-through door between the restaurants. My skin started to buzz as if I'd just taken a hit of her coffee. Which I had not done in several days, not wanting to see if she'd made it for me every morning as she had until she'd laid her lips on me and found out I was Benedict Arnold Daddy. Or whatever she called me in her private moments.

I didn't want to know.

Macy moved aside the boards we'd put up to keep her out and hacked through the tape we'd wrapped over the opening to stop her from peeking. She was using a machete or something smaller and just as deadly.

"I don't want to hear it," she said to the nearest crew member who tried to admonish her. "I pay the bills for this operation. From five to five, I own you, sucker."

Joe lifted his hands and shot me a glance as he backed away from the door. "You deal with her, man. She's a tornado."

"You better believe it, and he's not going to deal with me either. I am here for a status report. My restaurant is due to open in," she consulted a paper in her hand, "sixty-two days, and I want to know how things are going." She stopped stomping across the room and pointed at Lucky's built-in. "What is this for, a miniature dollhouse? I wanted big. That is too small."

"Same thing Lucky heard last night," someone called.

"He's been advised that's not to proper scale and will make adjustments."

Macy zeroed in on me. "Shouldn't that size issue have been noticed before he got that far?"

"Hey, don't be rude to the little fella. He's been dealing with those comments all his life."

Lucky ignored Joe and turned to Macy. "Look, you have a problem with my work, you talk to me. I'm not twelve."

"Okay then, let's chat." She stepped right up to him and got in his face as well as she could, considering he was more than half a foot taller than she was and tended to loom over people in an attempt to dominate them. But there was no using his size to make Macy submit. She would've gone toe to toe with the devil himself.

I didn't find that ridiculously sexy. Oh, hell, who was I kidding? She made my fucking head light, just from watching her jab her finger in Lucky's barrel chest.

"I was clear as a bell what size I wanted that built-in. So, fix it."

"I will fix it. I stand behind my work. There's no need for you to come in here like your balls are too heavy to carry and you need to throw them around."

Macy narrowed her eyes. For a second, I thought she might really haul back and hit him. Instead, she started to laugh. And she did hit him, but it was just a friendly jab in the shoulder. "All right, dude. Do your thang."

I wasn't sure which of us was more surprised. I'd been prepared to step between them if need be.

Maybe a blow to the head would knock some sense into me regarding Macy. Nothing else had.

Macy turned toward me and blew out a breath that ruffled the loose strand of hair that had escaped her braid. "I'm sorry, Lucky, but Calendar Boy here and his legion of admirers have me all messed up.

I've had to hire more staff, and we damn well know I won't have a use for them once he puts his cannon back in its holster."

"Oh, yeah, and what's going to do that? Since all he's done is sulk and fuck shit up all week." Lucky shrugged when I cut him a look. "Just saying. I don't see how us hiding in here as if they aren't all *attached* to the windows outside is going to help the situation. Gideon has to make a decisive move to put an end to this." He slipped a hand into the pocket of his overalls. "I do have about fifty of my business cards on me, if that'll help…"

Because I knew he spoke the truth—even Lucky had to get it right now and then—I strode to the door that faced the street and undid the locks. Behind me, I heard muttering and a few gasps and a couple of chuckles.

I flung open the door, and the walkway was not full of women, thank God. Instead, a woman in a trim navy pinstriped suit held a microphone in my face with a triumphant grin. "John Gideon, the DILF of the hour. What do you have to say for yourself?"

"Fuck off."

She blinked, glanced at her cameraman over her shoulder, and not so discreetly made a hand gesture by her hip. As if she'd summoned a murder of crows in a Hitchcock movie, a herd of women stormed toward the building, coming out from behind cars, trees, and even seeming to appear from the grates in the ground. That couldn't have been true, but a man's mind tended to play tricks on him when he was about to be swarmed.

"Call them off," I said in an undertone, not bothering to disguise my urgency. They were probably all very nice women, but people in groups made me edgy. "If you do, I'll give you your scoop."

"What scoop is that? Are you going to reveal on live local TV that you in fact placed your own Facebook ad, requesting, and I quote, 'a woman to be your wife who is better at cooking and cleaning than you are'?"

I squeezed my eyes shut as the sun beat down relentlessly on my scalp. I'd deliberately not read the "ad" Dani had placed, even though I knew I had to deal with it. I had to read it and process that my own offspring believed I was so hard up and desperate that she needed to do a mass post requesting female companionship for me—and had insulted my cooking and cleaning while she was at it. Yet she had gleefully consumed my apple pancakes even as she'd posted the blasted thing.

And I needed to ground her. For using the internet as a dating resource. For lying that I even wanted a date, never mind a wife. For covering up what she was up to with her phone.

Damn Jessica and her decision to give Dani her old phone in the first place. And damn her for calling me "sloppy" in Dani's earshot. I'd never been sloppy while we were married, and I sure wasn't now.

What I was, though, was pissed.

"I did not place an ad. Neither did my daughter. She simply wanted to find me a date. It wasn't advisable, but we were all children once, weren't we?" When the newscaster didn't reply, I shrugged. "Okay, maybe not you, but I was a kid and I did stupid things. Not this kind of stupid, but her heart was in the right place. She cares about me and wants me to be happy and not alone for the rest of my life because her mother cheated, and we got divorced." It was only when the newswoman's eyes widened that I realized I had seriously gone too far.

Since I never said too much—and many times, rarely spoke at all—that only proved how rattled I was by all of this. I needed to end it. Now.

The newscaster motioned for the circling women to stay back and for her cameraman to come in closer. "Lonely, lost, needing companionship, you appealed to your young child to help you find a woman. Is that what I just heard? If it is, don't be ashamed. Many of us have been where you are. We understand." She batted her dark lashes a few times too many at me, to the point that I wondered if the glue she'd used to stick them on had clumped.

I truly did not understand the feminine mystique.

"I didn't appeal to anyone. I didn't need to. You know why? Because I already have a woman."

To be fair, I was as shocked to hear the words come out of my mouth as the newscaster appeared to be. An actual gasp went through the crowd. Or that might just have been Lucky, who'd pushed me all the way through the doorway so he could grip the jamb and lean forward to survey the situation.

"Oh, you do, huh?" The newscaster studied me with her now suspicious brown eyes. "Just who is that partner, and how come your sweet daughter failed to realize you had one? Or are you having," she dropped her voice, "a secret romance?"

Another glance behind me just brought me face to face with a smirking Lucky. I grabbed a fistful of his shirt and hauled him out of the way, tossing him to the side like an offering to the assembled ladies in our midst. It was only sheer surprise that allowed me to move him so easily, since he was built like a freight train and stubborn to boot.

Once he was out of the way, Macy stepped forward. And I swear to God, I wasn't a fanciful man, but it was as if the heavens opened up and a chorus began to sing. I reached for her, pulling her against me, my only thought to get through the next minute with her by my side.

Then my gaze dropped to her brick-red lips, painted and scowling. She rarely wore makeup when I was around, and to be honest, she didn't need the warpaint. But at that moment, I'd never seen a more gorgeous sight. Especially when paired with her sizzling blue eyes, so wild and fiery that I couldn't have looked anywhere else if I tried.

Definitely couldn't have remembered another woman, despite being surrounded by them. All of whom were watching us avidly, I could just tell.

And I did not give one flying fuck.

"Right?" I asked softly, cupping her surprisingly silky cheek in my palm.

With Macy, you almost expected her skin to be lined with thorns. Instead, it might as well have been the finest satin. Her eyes flashed and I went for broke, because I really had no choice. She could make my lie into a kind of truth or prove it to be the story that it was, and I was entirely at her mercy.

"Right what?" She wasn't swooning in my arms, but she also wasn't pulling away. Her gaze raked over mine, and if I wasn't mistaken, she even turned her face into my hand just the slightest bit.

Enough for me to say the words suddenly burning their way from my chest into my throat.

"You're my woman." I dared to rub my thumb along the little dip under her lower lip, reaching upward when her lashes fluttered, and her mouth parted.

Not to admonish me. Not to tell me to go to hell. But to make the softest exhalation I'd probably ever heard. Barely audible. Just enough to cause me to angle my head and fuse our mouths together the way I'd been aching to do since she'd kissed me days ago.

This wasn't like that kiss.

Oh, the same aggression and frustration were there, layered under a sweet sensation of surprise that had me cupping her face and going deeper, dragging her with me whether or not she was ready to dive. That she'd take this ride even knowing there would probably be a collision with some pretty fucking hard rocks shook me to my core.

Then again, maybe she had no choice. Just as I didn't. There was only her mouth, so hungry and pliant against mine, her teeth razing over flesh and leaving a sting of blood that tasted like victory.

Hers *and* mine.

For a moment, only the battle counted. It didn't matter who came out on top, because the spoils were ours to share.

That *this* could exist beyond years of petty arguments and snarky comments and judgy looks was some kind of miracle, and I'd given up in believing in those beyond the sparkle in my little girl's eyes.

Then she drew back and sucked in a greedy breath before tilting her head in challenge at the newscaster. "What he said. Make sure you write all that down."

SIX

MACY

Deciding to decorate my café at nine at night wasn't the best idea.

Then again, I hadn't been able to stop thinking about Gideon's mouth on mine. Not only did we now have two kisses in our collective unconscious, the whole damn town and world had witnessed the second kiss.

That was the part that had me so wound up I couldn't settle. The idiot had just grabbed me. Oh, and instead of me hauling off and smacking the crap out of him like I should have, I'd kissed him back.

So freaking stupid.

The worst part? Now there were tons of videos floating around with me looking like a shellshocked moron. A bunch of entertainment shows had picked it up, thanks to Gideon's boneheaded mention about his ex-wife cheating on him.

If it had just been him and me, it would have blown over. Nope, now he had to bring in his famous ex. Before this week, I hadn't even known he had a wife, let alone that she was relatively famous. To add a little more acid into the wound, because honestly, salt wasn't nearly enough for how it burned when I got a look at this Jessica Gideon. She was stacked, currently platinum blond, and gorgeous enough to make feel like an extra on *The Walking Dead*—you know, comparatively speaking.

Just ugh.

Secondary kick? The kiss had actually killed the entire mass hysteria. All the extra foot traffic had disappeared like a puff of smoke. I mean, Brewed Awakening had served our regular Friday customers, but the town was almost back to normal. Disappointment reigned that John Gideon had a pseudo-girlfriend.

Aka me.

So, now I was the bad guy. I wasn't quite sure how that had happened.

What I did know? That my life needed some order. And the only thing that truly made sense to me was Halloween. So what if it wasn't quite September yet?

Of course now it was nearly four in the morning and I was at an all-time high for insomnia insanity. I'd been dusting and cleaning every crevice before putting out my vintage, kitschy, and sometimes ridiculous decorations. I'd covered the back counter in pastel pumpkins and a few of my Halloween-esque houses I'd been collecting since I was a girl.

I was aware I'd need to ease the town into my obsession. They already knew I was bad, but I usually waited until mid-September to deck the café out. End of August was definitely pushing it for the annoying biddies of the town council. So, the actual counter was pretty-in-pink style for now. Leaf garlands in pops of orange wound around the white and pink plastic pumpkins I'd been collecting since I'd opened Brewed Awakening. End of the season sales were golden for cheap decorations and I always stocked up for next year.

I made sure everything was still functional for counter space. One of the many reasons I'd used Gideon's talents during my first year. He'd created a maze of shelves and cubbies for me. It usually was full of Brewed Awakening merchandise. Now it was pumpkinfied with a selection of my favorite bats and skulls.

Before midnight, I'd attacked the front window with the pink and orange brigade as well. The first of October, the coffee shop would be transformed into my true nature of witchery, creepy bats, and skulls.

I just had one section left. I pulled down my bandana and took a long drink from my huge Jack Skellington tumbler full of water. I walked around the front of the counter and fussed with a trio of skulls on top of the bakery display. I'd commissioned Dahlia McKenna to do artsy, spooky florals in the skulls and had found a kindred horror spirit with an equally sad case of insomnia. The bonus round had included the fact that she was an interior designer. Collaborating on a themed restaurant seemed like the perfect storm.

We'd been working on plans for The Haunt for almost a year, and now it was so close to becoming a reality. Between obsessing over the progress of my restaurant and this ridiculous *thing* with Gideon—well, it was a wonder that I wasn't more of a basket-case.

I refilled my cup with the perpetual jug of lime water on the scarred table I was using for a decoration station. If I'd only lived on coffee like some people assumed, I would've probably ended up in the emergency room with a heart attack.

Picking out a few more bats, I tucked one of the furry ones into a mug. The creamer station was decked out in Rae Dunn Halloween items due to auctions on eBay, Facebook, and Mercari. I'd been buying since last Christmas when I found my first Spooky black mug. I didn't even care that I was a trendy bitch. Halloween was my jam and I wanted it all.

IKEA and I had enjoyed a date yesterday after the incident. I certainly wasn't going to ask Gideon to build me shelves for Halloween decorations.

Besides, the IKEA ones had ended up being super sturdy. Not everything from that store was blinding white. Who knew?

Instead, these were wrought iron and fake dark wood that would fool most people, me included. Gideon or August would probably sneer at the shelving, but it worked for me. And it made cleaning up the copious amounts of coffee that somehow seemed to spill everywhere far easier.

Crawling around under the structure, I found a few more spots for bats. I had a battery-operated black cat with ominous green eyes nestled in with bags of my special August coffee blend. It wasn't quite summery, and not yet filled with the spices of fall.

I yawned and contemplated curling up under the creamer station like Isis, my cat, but I backed out and moved over to my remotes. It was far too late to sleep now. I'd just have to make it through the morning rush then I could disappear for a nap.

I turned on my spooky playlist. Lana Del Rey's moody voice filled the empty café. Since I was alone, I twirled and swayed my way across the room with my big stepladder to tackle the best part of my Halloween transformation—the corner bookcase. It was my favorite place to sink in and make it as over the top spooky as humanly possible.

Well, that and to still be functional...*ish*.

I gathered my rags and cleaner and climbed up to the top to start dragging down the books and mugs I'd used as decor. Dust kicked up and I pulled up my bandana to keep from swallowing it all. I sang along with the whispery, sex-voiced Lana. Her version of "Season of the Witch" was one of my favorites.

My hips swayed to the beat as I tucked in a skull and a raven from my Poe collection. The old typewriter I'd found at a consignment shop in Salem held center stage. I'd typed up a few stanzas from *The Raven* and added a little slashy blood on the parchment paper.

"Daddy, what is she doing?"

I screeched and only my quick grab on the ladder kept me from tipping.

Gideon rushed across the room to stabilize my ladder with one hand. His other gripped the back of my calf. "Jesus, Mace. What are you doing up there?"

I glanced down at him. "Better question. What are you doing here trying to scare eight years off my life?"

His jaw was tight, and his eyes hooded as his gaze kept tracking to my ass then back to my face as if he couldn't decide where it belonged.

A strawberry-haired girl hobbled forward on one crutch. She twirled to take in the room, then seemed to realize Gideon was no longer next to her. She hopped double-time to get close to Gideon. Her eyes were huge. "Whoa. This place is so sick!"

"Um, thanks." I glanced down at Gideon's hand still gripping my leg.

He cleared his throat. His green eyes looked about as bloodshot as mine probably were. "Right. Sorry." He released me and stepped back.

"Hi." The little girl was grinning up at me with a tooth missing in the front.

"Hi." Then I turned to Gideon with probably matching huge eyes and tilted my head in the universal sign of *what the fuck?*

"Your mask is super sick. Can I have one?"

"My what?" I blinked before realizing what she meant and pulled down my bandana with the evil jack-o-lantern drawing on it. "Sorry." Dumbfounded, I didn't know what else to say.

I felt vaguely sick too and not from my inherent cool factor.

Gideon held out a hand and obviously, I was well past sleep deprived since I accepted it and let him help me down the stairs.

"What's going on?" I asked out of the side of my mouth.

Gideon didn't let go of my hand. "So, I have a huge favor to ask."

I tried to detangle our fingers, but he was holding on like I was a damn lifeline. "What are you doing here? And who's your friend?"

He frowned at me, one eyebrow raised. "This is my daughter, Dani."

She waved. "Hi. What's your name?"

I finally was able to get my hand away from his. Probably because I'd immediately started sweating like a prepubescent. I swiped my palm down my jeans. "I'm Macy Devereaux."

"Wow. Cool name. I'm just a lame Danielle."

"Still French, right?"

She gave me a gap-toothed grin. "I guess so." She hooked her hand around her dad's wrist. "Is my name French?"

He smiled warmly down at her and swiped his big hand over her shiny strawberry hair. She had uneven ponytails on either side of her head that she'd probably done on her own. "I do believe it's a French name. But your mom just liked it, I think."

"Oh." Dani shrugged, her attention already jumping from names to my large box of decorations. "Holy crap."

"Dani," he warned.

"I mean, wow."

He rolled his eyes. "My babysitter came down with something, either the flu or something far worse. She can't watch Dani today."

Dani pulled a skull out of the box. "Is this real?"

At a loss, and not really able to tell Gideon to fuck off in front of his kid, I cleared my throat. "Actually, it is." I winced as my gaze shot to Gideon. "Maybe I shouldn't have said that."

"So cool!" Dani carefully set it back into the bubble wrap.

"You'll find that my daughter is about as into Halloween as you are."

"I doubt that."

The crutch clattered to the floor as she dropped to her knees and dug in.

"Hey, be careful—"

Huge green eyes that matched her father's bugged out as she lifted out a book. I resisted the urge to snatch it out of her hands. "Is this *the Necronomicon?*"

Huh. I tilted my head. "What would you know about it?"

"Only that it was the coolest thing in *Army of Darkness*. Well, next to the chainsaw. I mean, Ash's chainsaw was fairly amazing if improbable because of the weight of it." She sounded so matter of fact, I laughed despite myself.

"Well, don't pull an Ash and screw with the book." I gave her *gimme* fingers.

She laughed. "Can't have that. Wouldn't want to get the words wrong like he did." She handed it over then picked up the skeleton head. "Then we'd be in real trouble." She held the head up to her father and stabbed the air with the mandible. "So much trouble."

Gideon hung his head. "Put that down, please."

Dani turned it back to face her. "Give me some sugar, baby."

He swiped his hand over his face. "I found her watching the movie at two in the morning."

I grinned. "I'm sure she's seen worse."

"Oh, I have," Dani said. "It wasn't even scary."

Gideon's jaw muscle ticked. "When she was seven. I wouldn't have let her watch it if I'd known."

I pressed my lips together against a huge smile. "Probably about how old I was when I found the movie. Now about this babysitting deal?"

"I'm in a jam. Karen, my usual sitter, is a college kid. She's great, but sick as a dog. With Dani's ankle, I can't really send her to the usual daycare."

"Dad. Daycare? Really? I'm eight."

"I know, kiddo. That's just what they call it."

I sighed. "Still have a lame nickname for her."

Dani winced as she moved to the next box. "He doesn't understand nicknames."

"Oh, and what would you name her, hotshot?"

"Obviously, Ash."

"Yes!" Dani grinned up at me.

"That's not her name."

"Yes, but nicknames are about moments. And now that I know she loves *Army of Darkness*, she's Ash, the lead in the movie. Until a better nickname comes around." Not that it would because I wasn't getting close to this kid.

He shook his head and raked his fingers through his hair. "Whatever." He tipped his head back and I saw the exhaustion dragging at him. "I wouldn't ask."

"Which is smart since I, you know, run a business. I'm not exactly babysitting material, Gideon."

"No, and I get that. But if she could just stay here in the café? I'm right next door working on The Haunt, so if she needs anything I can be close by. All she needs is a corner to watch movies or read. She's really no trouble."

"Ruff!"

"Danielle Alicia."

"Jeez, Dad. Stop talking about me like I'm a puppy. I told you I could stay home alone."

"As capable as you are, legally, it ain't happening."

"Rules. Ugh." Dani practically dove headfirst into my box of bats. "Can I help you decorate? Dad doesn't let me do it at home."

"You don't let her decorate?"

Gideon crossed his arms. "I let her decorate plenty."

"Lame decorations from Wal-Mart don't count."

"By the time I get out of work, the other places are closed. And by the time we get time to put them up, it's time to change to Christmas anyway."

"Okay, you need to go. Clearly, you've been abusing this child. I shall correct all past transgressions and get her straight." I turned Gideon around and pushed him toward the counters. "You owe me so big. *So* big," I said under my breath.

He pushed back on me, digging his heels in. "I promise I'll find someone this afternoon. Probably my father, but he is out of town until this afternoon."

"If she's a handful, I'll just start taking money off your bill for The Haunt."

"Seriously, Macy, I would never ask unless I was absolutely screwed. With all this nonsense that's been going on, we're days behind at the restaurant. I can't have her over there since we're ass-deep in the kitchen installation."

"I have no idea what that means, but a construction zone is no place for a kid. Just give me a holler when your dad can take her."

"Thanks." He turned and slid his arm around my lower back, his hand splaying along the curve of my spine. His gaze dropped to my mouth before lifting to meet mine again. "We still need to talk about yesterday."

"What's to talk about?" I tried to step back, but he held me fast.

"You know everything got way out of control."

"It was just an act, right?" That his mouth on mine tasted more perfect than coffee? Sure. Just an act.

"Was it?"

"Of course it was."

"Nothing has ever been easy between us, Macy. But it sure as shit hasn't been an act. Now that I've had a taste, you really think I can turn this off?"

My fingers twisted into his soft shirt. "You never pulled the trigger before. What stopped you?"

"Always with the hard questions."

I lifted my chin. "Always with the avoidance." Because God, if that wasn't the truth. And I was tired of the dance. I wasn't fucking good at it. "What do you want?"

"You."

I drew in a breath.

"Go out with me."

I frowned. That question did not compute. In fact, it was more of a statement than anything else. "I'm sorry?"

His lips quirked under the fullness of his beard. "I know we've been doing all this crap backward, but maybe it was the shakeup we needed."

I tried to wiggle free. Things with Gideon had always been more of a nebulous maybe and I rather liked it there. Like a celebrity crush—no basis in reality. He was the hot blue-collar guy with big working man hands. A little rough around the edges with a banked fire that made a woman wonder what would be unleashed.

I could say with absolute accuracy that he might normally stay on simmer, but there was a fuckton of heat waiting to bubble over.

But I wasn't sure I was ready to be brave. And that chafed more than I wanted to admit, even to myself.

"So much going on in that head." Gideon lowered his face to mine, but instead of a kiss this time, he just brushed his nose along mine. "Give us a try. Give me a try."

"You're still not actually asking me," I said in the rapidly dwindling space between our lips. His breath was warm and minty and I had the ridiculous urge to slip the pads of my fingers over his bearded cheek and pull him closer. There was something about his beard that drove me a little crazy.

"Macy Devereaux, will you go out with me?"

I didn't even think. I just blurted out an affirmative. He nipped at my lower lip quickly than stood up straight. "Great, I'll pick you up at seven."

"What?"

"Seven o'clock." His lips twitched with amusement, then his attention diverted to his daughter. "You all right, squirt?"

I blinked out of the fog he'd dropped me into. What the hell? "Wait."

"Nope, you said yes." He slid his fingers into the back pocket of my jeans for a quick squeeze before stepping away from me.

Who the hell was this man? Talk about a change of situation between us.

"Dani?"

She spun around with a skull in her hand. "Yeah, this place is so sick. You don't ever have to pick me up."

"I'm sure Macy would disagree, but please behave for her. I'll be right next door if you need me."

Dani waved him off. "I'll be fine. I'm going to help her decorate."

He glanced at me. "Well, that's that."

"Evidently." I crossed my arms since I didn't quite know what to do with them. Especially since leaning into Gideon was becoming more and more of an inclination. I scooped my flyaway hair out of my face. "Is she allergic to anything? Would you hate it if I plied her with chocolate and espresso?"

His jaw dropped, then his eyebrow quirked. "I know you're not exactly used to kids, but I'm hoping you're kidding. Sometimes I can't tell."

I lifted a shoulder. And the joke was on him, since I knew far more about children than he could even fathom. The old wound throbbed, and I pushed it back where it belonged—in the past.

"She's not allergic to anything," he said into the silence.

"Good, then she'll probably only be slightly high on chocolate by the time you get her later."

"Well worth it. My dad will be back this afternoon. He's a long haul trucker and will be making a stop in."

Hmm. Interesting tidbit of information there. And spoke volumes as to why Gideon was so…Gideon. Isolated sometimes, even-tempered most of the time, and affable always. He was a chameleon of sorts, and this past week had taught me more about him than the two years we'd spent sliding around one another.

I drifted toward the kid since she was in my box of favorite decorations. Gideon checked that Dani was busy and quickly spun me around to him one last time. The kiss was as fast as a rattlesnake and left my mouth just as swollen as a bite.

Then he was striding across the room without another backward glance, leaving me just as unbalanced as the day before, dammit.

I shook it off and headed over to the corner. Dani had a dozen skulls set up with little trios of decorations around each one. Kind of genius. Like little triptychs.

"What made you do that?"

She peered up at me. "Bit of glitter on this one looks like it would go good with—"

"Well," I interrupted instinctively. Jesus, I sounded like my mother.

She gave me her father's inquisitive eyebrow raise, only hers was a golden strawberry in hue.

"Go well. Grammar is important."

"Grumps says the same thing."

"Grumps?"

"Yeah, my grandpa. He's grumpy like you."

I laughed.

"Okay, so these go *well* together." She pointed to the little bit of pink and black in one of the skull's teeth. "So, that one looks cool with the pink and black boa with the bats."

"I like it. Take a crack at it, Ash."

She preened at the nickname I'd used before and went to work. I picked up the remote control and beefed up the music. At least things would move along a little faster.

And maybe a little different than last year.

She boogied to "Give Me Shelter" as she hopped around on one foot and moved books and mugs around to turn her skulls just so. I climbed the ladder to do the higher shelves, and we met in the middle.

Finally, one box was empty. I stood back and she hopped after me, mirroring my crossed arms as I took in the various shelves. "You have a good eye, kid."

"Yeah? My teacher says that too. I like to decorate."

"Guess I have to introduce you to my friend, Dahlia."

"Oh, I've met her. She works with my dad."

"She worked with me first." I moved to the water station and filled a mug with lime water before grabbing my own tumbler. I handed the mug to Dani. "You can pick a tumbler to drink from if you want. But for now…"

She took it and peered inside. "Water?"

"Hot chocolate is earned."

She gave me a gap-toothed grin. "Guess I need to do some more work."

"Guess you do."

She took a gulp and her eyes went wide. "What's in it?"

"Limes."

"Wicked."

I laughed. "All right, since you did okay with the skulls, let's see what you can do with my collection of bats."

"Excellent." She shoved the mug at me and hopped her way over to the boxes again. I couldn't stop the smile when I followed her over.

By the time Vee came bustling in, belly first, we were moving on to the dessert station and spreading cobwebs everywhere.

"Holy Halloween."

Dani turned around, fake cobwebs sticking to her hair. "Hi!"

Vee leaned on the door as she looked around. "Bit early even for you, Mace."

"I know. I had an itch."

"A rather big one. And a helper." Vee rubbed the side of her belly. "I'm Veronica."

"Dani." She hopped up and winced when she forgot that she was supposed to be being careful with her left ankle.

I moved to her and she leaned hard enough that I had to take a sidestep. She was sturdier than she looked. "This is Gideon's daughter. She's going to be hanging out with us today."

"Oh. Well, that's a first. We love your dad, but he hasn't been very forthcoming about you."

I gave Vee a hard look. "What Vee means—"

Dani picked a piece of the web out of her hair and made a face before wiping her hand on her cargo shorts. "It's okay. My dad's protective. It's because my mom is famous. He doesn't trust anyone with me really. Well, except for my usual babysitter, but Grumps told me it was after an FBI-level review."

I snorted.

Dani grinned up at me.

"Sounds like your dad."

She shrugged. "He's really weirded out with this girlfriend search thing. I kinda messed up."

"I'm sure he knew you meant well." Vee's soft heart went on full alert.

"Tell that to him. He keeps trying to figure out some way to ground me. Luckily, he forgets about it almost as fast."

I pressed my lips together. Sounded like Gideon was pretty well wrapped around this little girl's finger. I liked her even more already.

Vee laughed. "Happens to my husband all the time. My son, Bray, has his ways."

Dani hopped over to the couch. "I just got back from my mom's." She dropped down with an overblown sigh. "I get away with more right after the summer."

I wasn't sure what to say there. It seemed skeevy to pump her for information. I'd resisted the urge to Google the hell out of Gideon after Dani's Facebook post's wildfire, beyond doing an image search for Jessica.

Hell, the post had ended up on Instagram too. Probably even on

Twitter. All over the dang world, it seemed like. I still couldn't believe it had become as huge a deal as it had.

Her dad had an impressive physique for sure. I had intimate knowledge of just how good he felt up close and personal. But just how famous was her mom?

Ugh. So many questions. I really hated having standards in morality. A lot.

Vee seemed to understand I was at a loss. She jumped in. "Sore?"

Dani shrugged. "A little."

"You probably overdid it. How about I fix you some breakfast?"

Dani's eyes lit up. "What kind of breakfast?"

Vee picked up Dani's crutch. "We have a full kitchen. Why don't you come help me make something special?"

"Thanks, Vee."

"Sure." She glanced over her shoulder at me. "You can get the rest put away before we open."

"Isn't that my line?"

"When it comes to you and Halloween, you lose time."

That was definitely a true statement. I dug out my phone and checked the time with an inward wince. People would be showing up for their morning coffee soon, and I was way behind.

One more thing I could blame on Gideon.

SEVEN

MACY

I WAS LITERALLY DRAGGING WHEN THE NOON HOUR CAME ALONG. Enough that I called in a marker and asked Rylee to cover for me. And because I had to make sure everyone was covered—and I was at least two people's worth—I called in one of my new part-time girls.

Dani had been remarkably great the whole morning. She'd read in the nook for a good bit of the day. Somehow she ended up starting a children's book hour and entertained a sobbing set of twins with her hilarious rendition of *Where the Wild Things Are*.

The frazzled mom had been so happy she'd bought cake pops for the five kids that sat down to listen as well.

My cash register liked it just as much as my throbbing head.

Vee and Dani hit it off so well that she was shadowing my baker more than me. I wasn't nearly as interesting once the Halloween decorations weren't a factor anymore. That and I didn't exactly know what to say to her.

Hey, I'm into your dad—is that cool?

But not too into him. I'm not looking for stepmom status.

I shuddered. God, no.

All I wanted was my bed and perhaps a shower. Between sleep

deprivation and irritation from crawling around in the dust, I was overdone in the worst way.

And somehow I had a date tonight.

I'd taken my phone out of my pocket to beg off more than once. Instead, I ended up easing Gideon's fears about my babysitting prowess via text.

Rylee breezed into the café. "I'm here."

I shoved my phone back into my butt pocket. "About time."

"Hey, I had to drag Gage out from under his latest pet project."

"You?"

She gave me a saucy grin. "No, that was this morning. Once I sent him to work with a whistle, he was all about the '67 Impala he's doing for some *Supernatural* ultra-fan. And of course because Gage is Gage, we've been watching the show."

"There's worse ways to spend an evening."

She laughed. "That is a fact. He even let me call him Dean and I played his angel."

"Okay, too much info." I shoved my frayed braid over my shoulder. "Wait, which angel?" I watched the show. It had my catnip in the title, for God's sake.

"The redhead. That Castiel dude would be a whole different scenario."

I snorted.

Rylee tied her apron on. "Seems like I'm having a better day."

"It's been busy."

Not as busy as when the abstastic dude next door had gotten a zillion likes on his photos—the number of likes on the post was somehow still growing, I'd just checked—but we were doing okay.

"Didn't sleep, huh?"

"Do I ever?" I finally locked my espresso portafilter under the correct chamber. It took three tries.

Rylee shoved me out of the way. "Go upstairs before you burn your-damn-self. You look like death."

"Thank you."

She huffed out a breath. "Don't make me worry about you."

"I just need a few hours down. I'll be fine." I wasn't sure what I was going to do about the kid. I couldn't leave her alone here. I was responsible for her.

I dug out my phone and tossed off a quick text to Gideon about when he was relieving me. I didn't want to bug him, but I was nearly cross-eyed.

My phone buzzed in my hand.

2PM. Sorry, he got held up. I'll make it up to you tonight. Promise.

Yeah. About that date, buddy.

It'll be worth it. Don't back out—you already said yes.

I hung my head. When I looked up, Rylee was standing in front of me. "What?"

"You're on your phone."

"Yeah. So?"

She snatched it out of my hand.

"Hey."

She thumbed through the texts. "Date?"

I plucked it out of her hand. "What of it?"

"You have a date with Gideon? Holy crap. It's about freaking time."

"Would you help a customer or something? That's what I called you here for." I did not want to have a conversation about my date. I didn't even want to define what things were between us, let alone dissect it.

"What are you wearing?"

"Clothes."

She rolled her eyes. "What kind of clothes?"

I glanced down at my jeans and sugar skull fox shirt I was wearing. "Whatever is next in my drawer."

"You wound me on nine different levels."

"Yeah, well, my girl genes got ground up with my All Hallow's Eve blend three years ago. I had to sacrifice them to the dark lord." About the time my ex ground my heart to dust. Seemed fitting that I'd create my darkest and best coffee ever.

"Sounds like you. Us mere mortals rejoiced, because that's the only thing that kept me alive while Hayley was cutting her first damn tooth."

My chest tightened. There had been a time when I'd done the same. Sleepless nights, thanks to an ear infection or upset tummy. So damn long ago.

I slammed the door on those emotions. It was just easier to forget about that part of my life. Crescent Cove was my fresh start. God, I really must have been starved for sleep to let the memories surface after so long.

"Well, not even AHE can help me today. I'm going to take the kid upstairs with me. Trick will keep her appeased, I hope."

"Kid?" Rylee twisted around and scanned the café.

"Gideon's daughter is hanging with me today."

"Did I enter another dimension?"

"Shut up. I'm too tired to banter."

"No, seriously." She lifted onto her toes and craned her neck to look over the customers waiting at the counter. "What does she look like?"

"Guess."

Ry tucked her inky hair behind her ear. "Is she a mini-me deal?"

"Nope."

She dropped back on her heels. "You're not helpful."

I spotted Dani with her left leg draped over the arm of the couch. She looked bored as hell. "I'm good with that." I walked out from behind the counter to the dining room and did a sweep of mugs and plates on my way over to her.

I gritted my teeth through a few smiles at my regulars, but they were used to my less than chatty moods. Dani, not so much.

"Hey."

She sat up and swung her leg down, a blush firing up her neck. "Hi."

"Don't worry, you can't hurt that couch. Not sure a flamethrower could."

Dani giggled. "You're funny."

"Not to most people."

She giggled again. The sound of it was a balm. And again, my exhaustion had to be at epic proportions if that was a thought in my head. "What do you think about crashing upstairs with my cats and *The Princess Bride* for a few hours?"

"Cats?" She bounced up, hopping on her right foot. "How many?"

"Two."

"Cool. Dad won't let me have one. Says he would have to be the one to take care of it. I mean, I told him I would, but he doesn't believe me." She grabbed her crutch without me reminding her, which told me she was probably feeling the ankle deal more than she let on.

Could kids have drugs? What kind? I knew about baby Tylenol, but what if you were more of a middle of the road age like Dani?

Ugh. Why the hell was I in this predicament? I wasn't the mothering kind anymore.

She hopped along beside me. "What are your cats' names? What's *The Princess Bride*?"

"You know about *Army of Darkness*, but not the second-best movie known to man?"

"What's the first?"

"*Halloween*."

"Oh my God." She wrapped her arm around my waist and *Velcro*-ed herself to my side. "You are the coolest person I've ever met."

"You need to get around a bit more, kid." Her gleaming smile remained unchanged, but I hugged her back for a second before slipping away. "Can you do stairs?"

"Yes. As long as there's a railing."

"Then we're a go for my apartment."

There was a fairly decent network of apartments above my café.

The owner, Gavin Forrester, had slowly been renovating all of them. I'd taken one of the larger corner units.

In the end, it had been worth it.

I led her upstairs to my floor and down the hallway to the quiet nook I guarded like the cranky gargoyle I could be. It was my one oasis in a busy life. I tried everything to settle my brain against the incessant insomnia I dealt with.

On the door, a wreath of ivy had year-round bats nestled in the greens. Dani grinned as she reached for one of the fuzzy rubber pieces. I braced for her to mishandle it like any kid, but she only brushed the tips over her fingers along the wing before waiting patiently for me to open the door.

I unlocked the door and a black blur shot across the wide-open living area.

"Whoa."

"That's Trick. She's a little shy at first, but she'll come out." I tossed my keys in the smoky gray bowl inside the door and automatically set my cell on the recharging pad. "Are you hungry?"

She shrugged. "Depends."

I kicked off my sneakers. "I'm not Vee, but I can manage a few things."

Dani twirled on her good foot, taking in the high ceilings and web of twinkle lights I'd carefully woven through the rafters I'd convinced Gavin to put in. They were faux beams but gave the space a great structure and had given him plenty of ideas to use on the other apartments.

Instead of making them all carbon copies of each other, he was making each one individual. Another job that Dahlia had been working on in small doses.

She'd helped me with the café and my own apartment. She actually put me to shame with her gothic touches. It had taken almost two years to get my apartment just right, but in the end, it was pretty perfect for me.

"Are those...monsters?" Dani didn't seem to know the term for the corner statues I'd tucked on the floor-to-ceiling bookcases.

"Gargoyles."

"So cool."

I grinned. "I need a shower. Think you can amuse yourself for a few?"

She hopped her way over to my stereo. "You said movies. Where's the TV?"

I crossed to the projector tucked in one of the bookcases. "I've got one better." I flicked it on and the large white wall across the room was filled with the menu on my Apple TV.

"Holy crapballs."

I handed her the remote. "I bet you know how to use this."

"Yep." She plucked it out of my hand and hobbled over to my oversized beanbag chair and dropped into it with a laugh. "You have like every movie ever."

"Not quite." I crossed my arms and tried not to think about how cute she looked in my space. It had been a damn long time since anyone under twenty-four had been in my apartment. Even the new moms in my life rarely brought their kids over.

Mostly because my place would probably scare a lesser child.

I had a large collection of monster memorabilia as well as undying devotion to the macabre in its various forms. Anything from sugar skulls to antique glass. I had them all tucked in corners and on shelves like other women had knickknacks.

Dani Gideon looked damn comfy in my apartment though. She flicked through all my movies at the speed of a distracted teen, finally stopping on the *Saw* series.

"No."

"Aww, come on."

"No torture por—movies."

"I've seen worse."

"I doubt it, but good try."

She squinted at me.

"Don't make me try and figure out the parental lock. I'm very good at passwords. You'll never figure it out."

She sighed. "All right."

"Try *The Princess Bride*. I promise you'll like it."

She made a face but scrolled down to the movie and pressed play.

Making a pit stop in the kitchen, I found a bag of fruit snacks and peanut butter crackers. My fridge pretty much held coffee drinks in various forms, but I found a bottle of chocolate milk that was still within a good date.

I brought them back out to Dani, who was already engrossed in the movie. She was twisted around in the chair on her belly with her feet swaying as Trick slowly crept over to check her out.

I trusted my cat. She was the sweet one of the duo. Isis was still missing, but she probably wouldn't make an appearance. She didn't like strangers. Very much like her mama.

"This should keep you out of trouble. I'll be back in fifteen."

She accepted the chocolate milk with excited eyes. She Gumby-ed her way into a cross-legged stance and gave a delighted laugh when Trick hopped into her lap.

"She likes you."

"What's her name?" She coasted her hand down my onyx-colored cat.

"Trick."

The cat instantly began a motorboat purr. Her bright green eyes were mere slits as she accepted the small human's endless strokes.

"She'll let you do that for hours."

"That's okay. I can keep doing it."

"I bet." I set the snacks onto the table between the couch and the beanbag chair. "None for the cat. She has treats on the kitchen island though. She can have a handful."

"Cool." Not that they seemed inclined to move. Dani's attention was already back on the movie, and Trick had curled into a ball in the bowl of her legs.

I padded down the hall, my stocking feet quiet on the cheetah print runner. More antique mirrors lined the walls with stained glass accents. Some had little shelves that held tiny cat statuaries, as well as other animals like elephants and giraffes.

Whenever I went out to find things for the café, I always ended up finding something ridiculously miniature that ended up in my collection.

Isis wrapped herself around my ankles as soon as I entered my bedroom. I bent and lifted her, then absently tucked her onto my shoulder where she liked it best.

I took my huge purple robe off the back of the door and headed into the bathroom. She jumped neatly onto the black marble countertop and licked her paw.

"How was your day?"

She gave me her usual eerie yellow-eyed stare and continued her personal grooming.

"Mine was the same. Well, save for the little human I brought home. Be nice to her. I'm fairly sure her dad would be displeased with Dani going home with the same map of scratches that I own."

Isis rolled over onto her back and stretched herself out until she slid into the sink. She held her face under the faucet and stared at me.

"I have to take a shower."

She blinked at me and I rolled my eyes. I turned the tap on to the barest hint of a drip and she lapped at the water like the spoiled princess she was. I gave her a minute then turned off the faucet.

She batted at my hand, but I ignored her for the sheer heaven of my own shower. I turned both of my body shower heads onto full blast and stepped into the steaming water.

I flipped the switch to turn the rain hood on and simply stood under the water for a few minutes. Exhaustion weighed me down, and I swayed slightly in the stall.

I'd gone too many nights without sleep in a row. I needed at least four hours down, or I'd end up falling face first into whatever food Gideon picked for us to eat. Diner? Spinning Wheel? Maybe even the steakhouse at the edge of town.

I wasn't overly particular, but I wouldn't make it through the salad portion in my current state. If that was what we were doing. Gideon seemed a standard fare kind of guy.

Dinner. Awkward conversation. Maybe I'd invite him back here to bang it out.

I wasn't stupid. I knew that was where we were heading. The minute we'd gotten our hands on one another, I'd known it would be part of our future in some form or another. I just wasn't sure how the steps were going to go. Or the duration of it.

One and done? I tipped my head back under the water. Or a trio of secret bangs so our friends and neighbors didn't link us up like the other fallen idiots infesting this town?

I lathered my hair and the familiar honey and milk scent of my shampoo filled the steamy air. I wasn't like Rylee and her sister with their potions and weeping credit card to Sephora. I was more of a six-dollar bottle of shampoo and conditioner kind of girl. It did the job and didn't break the bank.

I preferred to put my extra cash into my dream projects like The Haunt. It was a legacy I could leave behind, unlike my parents who hadn't had more than a pair of pennies to rub together.

Between the medical bills for my father, and the shitbox apartment my mother could barely afford to pay for, we'd struggled most of my life. Eventually, my dad had withered away from his weak heart.

Nolan, my brother, had been the first to get out. He'd sent back money to help when he could, but he'd been more interested in his metal art sculptures that he made from pieces at scrapyards than keeping a steady job.

I'd stuck around to take care of my mom and had fancied myself in love with one of my brother's friends. I'd been too much in my own way to see I was falling into the same patterns as my mom.

Caretaker. Support system. Doormat. It was really all I'd ever known.

The burn of tears sideswiped me. I hadn't allowed myself to think about Chicago for a damn long time. I doused my tears with the spray as I washed away the conditioner and suds of my bath wash.

After my mom had died from exhaustion and her own heart issues —hers more of a broken heart instead of the corrosive damage of drugs and alcohol like my father—I'd turned to building a life with the one man I thought loved me.

Lou had taught me that pain was relative. I'd already grieved for my parents long before they'd found their way into their matching cemetery plots. Losing my parents had been nothing close to the sledgehammer of pain he'd provided. I'd left everyone and never looked back.

And that was where my damn memory lane ended.

I obviously wasn't fit for anyone tonight. I'd just tell Gideon the date wasn't happening. Maybe I'd even get more than four hours of sleep.

Right. I'd be lucky to get ninety minutes.

I rested my head against the glass door of my shower for a second before opening it and slipping into my fuzzy, ancient terrycloth robe. I took care of my usual post-shower routine as I drip-dried.

Isis daintily licked droplets of water off my ankles while I brushed and flossed. I'd definitely taken way longer than fifteen minutes due to my stupid brain.

I quickly wrapped my hair up in a towel and rushed down the hall to check on my charge.

She was curled up in the beanbag chair with Trick tucked behind her shoulder. Both were sleeping soundly while Wesley and Inigo battled in a test of wills and swordplay.

The quick rap on my door had me tugging on the tie of my robe. Then again, I didn't know how I was doing the handoff with Gideon.

I peered through the peephole and winced.

"Crap." I looked over my shoulder. The kid was still out.

I swung the door open as I gathered the lapels of my robe together tightly. "Hey."

Gideon's gaze swept me quickly. I wasn't sure if he was hard up or what. I was definitely not rocking an outfit to get that heated stare. I backed up, lifting my finger to my lips.

He tucked his hands into pockets, looked around the room and then backed up. "Shoes?"

I tried not to get gooey that he actually had enough manners to ask. "You're good."

He nodded and came in again. He smelled of paint and something with aerosol. Black and red spattered his white shirt and jeans, smudged his fingers, and dotted his beard.

I pressed my lips together. "Hard at work?" I whispered.

He looked down at himself. "Yeah. I texted you to bring her down, but you must have been in the shower." He took a quick step closer. "If I wasn't dirty as hell, I might ask what's under the robe."

"Wouldn't that be the definition of dirty?"

His lips quirked in that almost smile of his. "Don't tempt me to kiss you in front of my kid for a second time in the space of twelve hours."

"She's currently staring at the inside of her eyelids, so I think we're ok."

"So, I can steal a kiss?" He toyed with my purple belt.

"You smell like a paint can."

"Hazards of the job. Especially when my client likes blood spatter and black everywhere."

"Does that mean you're getting closer to done?"

"Closer than we were yesterday."

I huffed out a sigh. Ever the elaborator, that was Gideon. "Can I at least come over and see?"

"Nope."

"You know I am technically the boss in this situation."

His eyebrow hiked up toward his hairline, but he didn't answer.

I glanced down at his attire. "Is that what I have to look forward to tonight?"

"I promise to shower."

"No other details?"

"Nope."

It was on the tip of my tongue to tell him that the date thing was a bad idea. We worked together, and Crescent Cove had a habit of playing cupid whether it was well-timed or not.

In fact, I probably should rethink the naked mamba part of things with him too. The law of averages was damning for any and all of the couples I knew.

Especially since he was obviously potent. The proof was ten feet away from us.

He lowered his mouth to the line of my jaw and tugged my towel free from my hair. It tumbled in a mass of dark ropes around my shoulders, the cold strands going right into the neck of my robe.

I shivered. Obviously because of my cold hair.

That was my damn story and I was sticking to it.

"I like the scent of you fresh from the shower. Then again, I like when you smell like coffee too." He handed me the hair towel.

I dragged in a breath, but before I could step back, he retreated. And just like that, he went into dad mode, leaving me off balance as usual.

He crouched in front of his sleeping daughter. "Hey, sweetheart. Ready to go see Grumps?"

Dani tucked her hand under her cheek with a grumble. "Sleeping."

He tugged on one of her pigtails. "Come on, kiddo. We took up enough of Macy's time today."

Trick burrowed further into the space behind Dani's neck. "Looks like neither of them want to get up."

Dani giggled at the wriggling cat. "Can I have a cat, Daddy?"

"We've talked about it."

"I swear I'll take care of it."

He sighed. "We'll see."

She sat up and gathered the cat into her lap. "That means no."

"No, it means we'll see."

She pressed a kiss to the top of Trick's head. "Can I come see her again?"

"Sure," I answered before there was a meltdown.

Gideon looked up at me. "Don't make that promise. She'll never let you forget it."

I shrugged. "She likes the company. I mean, if you want."

"I want." She lifted Trick as she struggled to get her butt out of the hole she'd made in the beanbag chair. I took Trick from her before the cat got pissy.

Trick settled into the crook of my arm where she liked it best, and

Dani gave me the big cow eyes I hated. She stood on her tiptoes and gave the cat a kiss. "I'll see you tomorrow."

"Might not be tomorrow, squirt," Gideon said with a wince.

"What if Karen is still sick tomorrow? Am I staying with Grumps?" She hissed as she stepped on her ankle.

"We'll figure it out."

"She's fine at the café if you get in a bind."

Gideon stood. "Are you sure?"

I shrugged. "She created a whole children's reading hour today. There may be a riot if she doesn't come back."

"Is that so?" He ruffled Dani's bangs.

She batted his hand away. "Better than crying kids. Besides, she's got good books."

Brewed Awakening had become a bit of a local library since my patrons had been using it as a dumping ground for old books. I didn't mind. I'd stolen a few books off the shelves myself for the nights when sleep wouldn't come.

So, that would be a damn lot of books lately.

Between the stress of The Haunt and my own inability to turn my brain off, sleep was non-existent. I yawned as if on cue.

Gideon scooped his daughter up, somehow managing the crutch too. "Looks like you might need a nap before tonight."

"Yeah, about tonight." Trick wiggled out of my hold and zipped across the room. I didn't know what to do with my hands now.

"Nope. No renegging."

I twisted my wet towel. "I guess I'll see you later."

"Dad, I don't need you to carry me."

"Indulge me." He hooked Dani onto his hip, her long legs dangling even with Gideon's height. "Say thank you to Macy."

"Thanks for watching me. Even if I don't need a babysitter."

I tried to hide my smile. I understood how it was to want to be grown up before your time. I'd been the same to try to make things easier on my mom. "You're welcome."

"I'll see you later."

I rushed ahead of them to open the door. "Right."

Dani waved at me then at Trick, who'd reappeared to wind around my ankles. "Bye Trick."

With one more smile over his shoulder, Gideon disappeared down the hallway to stairs.

I looked down at my cat. She was obviously contemplating a trip after them. Before she could dash, I scooped her up and closed the door. "We are taking a nap."

Trick's green eyes were unreadable, but she seemed amenable. Five minutes later, were were all piled in my bed—Isis had joined the party now that the enemies had left the field. I'd traded my robe for an old Garfield nightshirt and blinked out before my head hit the pillow.

Ten minutes later, Rylee was shaking my shoulder. At least it felt like it. "There better be blood or fire involved."

"What?" Rylee hopped on my bed.

"Why are you waking me up?" I pulled the pillow over my head. It was so hard for me to actually sleep, but the fact that I'd blinked out half a second after Gideon left did not bear scrutiny.

Nope. Not at all.

"Uh, you have a date?"

"So." I lifted the pillow to look at my bedside clock. "I have two hours. Go away."

"Nope. I'm here to girlify you."

"I've been dressing myself for a long time. I'm good."

She smacked my ass. "Nope. We're going to go with something a little more impressive than a rude T-shirt and yoga pants."

I sat up with a groan. "I have a nice ass. Yoga pants work."

"Jeans work better."

"Jeans are binding." I yawned and pushed my tangled hair out of my face. Sleeping while it was wet was never a good idea.

Rylee put her hands on her hips. "I have more work to do than I thought."

"Gee, thanks."

She grabbed her ocean-liner of a purse off the end of the bed. "Let's get to work."

"God, kill me."

"Nope, we're going to kill Gideon instead."

"It's our first date. Can we wait to slay him until I at least get a steak out of the deal?"

Rylee yanked me off the bed and pushed me into the bathroom. "I make no promises."

EIGHT

Gideon

"You're going on like a real date? With kissing and stuff?"

I pulled on my jacket and narrowed my eyes at Dani. "Not all dates have kissing, young lady."

"Boy, he sounds like a proper fuddy-duddy, doesn't he, Ginger Snap?" My dad didn't even look up from his newspaper.

I wasn't sure where he still found them, because the local paper had ceased daily operations. Probably some national paper. Leave it to my dad to want to stay informed.

My own life was insane enough.

"Be glad you're even allowed out, Danielle." I was more than a little salty that apparently, I was the only one in the known universe who didn't have a cool nickname for my daughter. "After that stunt you pulled—"

"But you're going on a real date. And you kissed Macy on TV. Toby was almost sure you used *tongue*." The expression on her face revealed the depth of her disgust. In case I didn't fully grasp it, she crossed her eyes and mimed gagging. "That's totally gross."

"You like Macy," I reminded her. Which really didn't address the whole kissing thing.

I kind of hoped that her mother would have the birds and the bees chat with her, ideally when she was eighteen or so. Okay, no, I knew I couldn't wait that long, and I also knew I couldn't depend on her mother to handle such an important task. Especially since I had no way of guessing what she might say to her.

Then again, I had no clue what to say either. Thank God she was just eight. I still had a little while to think of the best way to describe flat out lust, the kind that Macy seemed to inspire in me on a daily basis lately.

"She knows basically every horror movie. Is she your girlfriend now?" Before I could answer that, Dani stopped coloring in the book her grandfather had given her and frowned. "If you get married, will she adopt me?"

I didn't know why I laughed. It was tinged with more than a small amount of hysteria. "Macy isn't the marrying kind."

"Oh."

It was my turn to frown. She wasn't, was she? If anyone had asked me that question a month ago, I would've said Macy was the only person in town less likely to get married than I was. I'd done it once, and that was plenty. More than. I'd let impulse and desire and the fact we were having a kid push me to the altar. When my dad had questioned my good sense, I'd insisted that I loved her. I had, but probably not enough. When you love someone, protecting that love should be worth any fight. It should be more important than any risk.

Jessica had cheated on me, and she'd asked for forgiveness. I'd shut her down and requested a divorce and that had been that. Throughout, I'd only felt sadness and a terrible sense of relief that I could never tell anyone. Our getting married might've been a mistake, but the daughter we'd made was a gift. She was still one, even as she gazed up at me with her eyes asking far too many questions.

Then her mouth joined in.

"Does Macy like you? I mean, besides kissing you."

That was the question of the hour, wasn't it? Although I'd just thought of another question, and that one had my response sticking in my throat.

Had Dani heard about what I'd said about her mother cheating on me? Or worse, had she seen the actual clip? I had to hope that maybe Toby had just described it to her, and the idea of kissing was so abhorrent she wouldn't go looking for the evidence herself.

Not that I wouldn't deserve it if she did go looking. But she didn't deserve to be confronted with my stupid off-the-cuff remark. True or not, she would never hear anything bad about her mother from me—even if it killed me. Some days, I was nearly certain it might.

"I think you should let your dad get ready to go," my father said, peering out from behind his newspaper.

I looked down at myself. I wore my standard uniform of jeans, white T-shirt, and boots, with the addition of a jacket because it was a cool late August night. Autumn would be here soon, which was why I'd managed to pull off this particular date in the first place. "I thought I was ready to go."

"You look like you're headed to work."

"This is what I wear, Dad." It was almost impossible to keep the impatience out of my voice. "We're headed to a hayride—"

"What, noooooo." Dani threw down her crayon and crossed her arms. "You always go on the first hayride with me."

It wasn't a lie. Guilt attacked me with fists and claws as it so often did. "Not with that ankle. Next time, squirt," I promised as she screwed up her face. "You wanted me to have a date, right?"

It was probably cheating to use that against her—and I still needed to give her a stern talking to about why what she had done was wrong, no matter how good her intentions had been—but I was a desperate man.

On about sixteen levels, not the least of which was that I'd packed fresh condoms in my wallet. Which might have also made me ridiculous, since Macy and I had barely kissed a couple of times, yet I already thought—hoped—it was time to level up.

"Yeah, but we do the hayride together." Dani's chin wobbled as she reached down to itch under the edge of the bandage around her ankle, kicking up my guilt to the max.

"We'll go twice. Maybe even three times. You know how the first night usually sucks. Remember that time Mr. Ronson couldn't even get his chainsaw working?"

She giggled. "Yeah. But it was funny."

"Macy won't find it funny. She'll get pissed. Maybe I should call Sheriff Brooks and have him on standby." I was only half joking.

"I could come and help calm her down." Dani's big green eyes lifted to mine hopefully. "She likes me. Everyone likes the cute kid."

I had to laugh as I ruffled her hair, even knowing she hated it. Some habits wouldn't die no matter what. "And the modest one too. Thanks for the offer, but you better hang with Grumps tonight. He's back on the road tomorrow and he'll be gone, what is it now?"

"Three weeks, give or take." My dad folded up his newspaper and looked at Dani over his reading glasses. "Sure you aren't ready to travel the States with me, Ginger Snap? Think of all the fun we could have."

He was only kidding, but I still narrowed my eyes. Danielle was an impressionable kid, and I really didn't need her deciding a life riding around in a truck all day making long haul deliveries was more interesting than going to school. And interfering in her dad's love life, which actually wasn't going too badly now that the hungry women had stopped circling.

At least Macy and I were kissing, with an option for condoms. Possibly, by the year 2023.

"No, I have to get all As to get into college." Dani resumed coloring. "But you can buy me stuff, like from where you go."

"Oh, can I now?"

"Yes, please. Thank you."

I shook my head and looked down at my clothes again. "Fine, I'll change my shirt."

They exchanged a glance as I shed my jacket and went back upstairs to my bedroom. It wasn't as if my dresser drawers held a ton of other options. I owned a couple of pairs of sweats and more jeans just like these, plus a black pair. Shirts-wise, most were plain white like the ones I wore to work. I did have a couple of concert tees, most of which hadn't seen wear since I'd last been to a concert about five years ago.

How pathetic was that?

I swapped my jeans for my black ones and my white shirt for a vintage Poison shirt that I'd had forever. Poison wasn't even cool anymore. Had they ever been cool? I wasn't sure. But it had to be better than wearing my work uniform on a date.

My dad had been right. As usual.

When I came back downstairs, Dad was sitting beside Dani on the couch, and she was curled into his side under the glow of the adjacent lamp. He was reading her a story, something about big trucks and ice demons. You know, your standard fare for an eight-year-old who had zero interest in fairies or princesses or handsome princes.

Thank God.

"Better?" I held out my arms wide.

"Yes," my dad said. "Though you should really try to improve your taste in music. What about The Beatles?"

Dani cocked her head. "Poison? Like to kill you? What a stupid name for a band."

I lowered my arms and grabbed my jacket off the chair. "Thanks for the vote of confidence, guys." I came over to Dani and kissed the top of her head before doing the same to my dad, mainly to make Dani laugh. "Wish me luck."

"Break a leg," Dani said seriously. "Though even a sprain hurts super bad, so I'm not sure a date is worth it. Also, can you bring me home a caramel apple?"

"Sure thing."

With that, I was off to Macy's, after giving my father a slew of assurances I wouldn't be late picking up Dani because he had to be up bright and early the next day. As if I didn't. Normally, Sundays were the one day I slept in then made breakfast with the kid, but the crew was behind on The Haunt after the clusterfuck of the last week. It was hard to keep to a schedule when your team had to constantly duck and weave due to single women wanting to snag a DILF.

Who knew?

I hit the open road in my truck and turned up the radio. It was a nice night, already chilly and would get chillier as the evening progressed. I could practically smell fall in the air and in the crunch of leaves under my tires. I wasn't one to rush summer along, especially considering how far behind schedule we were on the restaurant, but I couldn't deny that autumn brought with it a surge of new possibilities.

Including this one, that the impenetrable Macy Devereaux had not only kissed me a few times but had also appeared to actually enjoy it. She'd even agreed to a date. I didn't know if we'd just scratch our itch and be done with it, but right now, with the wind coming through the windows of my old truck and Springsteen on the radio, anything seemed in reach.

Grinning, I drove down Main Street in the Cove, humming along, tapping my fingers on the wheel. I was already eager to see Macy and get a full-barreled dose of her snark when we had an entire evening to be alone.

Well, as alone as we'd be with our fellow hayride attendees and Jason Voorhees and Michael Myers and whomever else lurched out of the darkness. I wasn't a huge horror fan like my daughter or Macy, but even I could enjoy a night of being entertained out in the woods.

And if that led to some making out in the woods…let's just say I wasn't averse.

My smile lasted until I pulled up in front of Brewed Awakening, already prepared to drive around back and look for parking. Like I usually did. I'd never showed up here to pick up Macy for a date, but otherwise, everything was like normal.

Then I glimpsed the white stretch limo gliding up to the curb. The driver stopped and climbed out to open the back door for his passenger.

Huh. Who the hell could that be? It was far too early for homecoming dances, and besides, did anyone take limos to those? I thought that was solely reserved for the prom.

And for my ex, who floated out of the car and stood on the sidewalk, patting her lacquered hair and glancing around as if she couldn't believe her spaceship—sorry, limousine—had landed in the center of small town, USA.

She wasn't the only one. I was finding it hard to believe myself.

"Jessica."

She didn't hear me at first, since she was bickering with her driver. Probably debating if this could really be the right place.

We'd met when I lived a few hours away from here, near New York City where Jessica had been filming a movie at the time. She'd bought a small place outside the city that she intended to use as a hideaway and had contacted me through a reference from a friend of a friend to redo her fireplace and the surrounding built-ins.

I wished I could say we'd had a lengthy courtship—if you could call it that—but we'd been lovers within a matter of days. I'd moved in not long after that. Within six months, she was pregnant with Dani and we were married.

Looking at her now, staring at me as if I was a stranger, I wondered how I'd ever been that young and naive.

Or just stupid.

"Jessica," I said again, and this time, she tilted her head, her gaze sweeping over me in that thorough way that had once heated my blood.

Now all I felt was cold.

"John." Her voice matched the chill at my back. "I drove by your place. Your truck wasn't there."

"So it wasn't, because I was on my way here." I moved forward, my steps measured and unhurried even as my heart thudded dully in my ears. "Have you stopped using phones?"

"We needed to chat in person." She stepped away from her driver and I half expected a hulking bodyguard to emerge from the bushes as she approached me. Imagine a star of her caliber walking around freely in a dangerous town like Crescent Cove. "Since things have changed recently."

I set my jaw. "Have they?"

She gestured to Brewed Awakening. "Does this place serve

espresso? The real stuff, not the watered-down kind most Americans favor."

Oh, she and Macy would get along so very well. "This is a very high-end coffee bar, so yes, they serve whatever suits your palate."

"Is that so?" Jessica wrinkled her nose as she stared at the Jason hockey mask hung over the ornate light adjacent to the coffee shop entrance. "I wouldn't have guessed, since it's so…quaint."

"As is the owner, whom you'll be meeting soon enough." I didn't glance at my watch, but I knew I wasn't more than a few minutes early.

If I wasn't at Macy's door right on the dot, she'd come down into the café and soon realize why I thought marriage was the gateway to certain doom. More precisely, marriage to Jessica Kyle. I wouldn't blame anyone else for my negativity.

"Well, then, let's go inside and chat." Jessica gave a quick nod to her driver. "I shouldn't be long. If anyone questionable approaches the car, deal with them as you see fit." With that, she flounced toward the café door.

I wasn't one to demonize people. In fact, my father had always accused me of seeking the good even to my own detriment. I'd obviously once believed Jessica had many positive qualities or I wouldn't have married her. But it seemed like those particular attributes had been hidden under fur and jewels and pretension, and I wasn't at all eager to find out what had brought her to my town.

I followed her inside and met her at the counter, where she was already ordering a quad shot latte and "one of those adorable little scones". A very pregnant Vee was helping her, and she arched a brow at me when I stopped at Jessica's side. There was plenty of space between us, but I wanted to get this over with as fast as humanly possible.

Preferably before Macy came downstairs and schooled Jessica on how out of her depth she was.

We chose a table in back, closest to the pass-through that led to the apartments upstairs. I didn't relish Macy coming downstairs and seeing me seated with another woman on our date night, but I also wasn't going to squirrel away in a shadowy corner.

If Macy and I were going to make some kind of go at this—or hell, even if we were going to fuck each other's brains out and part as reluctant friends—I intended to keep all my cards firmly on the table. That was the only way I knew how to be. Especially after my unintended near miss with Macy regarding not telling her right away about Dani.

"You don't want a drink?" Jessica sipped hers and made a face. "I see why. It's not total swill, but definitely not like Paris."

"I'm sure Macy will be heartbroken at your assessment." I leaned back in my chair and slung an arm over the back. Already I was antsy to get this over with. "So, why are you here with no warning?"

"What, I can't visit my own baby girl without scheduling it first?"

"According to the courts, no."

"You've always been so rigid, John. Were you this tedious while we were married?" Before I could respond, she hurried on. "All the more reason I couldn't wait any longer to visit. I have concerns."

My gut tightened as if it was being twisted by a fist. "Such as?"

Jessica trailed a glossy pale pink nail along the edge of her china cup. She must've asked for one like that, since Macy's collection of cups for in house drinks were on the funky, eclectic side. Not tiny and fussy with little roses. "What's this media circus you've subjected my daughter to? I have to say, I expected more from you than airing dirty laundry—ancient dirty laundry to boot. Irreconcilable differences are no excuse to potentially harm my child."

Out of the corner of my eye, I noticed Vee creeping closer with a tray of drinks precariously balanced on her baby bump. I nearly rose to help her, but she edged away before I could.

"Your child is our child, and I have no clue what you mean."

"Oh, really. You don't recall telling Tillie Neusbottom—what kind of name is that, by the way—that your ex-wife cheated on you while you were live on camera? I'm surprised you would be so tacky, but I suppose small towns have a way of doing that to you."

I leaned forward, narrowing my eyes as my muscles locked. A

common reaction to Dani's mother, but this time was worse than ever before. "What exactly do you want?"

"Are you denying you subjected my girl to a media firestorm thanks to your libido?" She looked down her ski-jump nose at me. "No wonder Dani was so worried about you and your hermit lifestyle, if you think the way to find someone is to announce your desperation on Facebook."

"Dani was worried about me, hmm? If you know that much, then you probably won't be shocked to find out *our* daughter decided to make that post for me. Also, I wasn't the one to give her your old phone, and I wasn't the one who was probably filling her head with God knows what." I clenched my jaw. "Like saying I looked sloppy. That was a particularly nice one."

"I don't recall using those exact words."

I shifted in my seat. It was taking everything I possessed to not take off. Hell, I'd prefer to meet Macy somewhere rather than sit here.

"Right."

"Well, for God's sake, look at yourself. Do you even shave anymore? And a Poison T-shirt? Are you actually serious right now? On top of that, you're blaming my child for what you obviously did because you're starved for attention." Her pursed lips as she looked me up and down told me her thoughts on that score exactly. "Which means your focus isn't where it should be—on my daughter."

"Starved for attention, is it? Is that what you believe?"

Macy's voice from behind me had my spine stiffening, although it turned to liquid when she took advantage of my sideways position at the table to slide onto my lap.

Macy Devereaux was on my lap. In public. In her own café.

She wore some killer outfit I couldn't quite process. Dark blue jeans with slashes in the thighs. A black off-the-shoulder top with her hair in an updo that left her neck distractingly bare, allowing her spicy cinnamon scent to tease me mercilessly. I couldn't imagine a cinnamon perfume, but such a thing had to exist because if I lowered my head and sniffed, she smelled like fucking sin.

"Hi, I don't think we've met. I'm Macy. And you are?" Macy

dropped her big purse on the table with enough force to make Jessica's china cup rattle, and she reared back in her chair as if Macy was a cobra about to strike.

Which it turned out she was, just not the way Jessica thought.

Before Jessica could reply, Macy shifted toward me and stroked her fingertips over my bearded jaw. Her fingertips glittered with some shimmery polish, which was the last thing I saw before her mouth touched mine.

Actually, no. She feasted on me as if I was a piece of chocolate cake and she'd missed dinner.

Did I mind? Hell no.

Did I understand? Absolutely not.

But that didn't stop me from tilting my head and kissing her back without the slightest thought for my ex-wife or the rest of the patrons who had to be eating this up. I was too absorbed in Macy. Drowning in her and loving every second. A quick nibble on her bottom lip had her moaning into my mouth, and fuck, I went as hard as a pike.

A bang on the table had us jerking apart. Macy blinked at me like a startled cat, her blue eyes hazier than I'd ever seen them. Surprisingly soft and unguarded. Was that how she would look at me if I was inside her?

When. It was becoming an imperative at this point.

"Damn, you join the party fast," she said under her breath before shifting toward Jessica. She lifted her ass deliberately off my lap and slid more fully onto my thighs.

It took me a second, but when I got there, I had to grin.

"Sorry about that. So rude of me. What was I thinking? It's just my thing, you know, to greet my man when I see him for our first date. Surely you've seen the news?"

Jessica's barely there brows knitted together. "He's your man yet it's your first date? You run fast in this town." She flashed Macy a Cheshire smile. "Then again, I didn't date John until after he was 'my man' either. So, I totally understand, girlfriend."

Behind Macy, I tipped back my head. I'd thought the hell Dani had unleashed was bad? This was running a close second.

"I'm not your girlfriend, and I doubt you understand much if you think Gideon," Macy stressed the word as if Jessica was unfamiliar with it, "had to go on Facebook trolling for dates. He just has a very concerned child. Wonder why that is?"

"*My* child, you mean. The one we share. You sitting on his lap doesn't change that fact. It also doesn't alter the fact that if my daughter was concerned, she probably had reason to be—whether or not some thirsty small-town Betty thinks she's got him wrapped."

"Hey," I said to Macy, gripping her hip as she started to rise. And it wasn't to walk away, I was certain. She would lay Jessica flat out without breaking a damn nail.

"I got this." Macy waved me off.

"I know you do, Killer, but this is my mess." I stood and planted my hands on the table to lean toward my ex. "You're going to want to apologize to Macy. Right now. You might also want to get your story straight. Am I a sloppy hermit or horny and desperate? Seems like you keep switching stories."

Jessica slid her gaze past me to where Macy stood beside the table with her hands on her hips. "Judging from your choice of companion, I'll go with the latter."

Macy cracked her knuckles. "I have a rule about not allowing fisticuffs in my place of business. But I don't think it counts if I start them—or finish them." She took a step forward.

My arm shot out to block Macy just as Jessica unwisely chose to speak again.

"This is your café? Nice Jason mask outside. And all of these cute little Halloween decorations a season too early." She made a show of looking around before tapping her nail on the handle of her still mostly full latte cup. "Might want to spend more time on your coffee though. Your beans are burned."

Macy lurched forward. "Why, you bleached—"

"Enough," I snapped, earning a look of pure malice from Macy. "You don't want to do this," I told her in a low voice, well aware her body was humming beside mine as if she was a stun gun set on decimate.

"Oh, you're wrong. I very much want to do this."

I didn't doubt it, but I was beginning to grasp Jessica's intentions—at least in the pit of my stomach if nowhere else—and I couldn't let it happen. Not if it meant we were playing right into Jessica's twisted hands.

"Why are you here?" I asked quietly, refusing to give my ex the satisfaction of knowing how rattled I was.

Jessica didn't make cross-country trips for no reason. She also normally wasn't obsessed with my dating life—or lack thereof. If she was circling around that pond, trying any number of lures until she found one that worked, there was a purpose. She wanted something, and it didn't take a genius to figure out what.

The real question was *why*.

"Isn't it obvious?" Jessica got to her feet and gestured wildly. "You're out of control. Spreading untruths to the media, casting around for dates and hanging out with women with anger management issues, not to speak of a basic lack of class and taste."

Macy cocked her head and crossed her arms. "Looking at you, I'd say that's a compliment."

Jessica arched an eyebrow. "What movies have you been in, honey?"

"None. I also haven't seen you starring as a good parent either, *honey*, since I've been in Crescent Cove for years and I've never seen your face before."

Even as Macy said the words with a perfectly charming smile, my fists locked into fists at my side. The gauntlet had been thrown, and Jessica wasn't one to let it lie.

"I'm glad you mentioned that actually." Jessica tucked her clutch under her arm and stared at me until my throat constricted. I knew what was coming, felt it in my bones. "I don't see my daughter enough, and it's time I fix that. I want to alter our custody agreement, John. Equal split. Fifty/fifty."

While I reeled and tried to breathe through the shock and pain arcing through my chest, Jessica zeroed in on Macy. "Or maybe seventy-five/twenty-five, considering negative influences."

NINE

MACY

I'd been on a lot of first dates. More of those than any other actually, since most guys weren't fit for a second or third. At least not fit to my way of thinking. I was sure a lot of the men I'd tossed back into the lake would make some other chick very happy someday.

Me? I was kinda like that Garbage song, "Only Happy When It Rains." I wasn't miserable by nature, far from it. But I rather liked poking my head out of my trash can Oscar the Grouch-style and lamenting the general state of the world.

Yeah, so I looked for reasons to stay single. It was easier that way. Safer. Less problematic.

But I'd never had a guy show up for a first date and split before we'd even made it to dinner.

To be fair, Gideon hadn't left the property entirely. I knew that because Vee and I were crowded at the window beside the back door, watching as he paced and kicked at nonexistent rocks and twigs.

"You should go talk to him."

"And say what?"

"Well, I didn't hear everything that was said—"

"You liar. You probably attached a listening device to her cup when you served her."

Vee blinked her big eyes at me in the perfect picture of innocence. "I don't have a clue what you mean."

I snorted. "Right. Look, I appreciate your finely attuned hearing—probably mommy ears, right?—because it's what brought me downstairs in the first place. Although I didn't exactly help. I tried," I muttered, shutting my eyes against the sour flavor in my throat. It tasted an awful lot like regret. "I got a little jealous, okay, yeah. I mean, I had a date with the dude. Have," I corrected, despite that not being at all certain. "Seeing him with his ex kinda knifed me in the guts a little, but I dealt with it. She's just a stone-cold bitch."

Who wanted to take his kid from him, for at least half the year. If not more.

"I'm not a fucking negative influence," I added for good measure. "I'm an upstanding businesswoman who has added extensive value to this community. And so what if I have a Jason mask on the light outside? Is that a crime?"

"Definitely not." Vee gnawed on her thumbnail as she strained closer to the narrow window, pressing her rather large belly against the wall to get the best vantage point possible.

I snatched her arm and tugged her back. "Be careful. You'll crush them."

She laughed at me. Actually laughed. "You know, you could try letting someone else see your gooey caramel center. Just for a change."

"I don't have a gooey anything." I sniffed. Except I did, a side of myself I kept not only under lock and key but armored guard.

"Liar. I saw you on Gideon's lap. I'd say you were plenty gooey after that."

"Whole different kind of melting going on there, chick."

"Look at him." Vee jabbed one of her short rainbow-colored nails at the window.

I looked and my heart ached. I didn't like to admit I had anything in the center of my chest, preferring to believe that area was concave and/or possibly filled with coffee grounds, since I mainlined the stuff. But even I couldn't deny that taking in the hunched curve of Gideon's shoulders and the quick clip of his pacing feet made that stupid organ physically hurt for him.

It was partially my fault. I'd helped goad the tigress with the dark roots. She'd deserved every word that I'd blasted her with, but Gideon didn't. Dani didn't. If anything, I'd done had pushed Jessica to demand custody, I wouldn't be able to live with myself.

Like, oh, sitting on Gideon's lap like he was a prized steer.

And antagonizing Jessica.

And taunting her over her lack of mothering skills.

Minor things, really. Except not.

"I gotta go out there." I pushed my hair out of my eyes and rued that I couldn't shove my hands through it in frustration.

Rylee would kill me if I ruined her handiwork. Then again, she was probably upstairs asleep on my sofa, enjoying every minute of her few hours of freedom, and wouldn't know the difference.

Besides, the whole date thing was now in question. As was the possibility of using the condoms I'd packed just in case.

Unless my vibrator became a whole lot more animated, I doubted they'd be necessary.

"Yes, you do."

"Any tips?" I fiddled with my earrings.

Yes, I'd gone all out for this man. Lacy matching bra and panty set, the newest pair I owned. Earrings that weren't bats or ghosts or grim reapers, but dangling silver ropes.

"Let him talk." Vee turned toward me and inched up to lay her hands on my shoulders. "Don't 'Macy' him. The guy needs support, not snark."

"I should be insulted by your implication, but right now, I'll just gratefully take the advice." I tipped my forehead down to hers. "Thanks. Now go put your feet up and call your husband so he doesn't march down here with that adorable baby of yours and get more ovaries exploding in the café."

I walked outside and let the door swing shut behind me. Outside, the chilly August wind batted me back, making me grip the doorknob. I could still go back in. Let Gideon find me when he was ready.

If he was ready.

Hell, I had a power charger for my personal pleasure wand. Who needed men?

Then he turned and glanced my way, and the overhead lights along the back of my building illuminated the stark lines of his face. The hollows of his eyes. His clenched jaw.

And I couldn't turn away.

I made myself go over to him. To just stand at his side, since he'd finally stopped moving.

"You don't have to take me out tonight," I said hoarsely.

So, we were going with that as our way of offering support? Okay, then.

He worked his jaw before glancing down at me with hooded eyes. "The fuck I'm not."

I shivered, and it wasn't entirely from the breeze kicking up again. I didn't have a jacket, but the chill wasn't what made me swallow hard.

"It's too cold for this top, much as I like it." His gaze moved over my bare shoulder as thoroughly as a caress before he whipped off his jacket and tucked it around me. "Don't argue, Macy. Just do not. Not now."

I didn't. I just concentrated on breathing and not letting years of walls and protective barriers crumble under his hot, unflinching stare.

It wasn't even entirely due to him. I felt guilty and worried about him and Dani and conflicted about doing any of this considering our working relationship.

Considering I already wanted to scale him like a fence and put his post to *very* good use.

I wasn't stupid. I knew extreme sexual desire could make people do dumb things. I just hadn't been in that position for a long time.

Then again, positions—and thinking about the wide variety of them—was half my problem right now.

"Don't look at me like that either."

His voice was like a sandpaper touch against my too tight skin. "How?"

"Like you don't care what I say as long as I use my mouth in other ways."

I cleared my throat. "What kind of woman do you take me for?"

"An incredibly smart, savvy, beautiful one. Who I very much want to take out tonight, come what may." He ran a hand through his hair and cursed under his breath. "But it's all fucked now, because she wants to take my baby from me."

The pure agony in his voice had me laying a hand on his arm. He glanced down at it as if he didn't understand what I was doing. I didn't either.

This was simply fumbling in the dark.

"I messed up."

"Macy—"

"Let me finish. A little birdie told me you were in a spot with your ex. I'm a jealous bitch when I want to be. I guess that includes when the guy I'm going on a date with is chatting with a gorgeous Hollywood blond he happened to once be married to. Although I think her color is a bit brassy, to be honest."

The corner of his mouth ticked up. "I divorced her after she cheated on me with the pool boy. Can a story be more clichéd?"

"Oh, you'd be surprised," I said faintly, locking down any sudden needs to go to confession.

I didn't talk about Lou. Only Vee knew the barest bones, and that was because she'd been around right afterward. And okay, so did Rylee, but she was my best friend. There also might have been threats of blood loss involved. She'd been pregnant at the time, so she'd been in full-on savage mode.

"I don't have feelings left for her. If I could vaporize her with my mind and it not affect Dani, I'd probably do it just to save myself the aggravation of dealing with her. But most of the time, she's like that gnat you ignore because killing her would be more trouble."

I blinked. "That's specific. And because I'm me, oddly hot."

"I like you being possessive of me." His spicy cologne wafted toward me on the breeze.

And those shields that were wavering in his presence held up tiny white flags.

"It wasn't of you per se." Even I could hear the breathiness of my voice. I wasn't flirting so much as trying not to forget how to breathe.

"Uh huh. I was just the guy who asked you out."

"Right."

"The guy you keep kissing in front of God and Jason."

"I'm more of a Michael gal myself, but he'll do in a pinch. Also, you kissed me last time." He moved closer and my gaze bounced up to his. "I brought three condoms."

His dark eyebrow winged up. "Did you now?"

"No. Forget I said that. So, what about those Yankees?"

"I also brought condoms. Only two. Sounds like we should be in for a good night." He exhaled and looked somewhere over my shoulder. "I swear, it's like she sensed I could be happy for five fucking minutes and had to destroy it."

"I hope that's not a cautionary tale about your prowess."

He didn't laugh. Didn't so much as crack a smile. I wasn't sure he even heard me.

Sucking in a breath, I tightened my grip on his forearm. His eyes flashed to mine in the near darkness, broken only by the scatter of lights along the eaves of my coffee shop behind us. "I shouldn't have provoked the bear. It's a bad habit of mine."

"She came here with that in mind. It wasn't because of you. Dani's told me some weird things she's said lately. It's like she keeps going back and forth between my reclusive ways and my new player status, thanks to the media. Since acting is in her blood, I'm guessing she's been running lines to see which stuck. Tonight, she decided she'd go with me being more concerned about my love life than my daughter."

"Which is utter bullshit. You don't even date."

"Thanks for noticing, Killer."

"Do I lie?"

"No, not ever. Unlike me. I'm the guy who didn't tell you I had a kid. Or an ex-wife."

"Those weren't lies. Not exactly. Look, I say things when I'm horny and frustrated. Which means you might not want to speak to me right now. I've already made a ginormous disaster of the night. I nearly fought your ex. Like physically." I flexed the fingers of my free hand. "And no, there would've been no mud involved. Sorry."

"I didn't even ask. Although I'd like seeing you in mud. I'd prefer not to see Jessica at all. Ever." He shut his eyes. "Dani loves her."

"An unfortunate side effect of childbirth, I've heard."

"I don't want to keep her from her mother. For fuck's sake, I've worried she doesn't see her enough. It's not like I can provide her with that feminine touch thing as she gets older. Even if I'm not thrilled with the life Jessica leads and the environment in Hollyweird, she's still her mother. She has a period and understands all that female crap."

"I've never thought of understanding a menstrual cycle as a positive quality before."

"Try being a dude and you would." I started to remove my hand and he clamped his over mine, instantly warming it. "Don't close off from me."

"I'm not." Surely my voice wasn't that high-pitched.

"Wanting Jessica in Dani's life for her sake isn't the same as me wanting Jessica. I don't, in any shape or form. I don't hate her either. That would be just as bad as loving her, because that would mean she still had a hold on me. She's just someone I once cared about and made a kid with. The best part of my life." His grip on me tightened. "I can't lose her."

"You won't. You'll just tell them she's full of shit. You don't have a crazy love life—"

"Minus the swarm?"

"The swarm is gone."

"Minus the news story."

"That was a one-time thing."

"Minus the super hot brunette who I keep kissing and who isn't my girlfriend in any official sense."

I looked over my shoulder. "Don't get your panties twisted. I don't usually wear skinny jeans."

He still didn't laugh, and all at once, it hit me squarely in the stomach how badly I wanted him to. He wasn't one of those guys who had a ready smile, but the rare moments one broke free were all the more appreciated.

Now his eyes were so heavy and dark, the spring green of his irises nearly swallowed by his pupils in the low light. And I wasn't one for metaphors, but that wasn't the only part of him getting lost.

"She's not going to take your daughter from you." Tentatively, I stroked the back of his hand, still possessively clamped over mine on his arm. "The reason you have custody of her for the bulk of the year is because you're a damn good father. Even I can tell that, and I've only seen you with her a few times. Although I think maybe grounding her over that Facebook stunt would've been wise. Next time, she might try to enroll you in *America's Got Talent*."

The faintest quiver of his lips eased the constriction in my chest, just a little. "I don't have any talents appropriate for that show."

He probably didn't intend for that to be a sexual innuendo but tell that to my out of control hormones. "You don't say."

"Jessica isn't entirely wrong. Maybe I'm not giving Dani the best example." When I started to argue, he shook his head. "I haven't brought a woman around her in years. I mean, she has her aunt Alicia, but she travels all the time for work, just like our dad. I haven't had a date in what feels like a lifetime."

"You're on one right now, remember?"

"Oh, I do." His fingers curved under my palm on his arm. Any minute now, my hand would start to sweat and not just from warmth.

This man had an ability to rattle me like none other.

"I need that whole Facebook mess to go away. It would help if I could present a calm, stable home life for my daughter to the judge if it gets that far. A balanced one."

"You mean like you actually have? Didn't see any evidence of you having wild swingers' parties, unless I missed something."

"No, but it wouldn't hurt for her to have a female influence. I didn't want to be the guy who brought strange women in and out of her life, and I still don't. But she already likes you."

There was no missing the note of hope he tacked onto the end of that sentence. "Yeah, and?"

"And I like you. And you like me, I think."

"I wouldn't run you over with my car, no."

Now he did grin. The sight of it after waiting so long for a sliver in the dark cloud that had descended over him made me release a long breath. "There's a sentiment you don't see on Hallmark cards."

"I offered to write for them, but I think my application got lost in the mail."

"I just bet." He lifted his hand and I thought he was going to touch my face, but instead, he brushed a loose strand of hair out of my eyes. My cheek tingled as if he'd caressed me just the same. "It would help a lot if we could date. Just in case Jessica follows through and contacts the judge, which I have to think she's serious about if she's in town."

The faintest bit of panic tickled the back of my throat. I swallowed hard to make it dissipate. Dating was fun. Lighthearted. No kind of commitment.

I wasn't good at those, and most men I'd been involved with definitely weren't. So, it was better if that word never came up.

"Well, since we are on a date right now, this should qualify. Though you kind of conned me into it, and we haven't actually done anything date-like yet."

"Conned you by asking you straight out?"

"In a manner of speaking."

Finally, he lifted my hand off his arm, but not to offer me any sort of respite. He brought it to his lips and kissed my knuckles, his gaze roving over my face. "I'll ask you this straight out then. Let's date. No pressure. No stress. No worries about dramatic breakups when I catch you cheating with the pool boy."

I narrowed my eyes. "It's almost fall, so pools are closing. I also don't even have one, never mind a 'boy.'"

"Even better."

I nearly replied 'or dramatic breakups after I catch you using the copier as a sex bench with your ex.' It wasn't exactly first date material either, but why stand on ceremony?

Except it felt like he had enough baggage that I might as well leave mine at the curb.

"I don't really get what you're asking. We haven't even had one date yet. And no offense, I know there are extenuating circumstances and all, but I'm not even sure about the second never mind agreeing to a string of them."

"You will be. I have plans."

I arched a brow. "Do they involve eating? My stomach is about to chew through my sternum."

"Sure. We'll date as long as it feels good—or until Jessica decides she isn't interested in any more parenting time than she already has." He kissed the tips of my fingers and the zing went straight up my arm and down into regions of my body that had no morals. "Or we can put a date on it, depending how things go. With an option to extend of course. Like Halloween."

"Put a date on it. A date for when we stop dating, although it might be before if Jessica climbs back on her broom and flies away." Even as I said the words, my brain was whirling.

He was setting up a scenario to prove something he shouldn't have to. So what if he didn't have a woman in his life? He was just as capable of raising his daughter alone as millions of women were without a partner.

But I was no dummy. I knew judges often sided with mothers in cases like these. And I didn't know if her money and possible influence would make a difference, but they usually did in most other things, so why not here?

Still, I was wary enough about dating. So, my first foray into it in how long would have artificial parameters that looked good to the outside world? Then again, no messy breakup. No concerns about having to kick his ass out of my personal life while he was still working to get my restaurant ready for opening day.

"It seems messy. Potentially dangerous. You can't put boxes around feelings. Stuff happens when you date. Why I don't do it."

"You mean you might get feelings for me?"

I couldn't respond fast enough. "No. Of course not. I mean you might get feelings for *me*."

"I'll take my chances. Besides, we're smart, logical people. We'll have fun for a couple months and go our separate ways after if it has run its course. You'll look very good for me in front of the judge. Successful businesswoman and all. Completely upstanding. Not a negative influence even a little bit."

Although I knew he'd said it to tease me, I instantly remembered how I'd helped to get him into this mess—or at least I hadn't helped improve the situation.

I kind of owed the guy. And I did like him. And his kid.

Fuck me.

"Besides, it's not like either one of us has time to find someone, if we even wanted to. Workaholics that we are. This makes it easy."

Easy, sure. When a swarm of locusts was about to take flight from my belly. Sure didn't seem easy inside me when everything was a riot of questions and needs.

A lot of the last one.

"You sure you want to hook my wagon to mine? Seeing me again might make Jessica go for blood even more."

"I'll take my chances," he repeated.

"What about Dani?" I hated to even ask the question. "I don't want to lie to her. She's a good kid."

"Who's lying? We're really going to date. I'm really going to take you out, hopefully many more times than tonight. I'm really going to lay you out and enact several of the filthy scenarios I've played in my head a time or two hundred. Assuming you're on board with that. That can be negotiated. Everything can."

Shut up, nipples. No one asked you.

There were any number of reasonable things I could have responded to that with. Instead, I asked, "You've fantasized about me?"

He nodded.

"Can you elaborate?"

"Before dinner on a first date? Not a chance. That's definitely dessert conversation. Or…demonstration."

The best part? He didn't wink when he said it. It probably showed my deep pathology, but I absolutely hated guys who winked when they flirted. It reminded me of Bob Barker from *The Price is Right* or my grandfather when he gave me a hard candy when I was a girl. Neither one stirred my loins in any shape or form.

With Gideon? I was stirred so hard I was basically a coffee milkshake.

"No hints?"

He released my hand and I wasn't sure if I was relieved or disappointed. "Definitely not. But I'm ready to go if you are."

"Wait." I stopped him with a hand on his arm. "You're sure you want to do this? This evening didn't have the best start. We don't have to make it into some big…thing."

"What if I want to?"

"Well, you're dead set on this dating idea—"

"Macy, I didn't get dressed up for you thinking Jessica would ambush me. I didn't plan any of this. All I did was ask out a woman I like. And call me selfish, but I'm determined to get my fucking date tonight. Okay?"

I had to smile. "Okay. But seriously, dude, you call that dressing up?" I shook my head at his shirt. "Bret Michaels does have a superior set of lips on him though. If you could ignore all the places they've probably been."

"Can't say I've ever thought about it."

I slipped my arm into his. "Just so you know, I'm touchy with seafood."

"Noted."

"Some of it is okay, some is slimy and gross."

"Gotcha. I pretty much guarantee you'll like dinner. At least the location if not the quality of the food." He glanced down at me. "Trust me?"

"Not even a little." But I squeezed his arm. "That's the kind of date I like best."

It was probably too much to hope for chainsaws and gore, but I'd settle for not knowing what the next step would hold.

In my business, I had to plan everything to the nth degree. Here? I could just be.

Assuming I could manage to forget Gideon and I were now dating.

Shit.

TEN

Gideon

"So, I figured I couldn't hope for chainsaws," Macy said as we walked under the arbor of lit jack-o-lanterns and spooky creatures hanging above us.

"First night of the season. They do a dry run before things officially kick off in a week or two. I did some work here for the owners, so they let me know for Dani. This is actually only the third year Happy Acres has done the hayrides. Every year gets bigger."

"You usually go with Dani?"

I shook my head. "Not you too. I figured at least you wouldn't give me guilt."

"Did she get on you for taking a girl instead of her? Because she so should have." Macy pointed to a line of booths set up near the hayride loading spot. "You better buy her a caramel apple at least."

I knew Dani wanted a caramel one, but I was curious about Macy's choice. "What about a candy one?"

"Ugh, no. And skip the nuts."

"I'll take your word for it. But Dani claims she likes both." Didn't she? Now Macy was making me wonder.

"She's lying to you."

"Thanks for the vote of confidence." I jerked my chin at the hot dog stand. "Want?"

"Definitely didn't expect this kind of fare tonight, but I'm up for it." Before I could take out my wallet, she marched up to the counter—a feat over the scattered hay since her sexy black shoes had a thin stiletto heel—and asked for their footlong dog with extra relish, a side of spicy curly fries, and a soda.

"A woman after my own heart," the guy behind the register said with a slow grin. I recognized him as one of the family members who worked at the farm.

"Hey, Beckett. Nice to see you."

"Oh, hey, John. Didn't see you at first." He tipped his cap at me. "Where's Danielle? She getting too old for this stuff?"

I let out a laugh. "Hardly. We'll be here for the real opening day." I rested a hand on Macy's lower back. She sent me a look, but I pretended not to see it as I ordered—and paid.

"I thought we would pay our own way."

I brushed a kiss over her temple in a possessive move I wasn't used to from myself. The bonus was inhaling more of cinnamon and honey scent. An odd, alluring combination. "You thought wrong. I'm old-fashioned."

"Too old-fashioned to screw on the first date?" She lowered her voice to ask the question but not quite enough for Beckett not to grin as he loaded up her dog with relish.

"Have you ever gotten hay in unspeakable places?"

"No. Is this the night I get to check that off my bucket list?"

I laughed and lifted my hand to the back of her neck. I don't know why I cupped her there, just something about her warmth under my hand with tendrils of her hair teasing my fingers felt like foreplay. She obviously agreed, because she slid me another look, this one under her lashes.

"I have a feeling you're a big ol' tease," she said once we were straddling a picnic bench next to the candy apples and fritters booth. I'd have to make sure I didn't forget Dani's treat before I left.

Yeah, I did feel guilty. But it was hard to regret much when Macy was digging into her fries with a gusto I had to appreciate.

"I was afraid you'd ask for a salad."

She snorted. "The only salad you'll see touch these lips is Vee's chicken salad that is loaded with mayo. I barely recognize lettuce, forget eat it."

"Thank fuck."

"I never would've guessed you were the haunted hayride type. Too serious and stoic to put up with faux Freddies leaping out of the woods." She offered me a curly fry and I intentionally nipped her fingers as I took it.

"Oh, this isn't your usual corny hayride."

"No?"

"I mean, there's some of that. But it has its share of genuine spooks. And once you make it through the main course, they take you along the perimeter of the corn fields where there's the most stupendous view you could imagine."

"Oh, I heard about that view. Ivy told me she and Rory rolled in the corn."

I nearly choked on my own very ordinary mustard-laden hot dog. At least I'd skipped the onions. "Excuse me?"

"Well, not literally, just in that general area. You know how people are in this town. Hornier than drunk bunnies. Plus, she was already knocked up, so there's that."

I took another bite and chewed as I tried to imagine the level of detail Ivy had shared with Macy—because I knew it was far more than Macy was letting on—and if I'd ever done similarly with my guy friends.

Nope, definitely not.

"Why are you shaking your head?"

"Do women share everything about sex?"

"Only if it's not embarrassing."

"Hmm."

"If the guy sucks, it depends how much. Like if it's just garden variety crappy, then that's a gloss over and forget it story. If he's really bad—like two-minute fireworks that sputter out all over your leg—then that's probably also not a share. Unless the chick is a catty bitch. Why?"

I blew out a breath. "I'm sorry I asked."

Macy flashed a grin. "Scared?"

"No. I have no reason to be. But I do have a daughter. And the closer she gets to her teenage years, the more afraid I become. I'll probably start looking for a therapist soon." I grabbed another of her fries. "Then again, that might happen after this date."

She tossed a wadded-up napkin at me. "I was being straight with you. Isn't that what men claim to want? No games, remember?"

"I definitely want no games. And I want you straight. And bent over. And sideways. And every other way in between."

She lifted a brow. "Definitely a tease."

"It's not a tease if I deliver."

"We'll see. Hey, is that cotton candy?"

I grinned as I looked over my shoulder at the telltale plastic bags hanging from the eaves of the candy apple booth. "Should I be insulted you're more interested in that than discussing my sexual appetite?"

"No, because you have no clue the kind of dirty things I can do with cotton candy and proper motivation." She rose and dusted off her hands. "I'm going to get that blue one on the end before some bratty kid steals it. Want any?"

I was still stuck on inappropriate images of Macy with her mouth full of blue cotton candy—and other things. Christ.

I ran my hand down my face. "I'm good."

"Sure about that?"

She was gone with a grin before I could reply.

Evil woman.

When she returned, she opened the bag and shoved a handful in my mouth before I had any warning. I laughed as I choked and swallowed, surprised that it was better than I'd expected.

Then she leaned down and gave me a quick, hard kiss, pulling back before I had a chance to enjoy it. "Thought I'd give the snoops something to talk about."

"What snoops?" My head reeled a little as I glanced around. Okay, a few people were looking this way, but it was a busy place. Lots of couples and families roaming around.

"You haven't seen all the stares we've been getting?"

"Uh, no, other than Beckett's eyes popping out of his head at the sight of you."

"Oh, is that why you put your hand and your mouth on me?" She took her seat on the other side of the table. "Not that I minded, by the way. Momentary possessiveness hits us all."

"What if it's not momentary?"

Saying nothing, she ate cotton candy, her gaze steady on mine. That was Macy. Utterly direct and unflinching at all times.

She was unlike any other woman I'd ever been involved with. She didn't know how to be coy. If she wanted something, she asked for it. If she didn't like what was happening, she didn't disguise her feelings. There was no subterfuge with her.

It was refreshing and scary as hell.

"Hey, John." Hayes Manning, Beckett's younger brother, stopped beside our table. His hair was wild around his head and he'd tucked his usual glasses in the pocket of his shirt. Probably why his eyes were a little unfocused.

"Hey, Hayes. Have you met Macy Devereaux? She runs Brewed Awakening in Crescent Cove, along with—"

"Oh, you're the one who runs that rocking Halloween all year place?" Hayes eagerly pumped her hand. "I had the best coffee of my life there a few weeks ago." He glanced over his shoulder. "Don't tell my ma or my Aunt Laverne that though. They'll stop making a mincemeat pie for me at Thanksgiving."

Macy laughed. "Mincemeat is gross, but thanks for the compliment. Someone else said today that my beans were burned, but she's batshit crazy so she doesn't count."

"Yeah, damn straight. Your beans are perfect, far as I can tell."

I cleared my throat, and Hayes coughed into his hand. "Anyway, I thought you were probably doing that Trick or Treat shop too that's just going up. Same theme and all, but that's candy—"

"Going up where?" All humor fled from Macy's face.

"Edge of town. Just starting building now. My brother-in-law Ian stumbled across it online and he has the worst sweet tooth known to man. I figured I'd—hey, are you okay?"

Macy's cheeks flushed as she yanked out her phone from her purse. Her fingers flew across the keys. A moment later, she dropped the phone on the table. "Motherfucker!"

Hayes coughed into his hand again. "Okay, well, that's my cue. Hayride coming up. You're joining us, I hope?"

"That's the plan," I said under my breath.

"All righty, enjoy." Hayes practically sprinted from the table.

I might not have noticed anyone paying much attention to us before, but that wasn't the case right this second.

"Some assclown is trying to build a Halloween-themed candy joint in my town. Not far from my place. Can you believe the brass balls that takes? And look at this monstrosity." She shoved her phone at me, and I blinked at the twisted metal oversized scarecrow in the parking lot holding up a crudely lettered sign bearing the establishment's name. Some half-filled balloons were wrapped around the scarecrow's other hand. The metalwork was impressive, even to an untrained eye like mine—definitely not my area of expertise—but everything else was not. At least so far.

Including the ramshackle building near the sign. It was clearly being remodeled, but the project hadn't gotten far off the ground yet. Or it had been abandoned.

Kind of fit the Trick or Treat theme actually. Dilapidated candy shop, luring in unsuspecting kids…

I shared my theory with Macy, and she glared at me, clearly not amused.

"Maybe they aren't even finishing it." I gave her back her phone. "Perhaps they didn't realize you had something similar going on up the street and—"

"Similar? You call that low rent operation similar to my business?

I've slaved over every detail, and I'm paying top of the line to make sure everything is to my exact specifications. Paying *you*," she reminded me as if I'd somehow forgotten.

Rather than snipe back at her, I decided to let her wind herself up and then simmer down once she'd gotten it all out. I understood it must be a shock to have something of a niche you'd made your own, but by the same token, candy and coffee were not the same things. Nor was a restaurant. To me, it seemed as if the businesses could work together to send customers to each one.

Obviously, Macy was not in the same headspace.

"You have no clue who own the place, and it could be a simple mistake. Although I'd seriously consider seeing how you could create cross-traffic between your shops. Why cut off your nose to spite your face?"

She narrowed her eyes at me then stared hard at the balloons strung up where people were already lined up to board the first hayride of the night. "Did you know condoms can be used as inflatables in lieu of balloons?" she asked, propping her chin on the back of her hand.

I hid a smile as I gathered our garbage. "You ready to be scared?"

She made a face. "These things never scare me. I watched *Texas Chainsaw Massacre* as a bedtime story one night."

I rose to dump our trash and returned to the table. "Somehow that doesn't surprise me."

"Just saying, I don't scare easy."

When she tugged at the shoulder of her top, I reached for my wallet. She'd returned my jacket before we rode out to the farm.

Stubborn, sexy as hell woman.

"Want a hot cocoa? Or a hot cider?" I gestured at the booth beside us. "They sell both. Pretty good too. Can add a flavor to your hot cocoa."

"Ooh, can I?"

Rather than getting annoyed at the edge to her voice, I just pulled out a ten. I'd buy her a drink and she'd drink it. If not, I would. I had an eight-year-old. Temper tantrums didn't faze me.

Even if Macy used possible condom destruction as a weapon.

"I'll take a cider." Macy stood and heaved out a sigh. "Thanks. I'll go grab us a spot in line. Damn children keep jumping ahead."

I nearly reminded her that these hayrides were promoted heavily to children—well, those seven and up anyway, since the scares were a bit much for the littler ones—but decided she was dealing with enough right now.

After I paid for her cider, I met her at the back of the line. She was blowing on her hands, so I nudged the cider between them. She took a long sip, her eyes nearly rolling back in her head.

"You didn't mention it was caramel apple cider."

"I didn't know. Isn't it all the same?"

"Taste." She shoved it at me, and I took a drink, watching her all the while.

"It's good."

"Ugh, men." She yanked back the cup and took another long drink.

As soon as she drew the cup away, I tipped up her chin with my thumb and took her mouth. Slowly, sweetly, letting the tart apple and sweet caramel swirl together on my tongue. Under both was Macy, all sharp words and flashing blue eyes, even as I sipped from her lips. Then finally, she made a soft sigh of acquiescence and leaned up on her toes, fisting my shirt with her free hand.

"Here they go again," someone said.

I started to ease back, but Macy dove in for round two. I couldn't say I minded. The cool breeze tickled the back of my neck, but her mouth was an inferno against mine, all need and hunger. The kind I'd repressed for so long that I'd believed I wasn't denying it. But here with her, that part of me came roaring to the fore.

Still, there were children here. And while we were just kissing, it wasn't the sort that was appropriate for young gazes.

Someone bumped hard into my back as the line moved forward. I tugged Macy with me, sheltering her in the circle of my arm. She drew away and laughed as she looked down at the cider cup she'd nearly crushed, licking a little of the liquid now flowing out of the triangle opening on the top.

My cock lurched painfully against my zipper. So, I was going to spend my night in a state of personal agony.

Good to know.

"Guess we aren't doing so well at diverting attention." She inclined her chin at a couple of women I would've sworn had circled around The Haunt right after Dani's post. "Think they're thirsty too, but don't offer to buy them any cider, okay?"

"I'll try to control myself."

She took another sip. "Not doing awesome at that either, pal."

"Oh, you have no idea."

We reached the head of the line and paid. The first group was just coming back, so we were able to load fairly quickly, although they overpacked the rides. This occurred despite a kindly-looking grandmother I recognized as Laverne Ronson, one of Happy Acres's owners, yelling out, "Safety first!" before dropping a creepy clown mask over her face.

Macy shuddered beside me. "Fuck."

I had to grin. "I thought you were so badass."

"Everything but clowns. Freaking hate them. I'm surprised they don't have a fake sewer grate so one can pop his head out and give me a damn heart attack."

"Last year, there weren't any. No promises this year."

"Definitely no promises," Laverne agreed with a cackle as she tore off the ends of our tickets and gave us back the stubs.

Macy leaned closer to Laverne. "Can I pay extra and our ride skip that attraction?"

"You don't have that kind of cash, young lady. We don't make changes to the route for anyone. If you can't stand the heat, stay out of the kitchen." She pointed at me. "Or have your big strong fella protect you. That's what they're for. That, and unclogging pipes, and carrying heavy objects, and killing snakes."

Macy's lips twitched as she tossed out her cider cup and the last of her cotton candy. "Anything else?"

"Nothing that lasts more than a commercial break." Laverne motioned for us to keep moving. "Have fun, kids."

The ride was crammed with families and kids, so we ended up in the very last seats—which in this case meant wedged on the edge of the hay bales stacked side by side. The people behind us whined that they could squeeze in, but they must've missed that Macy was basically on my lap.

A fact I couldn't say I minded.

"Not sure this is safe," she said against my ear, looping her arms around my shoulders and settling in for the ride.

Justin Manning, yet another one of Beckett's siblings, called out a greeting to all of us. He was dressed like a farmer, except he had a bloody fake eyeball affixed to his cheek and bleeding slashes on his plaid shirt and jeans.

"This is one helluva first date." Macy wound her fingers through the ends of my hair. "If we had a bit more privacy, I'd give it an A-plus so far."

"I can agree with that one." I rubbed her jean-clad thigh near one of the rips in the denim, well aware that children were all around us. Thankfully, most of them were near the front of the ride, clustered on hay bales near the giant pumpkin head scarecrow with weird hollow eyes. He was clad in a similar outfit to Justin's—plaid shirt and jeans, except his ensemble included large brown stitched-on gloves with hay sticking out of the wrist holes.

"Seems like a waste of a space." Macy nodded at the pumpkin scarecrow as the hayride rumbled into gear. Already we could glimpse the lit jack-o-lanterns made into literal lanterns hanging and swaying from the trees we were about to drive around and between. Ghosts swayed in the breeze from the uppermost branches, and fun monsters and other frightful characters were attached to limbs and even staged along the ground.

I couldn't wait to bring Dani. I was already missing her, but it was smart we hadn't chanced it with her ankle just in case. In a couple weeks, she'd be completely healed, and she would love every second.

"You guys ready for some speed?" Justin called.

The responses ranged from "yes!" to "hell yeah!" so he gassed it. Well, relatively speaking. This hayride only went so fast. But even with his low speed, the chilly wind was just enough to make Macy shiver, giving me an excuse to haul her that much closer. I expected her to make some snarky remark, but she just rested her head against mine and tucked her hands between my jacket and my T-shirt, creating a pocket of heat that made my breath catch.

"You're so warm," she said near my ear, and it might as well have been dirty talk for the effect her husky voice had on my libido.

"Would I lose points if I said you're so hot?"

"Probably."

"Okay, I didn't say it."

Kids yelled and laughed as the first spook leaped out of the darkness. Macy laughed and shook her head. "Not scary."

"Just wait."

We rumbled along in the darkness, the chatter on the hayride growing louder as time passed with no one jumping out from between the trees. We went through a particularly dark area where the thick branches above obscured the light from the moon and the nervous comments intensified.

"Nice night for a ride." The edge of Macy's short nail crept up to trace along my collarbone and the thin chain I wore.

"It is. All kinds of rides."

"Perv." She dug out my chain and examined the thin gold disk in the shaft of pale light from the pair of glowing eyes dangling from the trees. "Is this…oh."

I took the disk from her and tucked it back under my shirt, surprisingly embarrassed. Thank God the light was almost nonexistent, because my flushed ears would've given me away.

"Dani's baby footprint?"

"Yeah."

"That's so sweet. You really wanted her."

"Want," I corrected, and it all hit me like a sledgehammer to the forehead again.

Jessica showing up without warning. Jessica fishing for information and accusing me of anything that popped into her head. The words between her and Macy.

"She belongs with you." Macy rubbed the spot through my shirt where the disk sat against my chest. "And just ignore me, because my mouth is like *Jaws* and I suck up all good times—holy fucking shit!"

A Grim Reaper jumped out of the darkness and nearly dove into the hayride, which was freaky enough. But then the pumpkin scarecrow that everyone had assumed was a decoration lumbered to his feet and let out an inhuman roar, making the kids and even some of the parents shriek and cover their faces.

I just laughed and laughed while Macy glared at me, her lips twitching as she fought not to join me.

"Asshole. It just surprised me is all." She poked me hard in the ribs before covering my grinning mouth with her own.

Just like every other time, it was akin to going deep diving. Loss of all sense of time and space. Nothing registered except the warmth of her lips and the slide of her tongue against mine as she shifted across my lap, crawling closer until we were wedged together.

And then the clearing of a throat about six inches away.

"Not the place for this, you two."

The deep voice caused me to jerk back and turn my head toward Jared Brooks. Also known as Sheriff Brooks, who was seated a few feet away from us on a nearby hay bale and leaning forward without a whit of amusement on his face.

For fuck's sake, he even had his official hat on. How had I missed that?

Distracted much?

Macy gave a minute shake of her head. "Got me."

It was my turn to clear my throat. "Sorry, Sheriff."

"Seems like I've had reports of you two doing this all over town."

"Reports?" Macy demanded. "From who? Give me names, numbers, and times."

The sheriff wisely ignored her. "Including on TV. I'd say get a room, but I'd assume that between the two of you, you have access to proper facilities."

"Yes, sir." I clamped a hand over Macy's mouth when she would've spewed God only knows what with children nearby. As it was, more than a couple of them had turned to watch us with curious eyes.

Their parents, however, didn't seem nearly as interested. More like pissed.

Oh, yeah, I was definitely setting a great precedent to go before a judge to prove how upstanding I was. Seemed like I better get on board that train fast.

Then Macy decided to bite me.

I yanked my hand away from her mouth and shook it out. "You've had a recent rabies shot, right?"

Even the sheriff winced. "On second thought, don't think that room will be necessary, after all."

ELEVEN

MACY

I WAS THANKFUL THAT GIDEON HAD TAKEN US OUT OF TOWN FOR OUR first date. Since then, only every third customer stared at me a touch too long. Because of course the whole town was already talking about us, thanks to my little stunt on his damn lap.

I still wasn't sure what the hell I'd been thinking.

And now I wanted to add extreme sexual frustration to my list of grievances. Add in some guilt due to his happily chattering daughter in the reading nook, and I was ready to take a scythe to the entire dining room.

Okay, maybe minus Dani.

It wasn't her fault her father was an idiot.

It had been a week since our first date. A minor emergency at the work site had kept him busy. That did not help my current state. Especially since he wouldn't let me over there to see what the hell went wrong.

He'd practically patted me on the head and told me not to worry about it.

He was very lucky that murder was illegal in New York. Okay, so it was a federal offense as well, but I was very creative. Besides, all I had to do was ask Vee how to hide a body. She listened to enough serial killer podcasts to give me a good lead on how to make sure he was never found.

Thankfully, the dinner crowd wasn't as heavy as my lunch crowd. Most people shuffled off to the diner for full meals or went to the handful of eateries around town. Exactly why I was excited to get The Haunt moving.

I wanted to feed people coffee and light lunch fare by day and full food by night.

With the specialty nature of the restaurant, it seemed fitting that it was a nighttime venture. As with most horror features, the light of day wasn't nearly as kind to monsters. Which suited me. If it really took off, I could always extend the hours.

Then again, I'd like to actually just get inside the freaking place and get my staff trained.

"You're going to literally burn people where they stand if you keep staring people down like that," Rylee said out of the side of her mouth.

"I'm just frustrated."

"They have toys for that."

"You need them? Thought you had a strapping man in your life these days."

"I'm not the one growing laser beams in my eyeballs. Besides, toys enhance. You should try it."

"Can you just make that latte, please?"

She shrugged. "I can do both at the same time."

"Obviously not, since you're still flapping your lips and not moving your hands." I swung around the end of the counter with the plastic tub I used to bus tables.

Rylee was whistling like the asshole she was as I returned to dump the first load of dishes. Damn her. And damn Gideon for leaving me so worked up.

Luckily, it was too busy for me to think much about next door. All I could focus on was the next customer in line and badgering Vee into making another batch of the sold-out double chocolate bat cupcakes.

Just as the crowd started thinning, Kinleigh Scott, from Kinleigh's

Attic across the street, muscled her way through the door with a huge wagon of pumpkins.

I was scrubbing a table near the window and rushed over to help her. "What the hell?"

"I didn't know what else to do with them. One of my deliveries included a gorgeous armoire that I'm going to be convincing August to help renovate with me."

I grabbed the side of the wooden-slatted wagon before it tipped. "What does that have to do with a dozen gourds and six weird looking pumpkins?"

"They were in the armoire."

"You do know you have a window as well."

"Yes, but this is more your thing than mine." She flicked her fingers over the Halloween decorations from floor to ceiling.

Dani wandered over, her huge eyes brimming with trouble. "Oh, wow. Can we carve them?"

"No."

"But they're pumpkins. That's what you do to them."

"In October, sure. Now? They'd be mush before we get out of September. We haven't even hit Labor Day yet."

She activated the puppy dog eyes.

"Nope. Don't give me that look, kid."

"Well…"

I gave Kinleigh a bland look. "You don't think you've caused enough issues?"

"Well, come on. I mean this is your thing, right? But I saw this thing on Instagram. Galaxy pumpkins." Kinleigh gave me a hopeful grin. "I kinda wanted to try it."

Dani started bouncing next to me. Her sprain was getting better every day and I knew she was bored as hell. It was almost time for the kids to go back to school and the holiday weekend would be in full swing in mere days.

But there were still two more days left in the week.

"Well, you started this insanity." I reached into my back pocket and pulled out my credit card. "If your dad's cool with it, you can go with Kinleigh to get some supplies."

Dani threw herself at me, hugging me around the middle. She tucked her chin into my ribs as she peered up at me. The child had no concept of personal space. "You can talk to dad, right? I mean, he listens to you."

And that was a fallacy if I'd ever heard it. Gideon hadn't listened to me at all this week. I should actually charge the craft supplies to him, but I wanted the pumpkins for my window. And dammit, galaxy sounded cool and witchy.

Dani linked her arms at my back. "Please."

"You are an evil child."

She rolled her eyes. "Dad says the same thing. Not that he calls me evil though. He likes brat."

"Fitting."

She squinted her eyes at me. "So, is that a yes…"

I sighed. "You don't have to sit in a weird seat or anything, do you?"

She let me go, her face affronted. "No. Just have to ride in the backseat."

"How am I supposed to know? Rules have changed since I was a kid."

Dani let me go and jumped around Kinleigh. "Can we go to Michael's?"

"How did I get roped into this?" Kinleigh sighed, but I knew it was all for show. Her eyes were already sparkling in that way she had when she had a new project.

I made a Vanna White wave over the pumpkins.

"Right. Hmm. Do I have a budget?" Kinleigh tucked a wild strawberry curl behind her ear.

I sighed and took my phone out of my back pocket to text Gideon.

I'm sending your kid off to the salt mines of Michael's with Kinleigh for some crafty shit. Is that cool?

Does she have outstanding warrants?

Dani? Not sure. She's kinda shifty.

I got a middle finger as my reply. I laughed. Another message came through a second later.

That's fine. I'm sorry it's taking so long today. Karen still isn't cleared to watch her by her doctors.

We'll figure it out. By the looks of the crowd gathering around this new craft situation, I think she'll be busy for a while.

Thanks. I'll make it up to you.

You damn well better.

I shoved my phone back into my pocket. "Looks like it's a go."
Dani jumped up and down. "Yes. Thank God. I'm so bored." The tone of her voice ended with the dramatic flair that only an eight-year-old could provide.
"Go wild. Just make sure to bring something to protect surfaces if there's painting."
Dani's ecstatic dancing brought Vee out. "What's going on?"
"Guess we're getting a craft corner tonight."
"Oh. That sounds like fun. I'll make paninis."
At least I'd get fed. "Should I leave the café open while we're working?"
"Nah." Vee nudged my shoulder. "Let people be jealous."
I liked money, but I was peopled out today, that was for damn sure. "Works for me."
I went about doing my closing duties. Dealing with money, reports, and other sundry tallies always took a good chunk of my brain. It was easier then overthinking every-damn-thing going on next door.

Cleaning up soothed and evened me out. Putting my little world back together after hours full of chaos was secretly my favorite part of the day. The chattering between women faded to the background as my current riddle invaded my thoughts again.

Who was opening another Halloween-themed place in my town, dammit?

Something about the sign niggled at me. Like when I couldn't name a character in a movie. It scratched at my brain. Unfortunately, there was no IMDB to help me with this particular quandary.

I tried an online search. I dug out a business license in process, but there was no name attached to it yet. Fucking annoying.

All the windows were blacked out with newspaper and black paper. To add insult to injury, that part of the street was too busy for me to figure out if there was a new car attached to the owner. There had been a new motorcycle spotted by a few of the customers doing their regular rounds of gossip. Unfortunately, there was always a new motorcycle in town since Tish did specialty designs for anything on wheels.

So, I was back to square one with the questions. I would figure it out.

No one would screw with my opening. No one.

I moved on to scrubbing the tables with renewed fervor. By the time Kinleigh returned—this time, with another pregnant woman in tow—I was working on the last table in the dining area.

"Look who I found at Michael's."

Vee waddled across the room. "Oh, Ivy, what are you doing up and around?"

"I have weeks left still." She rubbed circles along the side of her belly. "I'm going stir-crazy. Rory had to fly to California for one last recording session before the baby comes. I thought buying stickers for my planner would make me feel better." She was hugging her journal to her chest like a life raft.

"Come on, let's get you settled."

Vee wasn't much farther behind her to be honest, but she was in full mama bear mode.

Kinleigh dropped the huge sacks on the large worktable that students sometimes used for papers and homework. Since summer was still technically in effect, this part of the café had been very empty for the last few weeks.

She also had a brown paper bag that interested me.

I wound my way around the tables to peer inside. "You brought some adult juice."

"I did. I deserve it after today."

"Make sure you fill my sippy cup too, Cinnamon."

Kinleigh grinned. "You got it."

I checked in with Gideon. He was happy to have the extra few hours to get some woodworking done now that my crisis was averted.

And still, I wasn't allowed to see.

I helped Vee with the tray of sandwiches and paninis she made. I managed to heat half of one before the vultures descended. Namely, a certain eight-year-old that seemed to have a hole in her stomach. That or a hollow leg.

We all cleaned up after mowing down the food. Kinleigh spread out a tube of brown paper over the table and taped it down. Dani kept flashing me pictures of the galaxy pumpkins on her phone.

She was very organized with the steps we needed to take for each layer of the pumpkin. I went into the back and got some old aprons so we could keep the splatter to a minimum.

Of course they didn't wait for me.

Laughter and the familiar sound of ball-bearings rattling in a spray can swamped me with memories. My brother had always been working with that kind of paint. Nothing as traditional as brushes and tubes of color for him.

But the things he'd created with tag art and the finicky medium of spray paint had always amazed me. It had been years since that smell had filled my senses. The sudden flood of sadness was staggering. I'd walked away from so much more than just a broken heart.

I spotted Kinleigh pouring wine into a cup with a straw for me. Thank God.

"I'm making a pink one," Ivy announced with a white mask over the bottom half of her face.

I took my cup to supervise a little further from the line of spray. I wasn't sure if the paint was a good idea for her advanced pregnancy. Kinleigh came up next to me and tipped the wine bottle against the rim of my glass and refilled my rapidly draining cup.

Maybe I had a hole in it.

"Non-toxic spray paint, but I propped the front door open for some air."

"Thanks for helping out with Dani."

Kinleigh smiled. "She's a good kid. Not sure why Gideon was hiding her."

"Mother's a real peach. Famous," I said under my breath. I didn't want Dani to hear me say something about the piranha. Gideon was pretty adamant about keeping a positive spin on how they interacted.

"Oh, have you met her?"

"You haven't heard about my little Mexican standoff with his ex? I all but licked Gideon and called him mine."

"Is he yours?" She crossed her arms.

"Yes," Rylee called from the table.

Damn bat ears. She always heard everything. "We're dating," I admitted gruffly.

"About time." Kinleigh blotted her dewy forehead with the back of her hand—the only part not spattered in black and purple paint.

I took another long drink from my straw in lieu of an answer.

"You guys have been tossing off so many sparks, I'm shocked we haven't gotten a brushfire."

"Yeah, well, it's complicated." I nodded to Dani, who waved and gave me her shiny-eyed, deliriously happy gap-toothed smile. The one that made my chest ache with old ghosts and new anxiety. Damn kid.

"I mean, I know you aren't into kids—which hello, I don't understand. I want to have like five."

"Good God."

"What?" She picked at paint spots on her ringed fingers. "I want a big family. I never had one."

I recognized the sappy look on her face. Many a woman wore it in this town. Because I didn't know how to reply, I took another drink until my straw was slurping on nothing. I moved to the wine for a refill.

"Well, we're just doing the dating thing. His ex is being a bit of a... problem." Bitch. Narcissistic. Stone-cold cunt.

Kinleigh rushed over for her own mug of wine, keeping her voice low. "Do tell."

"I've said enough."

"Have more wine." She lifted the bottle.

"I'm still technically babysitting."

"We have actual mothers here, no need to be sober. Well, Vee is heading home in a few minutes, but you should drink some adult juice and dish more information."

"There's nothing to dish. We just started." Hadn't even really started. Just talked about starting with a side of eye-crossingly amazing kisses.

Evidently, I'd had enough wine. I put the tumbler down.

Kinleigh picked it up. "Nope. More truth juice."

"It's been a weird week." Weird enough that I wasn't sure if he was wrapped up in work or weirded it out like I was. Did he not want to get me naked? He'd seemed awfully into me at the damn hayride and now...

Well, now I couldn't get him alone in a goddamn room.

"So, go over there and give him a little...push." Kinleigh wiggled her hips in a distressingly inaccurate parody of getting laid.

"How long has it been for you, Cinnamon?"

She gave me a bland look. "Too long, obviously."

I hid a smirk behind the lip of my cup.

Rylee got up and crossed to us with her cup held out. "What am I missing?"

"Nothing," I muttered.

"Macy needs to ride that pony."

"Dear God." I took a larger gulp.

Ry grinned and took a marginally smaller sip from her wine. "You are so overdue for some adult recreational activities that it's laughable."

"I seem to remember a certain conversation where you told me to butt out of your business too."

"Yes, but I had other problems. You are a wide-open field."

"Who says?"

Rylee rolled her eyes. "You two have no reason why you can't." She held up her hand. "Yes, he's working for you, but he's always working for you. There will always be updates that need to be done on the restaurant or café. You're just making excuses now."

I huffed out a breath. "It's not just about us."

"Dating a single dad is not the problem and you know it. You're just using it as the excuse. Besides, he could suck in the sack."

"Doubt it," Kinleigh and I said at the same time.

I gave Kin a side-eyed glare.

She shrugged. "Can't say I didn't think about it before. He's a big, strapping dude with that lumberjack-hot thing going on." Her giggle only intensified as my growl grew. "See? You're so into him. What the hell are you waiting for?"

I set the tumbler down. I did a cursory check in with the kid. Dani was grinning as she shot white paint at the midnight gourd she had moved on to.

I unwound my messy braid.

"Oh, here we go." Rylee grinned. "All it took was another woman mentioning she was into your man."

"Shut up." I whipped off my apron and tossed it at Rylee's face. "I'll be back in a few."

"Don't do anything I wouldn't," she called at my back.

I stalked across the darkened half of the café to the pass way between the two buildings. I didn't even bother trying to be gentle with the nailed-in board this time. I ripped it free and let it swing down, then I ducked into the slim crevice and let the chipboard snap back behind me.

Music was playing. Televisions were up on the walls now, and the darkened Myers house filled multiple screens. Gideon was half hidden by a wall-mounted television he was screwing into the wall.

This one was still black, so I knew I wasn't in any danger of stopping him in the middle of wire work. He was distracted and definitely didn't see me. Things had progressed hugely since the last time I'd been in the room.

Booths were uncovered, walls were painted, and the floors were still covered in drop-cloths, but I was pretty sure that was more to protect them than anything else needing to be done. Speakers were stacked around and empty television mount kits were stacked on top.

But it punched me in the gut. This place was real. It was mine.

It was more than I ever thought it would be.

He turned to me, the quick, startled look giving way to worry. "Is something—*oof.*"

I leaped on him, locking my legs around his hips. "You've been ignoring me."

He grunted, but the hold on my ass never wavered. "I've been working." His gaze dropped to my mouth before returning to lock with mine. "You keep ruining my surprises."

"I don't care about surprises." My short nails bit into his neck and shoulders as I closed the last bit of distance between us. He was one of the few men taller than me by a good chunk and I loved it. He growled into my mouth as we drunkenly swayed, banging against the closest booth. I barely felt the glancing blow, then he righted himself and stalked to the bar with me wrapped around him like a damn monkey.

He shoved a dirty drop-cloth away and set me on the firm bar top. "We need to slow down."

"If we get any slower, it's going to be 2027 before I fuck you. I'm not waiting anymore, dammit." Our tongues tangled and the low frequency hum I'd been living with finally kicked up a notch. I hummed at the taste of him. My coffee and something hotter, bolder —Gideon.

I'd never experienced it before or since.

"I didn't want the first time to be here, dammit," he said against my mouth.

"It really had to be, don't you think?" I lightly scraped my fingers down his bearded cheeks.

I was slightly above him due to the height of the bar. His eyes were dark in the shadowed room. Pendant lights were the only illumination save for the movie. He dragged my shirt down my shoulder to get to my skin. His mouth raced across the space between it and my neck. He scraped his teeth over the high curve of my shoulder while his other hand tunneled under the bottom of my shirt. His roughened fingertips tickled over my ribs to find the sturdy cotton of my bra. Too bad I'd wasted my hot lingerie on our date night and he'd barely copped a feel. He swiped his thumb over the tip of my nipple unerringly. He tugged at it through the material, making me hiss.

He dragged my shirt down enough for him to cover the tight center with his mouth. He watched me as he made a wet spot through the black cotton before finally jerking the cup down to release my breast to his hot, hungry mouth. I arched back to give him room and gripped his hair to keep him there, letting him know that was right where I needed him.

I lifted my knees to clasp his ribs. He might've been tall as hell, but it was still a bar. Everything was just a little bit off for this.

Frustration arced between us. He shoved up my shirt so he could move between my breasts, his beard scratching and heightening the sensations with each nip and bite.

He wasn't easy—wasn't sweet. I'd half expected it from his personality. He always seemed so careful around people due to his size.

For once, being a tall and sturdy woman was to my advantage. If only we could get lined up.

I slid forward on the bar until my legs dangled and denim finally rubbed against denim. He was a hard column of need between my legs. Thank God. I ground against him, fire leaping between us. It wasn't nearly enough. Nothing would be enough until he was inside me.

It was only fitting for it to be here—in this place he'd created for me. He'd taken my schematics and insane sketches and made sense of them.

He'd taken my dream and made it real.

We were so tangled up after years of working together and keeping a barrier firmly between us for so long. But here and now, he was mine. Even if it was just for a short time. I'd take it. Allow myself to be greedy.

I didn't know how to accurately convey just how amazing this place was. Just how much I'd needed this man to be with me in this moment. To finally let him in. To finally trust that I could share something with another human.

That he could know me so well. Understand me like no one else ever had.

I dragged his mouth back up to mine. Our eyes locked, the shock of what we were doing seemed to be dawning in his eyes. I tugged on his lower lip with my teeth. I watched him as I lightly traced his lips and brushed my nose along his.

"I want this." God, was that my voice? Practically thready with need.

He seemed to look over my shoulder for a moment, his brow furrowed. Want warred with worry.

"She's fine. She's painting pumpkins and getting spoiled by four women."

His gaze refocused on me. "We actually have time?"

"Only if you don't waste it."

He touched his forehead to mine with a laugh. "Here?"

"Here." I nodded and whipped my shirt over my head, leaving me in only my bra. "Here is perfect."

I could've brought him upstairs, but that didn't feel right. This felt truer than any bed could be. Besides, he might change his mind, and then I'd have to kill him.

I pulled his hand up from the grip on my hips to cup my breasts. He pushed the two little mounds together to pop out of the confines of my flimsy bra. I wasn't exactly blessed in the breast department, but it didn't seem to matter to him. He scraped over the softness to find the hard tips.

I twisted my hands behind me to unclasp the stupid bra then it joined my shirt at the end of the bar.

All that mattered was that he was touching me.

He wasn't going to stop this time.

I fumbled between us for his belt, undoing the heavy buckle and peeling his jeans open to find the thick length of him already springing into my hand. He groaned against my neck as I freed him and stroked the very lovely and impressive length of him. Thank freaking God. I mean, I'd work with whatever he had, but damn, it was nice to see he was as blessed in the front as he was in the back.

Good goddamn.

I reached lower for his balls and gave him a good tug. He grunted and pushed me back until I was flat on the bar. "Watch what you're doing down there."

I lifted myself up on my elbows. "Or what?" I lifted my foot to dig my heel into his ass, drawing him against me.

He went for my zipper. "Lift that perfect ass of yours."

I grinned at him and obliged, thanking the yoga classes Rylee had been making me go to. I could hold this pose for a good minute—maybe two. Enough to kill him if I really wanted to.

From the look in his eyes and the heavy swallow working the long column of his throat, it was working.

I laughed and threw my head back as he stripped me of my jeans and then there was no more laughter. Nope. Not with that clever, busy mouth of his.

He hooked my knee over his shoulder and spread me open to give me one long, lazy lick. His gaze was a little wild, a lot hot, and just a touch scary.

Then he went on the attack.

I didn't have anything to grab onto, so his shoulders had to do. I arched under his touch as his tongue found my clit with an accuracy I never imagined possible. Most guys needed a little guidance, especially when the room was this dark.

But nope. He seemed to know exactly what to do. And holy fuck, was I forever grateful.

I curled around his head as my body wept and my mind cleared for the first goddamn time in too many years for me to count. It was bliss. It was heaven. It was perfection.

It was a perfectly built latte with extra sweet foam with a sharply rich coffee blend hidden under the wispy clouds of orgasm. His name was a prayer on my lips as I literally died.

I collapsed back against the wood, my feet sliding away from him as my arms splayed wide.

He straightened and grinned down at me, his mouth still wet. "You didn't think that was all, did you?"

I laughed, my chest heaving with exertion and the need to find oxygen. "Nope. That was just the qualifiers, right?"

He nipped at my inner thigh. "I've been dreaming about this pussy since the first day you told me off. There's probably something wrong with me."

"The only thing wrong is that you waited this goddamn long to get me horizontal." I rested my black socked foot against his shoulder and pushed him back. "Now show me what you've got."

He nuzzled his beardy chin against my ankle. "Cute socks, Mace."

I glanced over at the black cat socks with a shrug. "Love me a good pair of cat socks."

He scraped his blunt-tipped fingers down my inner thighs before swiping his thumb through my drenched folds to find my clit once more. As large as his fingers were, they were achingly accurate. "You're sure about this?"

I resisted the urge to roll my eyes back into my head and snap my legs closed over his hand. Sensitive didn't cover it. My lingerie drawer wasn't the only thing with cobwebs. "Not that I don't love a man who is willing to give head with no reciprocation, but get that cock suited up. I'm not done with you either."

He tipped his head back. The hair of his beard was tightly groomed, but a line of shadow snaked down to whorl around his

Adam's apple. "Christ, what am I doing? My daughter's in the next room."

"Pretty sure parents across the Cove have done the same thing." I sat up and reached for him, giving his rock-hard length a good stroke. "It had to happen here." I nipped his lower lip. He tasted of me. "Unless your horndog of an employee got down and dirty in here, I damn well should be christening it. *We* should be christening it."

He groaned into my mouth, our tongues tangling. "Fucking hell, Mace. You never say anything I'm ready for."

I arched a brow and swiped the perfectly silky head of his cock through my wetness. "Damn right."

He kissed me hard and dug into his pocket.

I teased him along my entrance. "Hurry up. I need this inside me."

"Jesus." His warm breath burned my tongue along with the nip of his sharp teeth.

My face was going to be all beard-burned, but I didn't even care. I cupped the surprisingly soft hairs on his cheek and scraped my nails through the shorter, trimmed ones around his chin. I licked around his lips, getting a more thorough mix of myself and his unique taste.

I moved to nibble on his ear. "You're going to wear me home tonight, Gideon."

"I'm never going to wash you off. You taste fucking perfect."

I swirled my thumb around the head of his cock and leaned back enough to watch him. "Should I take a taste of you too?"

"Sweet fuck, you're going to kill me."

I slid closer to him, shivering as I drew my pussy along the lower part of the shaft of his dick. "What a way to go."

He stepped back, slapping his wallet on the bar. He gripped the lip of the bar on either side of me as he bowed his head. "Give me a second."

I slid my fingers through his hair to cradle the back of his skull. "What's wrong, Gideon?"

"You're going to kill me, and I want to enjoy the first stroke inside that perfect pussy. Not blow my load like a goddamn bottle rocket."

I laughed against the crown of his head. His scent had sunk into me already. It really didn't matter how it went from here on out, this was perfect. Right now, if he was a two-pump-chump, I wouldn't hold it against him.

Then he locked his gaze with mine as he rolled the condom down his length. "At least I'm slick with you inside this rubber."

My heart rolled and flipped in my chest. Then he was there, between my legs. He yanked me to the edge of the bar, so my ass was barely on it before he slowly, effortlessly, invaded the last part of me.

He'd already chased me in my dreams.

He'd already haunted my endless insomnia-fueled nights.

He'd already distracted me on a daily basis.

And now, he was the perfect key into my lock.

His fingers snaked into my braid and he gripped my head to keep eye contact as he thrust into me again and again. Long, measured strokes that touched every part of me. He widened my legs to get us closer, then pulled me into him until there was no space between us.

We were chest to chest, belly to belly, and breath to breath. He burrowed deeper as if he was going to fucking climb into me. I curled my arms around his shoulders, my nails digging for purchase as the freefall started.

I tried to break away from him.

The connection was too deep. Too everywhere.

But he wouldn't let me go.

He surrounded me, enveloped me, and overwhelmed me.

Sweat poured between us as the friction ratcheted everything up to another level. His huge hands held me tight and safe. His arms wouldn't let me fall.

The soundless scream traveled up and strangled me as our hips found a synchronicity unlike any other. The angle had him dragging against some part of me that had never been touched each time he left me. When he filled me again, there was nothing but warmth and fullness.

For the first time, I didn't feel alone.

For the first time, I felt part of something—someone.

I shuddered around him, my lips trembling as he slowly, sweetly kissed me before the end opened up before us. His hips slammed into mine as we both raced for the finish. I held on and buried my face in his neck while my orgasm obliterated me.

As the world stopped for just one beat, maybe two. Silence and calm flooded my jangling system before I was slapped back into reality—the end credits of the movie still playing all around us.

Finally, he lifted me off the bar, somehow still inside me, and we landed in a heap of drop-cloths and laughter. The heaviness of the moment popped like a soap bubble.

"It's probably not manly to say my knees liquified from coming, right?" He stretched his arms over his head, arching his back as if to get the kinks out.

For God's sake, he hadn't even taken off his damn T-shirt. An arrow of dark, silky hair climbed up from where we were still tangled. His abs were a damn work of art. Not the perfect gym rat kind, but the working man kind.

I wanted to crawl all over him and find every ridge and curve.

I inched his shirt up, scraping my teeth over his muscled chest and finding a nipple in the fur.

He growled and seemed to firm again as I slid down his length. His fingers dug into my hips. "Don't start something you can't finish."

"Who says I can't?" I undulated my hips to hold him tight inside me.

He lowered his mouth to my neck, finding some insane combination that only he seemed to know. The edge between tickle and pleasure made my blood thicken and slow. I slid back just enough that he could get his hand between us, his thumb swirling over my clit. "Jesus, you're so fucking sexy."

I arched my back as the next trip started.

Jesus, how long had it been since I'd had an actual string of orgasms?

Then both our phones went off and thunder erupted on the chipboard doorway between The Haunt and the café.

"I'm sorry to interrupt," came Rylee's voice.

"Then don't," I yelled back as I rocked against his hand.

"Sorry! Emergency!"

I groaned as the climax started to dissipate instead of escalate. "No." Was that my voice coming out in a whine?

"Baby on board! Ivy's in labor!"

Both of us went as still as statues. We both shouted, "What did you say?"

"I hope you two managed to get the job done, because time is up!"

We both scrambled apart, legs tangled. Gideon tripped on the drop-cloth trying to get up and I slid back onto him, my knee jamming into his thigh.

He instantly rolled me so his dangly bits were safe. "Please don't unman me just after I've finally gotten you naked."

I snorted. "You think you'll get to do it again?"

"I fucking better," he muttered as he rolled off of me to take care of the condom and zip up.

I relaxed onto my back, the giggles coming up faster than I could breathe. "Can you find my pants?" They came at my head a second later. I couldn't stop laughing like a maniac.

"I hate you so much."

Nah, you love me.

Holy crap, I'd almost said that out loud. Suddenly, the giggles dissipated like my orgasm.

Gideon was standing over me with his hand out. "You all right?"

Nope. So far from fucking all right.

"Yeah. Time to add another mom to the collection, right?"

He helped me to my feet. "Is there a reason why you are so against kids?"

I opened my mouth to reply when another floor-rattling knock interrupted us. "Guess we'll have to wait for that story until another time." I hopped my way into my jeans and stuffed my feet into my shoes.

I found my shirt at the end of the bar and waved Gideon ahead. My racing heart needed another second. It had to be the orgasms. They were messing with my head.

TWELVE

MACY

"You couldn't wait for Lucky Charms to get home?"

Ivy let out a half laugh as she did those weird breathing exercises. "Nope, just like her dad, this one wants out early."

I tried not to wince. Ivy was on my couch. Evidently, that would be going into the scrapyard behind Dare's shop. Maybe I'd have him make me one of those fancy truck bench ones like he and Gage made for Rylee.

People were always fighting over it.

I made a mental note to put my order in over there. They were always so damn busy. It had taken me six months to get the stools for the bar on his order list. Then again, I'd been building The Haunt in my head for a year.

"Her?" Rylee asked.

"Shoot." Ivy blew out a rapid succession of breaths. "I'm supposed to keep it a secret."

"Does Rory know?"

"No, he wants to be surprised." She let out a long moan. "Actually, funny story, I wanted to be surprised, and he played along." She groaned and rubbed the side of her belly. "Then when he was talking to the doctor, I accidentally heard the tech say girl." She tipped her head back and shouted out a laugh and cry combo that made all my girl parts shrivel. "So, here I am with a big secret because my husband has been trying to play along with me. Oh my God, I can't do this."

Rylee came to sit by her side. "The ambulance is on its way."

"Kinleigh! Where is my husband?!"

Kinleigh was on the phone near the window, her shoulders hunched. She held up a finger and spoke urgently to someone on the other end who was definitely not Rory.

Gideon came up beside me, Dani in his arms. She was covered in paint, but her wide green eyes were worried. "Is Miss Ivy going to be all right?"

He rubbed her back lightly. "She's going to be just fine."

"Is the baby coming?"

"Possibly in my café."

"Cool!"

I glanced up at her with her arm wrapped around her dad's neck. He didn't cringe away from the paint she was wearing.

"Are you done working now, Dad?"

My neck felt really hot. I was pretty sure the whole room was looking at us. I glanced down at my shirt to make sure it wasn't on backward.

"Yeah, kiddo. We're good to go home as soon as we make sure Ivy's okay. Is that all right?"

"Can we go to the hospital with her?"

"You're all going to the hospital with me if Rory isn't here." Ivy slapped the back of the couch and arched up off the cushions like a demon. Dear God.

Gideon caught my gaze, his eyes wide with actual fear.

"Weren't in the birthing room, Dad?"

He swallowed. "Jessica actually went into labor on location." Gideon tipped his head against his daughter's. "I didn't get there in time."

I found myself rubbing his arm in sympathy before I dropped my hand back to my side. What the hell was wrong with me?

A knock on the door had me whirling around. I patted my pockets then ran back to the counter for my keys.

Chaos reigned after that. Rylee, Gideon, and I moved tables to get the stretcher into the dining room.

Kinleigh came back over to Ivy with the phone and held it out in front of her. "He's trying to get on the next plane, but I got him on video."

"I don't want video, I want him here."

"Ivy, love." Rory's voice came through the speaker loud and clear. "I swear I'll be there as soon as humanly possible. I never should have left you." His voice was out of breath.

Ivy snatched the phone from Kinleigh. "I cannot do this without you."

"You are strong and perfect and I know you'll make sure that little girl comes into the world safe and sound."

Ivy instantly burst into tears. "You know?"

"Of course I know. I've been trying not to say it every bloody day."

"Okay, miss. Let's get you on the—"

Ivy let out a scream that made the whole damn room go silent. She sat up. "I'm going nowhere."

"You are not having this baby in my damn café."

The paramedic pushed the stretcher out of the way to get to Ivy. "Okay, let's just calm down a little. Is this your first birth?"

"Yes." Ivy wiggled on the couch to get into a better position.

"Ivy," came Rory's tinny voice.

"Yes." She held the phone up in front of her face. "Yes, I'm here."

"Let the nice people take you to the hospital."

"I don't think I'm going to make it to the hospital." Ivy's huge eyes were full of tears. "I've had that backache thing all day. And you know those Braxton Hicks? Yeah. Those doctors are liars."

"Jesus." Gideon took a step back.

"Wimp."

"Yes, ma'am."

"Next time you do the kid thing, that's not going to fly."

His eyes locked with mine. "Is that so?"

I looked away quickly. "Hey, is there anything I can do to help? Towels? Hot water?"

The female paramedic started unpacking a kit. "We should be okay to take her. We'll just check her vitals and see how things are going."

"Down there?" I swallowed. I really didn't want to see it. The last time I'd seen pieces of a birth had been in health class. I was still haunted.

I could watch a head get severed, no problem. A head coming into the world? Nope.

No, thank you.

"Yes, I need to see how far she's dilated. Lucky for you guys, I'm a doula on the side."

"I don't know what that is." I held my hand up. "Don't want to know either."

She laughed and took out a few things out of her kit and went to Ivy. "Okay, mom-to-be, what's your name?"

"Ivy." Her voice was breathless, thanks to the breathing thing and sheer panic.

You know, because there was a human coming out of her.

Jesus. I bent at the waist to get my own breath for a second. I really couldn't have all these emotions swinging around like this in one hour. From orgasmic bliss to terror seemed a little cruel.

"Are you okay, Macy?" Dani patted my hand, then tucked her fingers into mine.

The floor shimmered once before I blinked back the tears. "Yeah, kid, I'm good." But I held on because the kid looked just as scared as I felt. I glanced up at Gideon, who was standing right by me. "Maybe you should take her home."

Dani lifted her chin. "I can stay. I want to see Miss Ivy's baby."

"Hopefully, she's going to the hospital to have the baby."

"Then I can go to the hospital. Right, Dad?"

"We don't want to be in the way, sweetheart."

Ivy let out an ear-piercing scream. "I need my go-bag. I need my husband. I need August!"

"I can do two of those things." Gideon put his hand on Dani's head. "You'll be okay with, Macy?"

She nodded. "I'll help."

I waved him off. "I've got her."

Dani dragged me toward the counter. "We can get towels. I'm thinking this is going to be yucky."

That was an understatement. I looked over my shoulder to find Kinleigh explaining where the go-bag was at her apartment. As usual, Gideon was taking charge. He was good at it with his men and here. And I didn't want to analyze why that made my chest tight.

He pushed up his sleeves on his cotton shirt. The neck of it was a little misshapen from…well, from me dragging at his clothes. Otherwise, no one would know I'd had a religious experience next door.

Cripes.

I pushed open the door and flicked on the lights. "Okay, Ash, go to that cabinet and get as many big towels as you can find."

"Okay."

I pulled down my biggest pot to boil water. I didn't know if that was really a thing, but if the baby was coming, shit was definitely going to get yucky as Dani had said.

"Okay, I got 'em."

I turned on the burner and twisted around. The stack of towels was past her head. I took two off the top. "Is your ankle okay?"

Her green eyes were sparkling. "I'm good."

I narrowed my gaze. "Are you sure?"

"Okay, maybe you can take half."

I took three more and turned her around, pushing the swinging door open to let her go ahead of me. "All right, let's go."

"Jesus." Chaos had changed over my café into some scary triage unit. Considering a metallic blanket was now tented over Ivy's knees, I had a feeling things were going even quicker than Ivy thought.

Dani took off like a shot and I hurried after her.

"I need my focus bunny," Ivy said at the top of her lungs.

"Ivy, I need you to take some deep breaths."

"I need my focus. I need it."

Kinleigh was sitting next to the couch, her hands clasped around one of Ivy's. "Gideon's getting my backup go-bag. He'll be right back."

"I need it now." Her face was ruddy and sweaty, her panic rising as Rory tried to talk to her.

I dropped the towels on the table by the second paramedic, currently on the phone with the hospital. I didn't know much about the baby thing. My limited knowledge of children was past the toddler days.

Memories of Malcolm and his favorite toy bombarded me. I shoved them down ruthlessly. Now was not the time to remember him. But maybe the focus thing was almost the same.

"Does she need something to focus on for the contractions? Is that what she's talking about?"

"Yes." The doula-slash-paramedic looked up from between Ivy's legs. "If you had something small for her."

I turned to my corner shelving unit full of bats and pumpkins and spiders. Nothing that Ivy would enjoy. But maybe…

I shoved aside books to find the little stuffed bat she'd given me that was perched on top of an ice cream sundae.

I held it up. "Will this do?"

Ivy's eyes were bloodshot from doing God knows what to get that kid out of her. "I need my focus bunny."

Kinleigh sighed. "Honey, we're getting it, but I just sent a man to find something in my shop."

Ivy laughed and cried at the same time. "I'm never going to get that bunny." She held her hand out. "Give it to me." She snatched it out of my hands and set it on her belly.

"Okay, love, just deep breaths." Rory's voice came from the same area. The phone was tucked beside her in heaps of clothing and tablecloths.

Dani rushed over to the female paramedic. "Here." She stacked towels next to her.

"Thank you very much. You're such a good girl."

Dani flushed, her freckles glowing. "Sure. No big deal." She rushed back over to me.

The door banged open and August came flying in with the bag. "I'm here."

Ivy's other hand popped up. "Auggie. Oh, God. Rory isn't here. I mean, he's here on the phone, but—" Her sobs started up again. "God, it hurts."

August Beck, her older brother, leaned over the back of my couch, frustration etched in his face. "Is this the best place to do this? Can't we get her to the hospital?" He glanced at Kinleigh helplessly, then at the paramedic.

He was a hulking, dark-haired guy who looked like he was just about to lose his lunch at the things going on at the end of the couch. He moved up to his sister and pushed away stray bits of hair from her braids. "You always like to make a splash, Ive."

"At least I didn't have her in the truck." She arched as another contraction slammed into her.

"Can't you give her something?" August gripped the back of the couch.

The paramedic shook her head. "Sorry. She's way too far along and we don't have those kinds of medications in the ambulance."

"Okay, Ivy. I'm going to need you to push when the next contraction comes around, okay?"

She shook her head. "No, I can't. I can't have her now. I need Rory."

"Nope, you are going to do this with all of us. Great energy in this room, right? Strong women all around and even males who haven't passed out yet."

Ivy collapsed back against the arm of the couch. "That is a miracle." She let August's hand go to grab her phone. "Rory?"

"I'm here."

She laughed weakly. "I don't want to do this without you."

"I'm right here. You'll never be alone, I promise you. Thank God for technology. My mum is even on her way over. She can't wait to meet her grandchild."

"Oh, is she?" Her eyes went wide and suddenly, she tensed again. "Here we go."

"I need you to push now."

"Now?"

"Now!" The paramedic's voice was stern and calm. It seemed to snap something to attention in Ivy. She immediately grabbed August and Kinleigh's hands and bore down.

Holy shit. I couldn't move. Dani ran over to me and hugged me around the middle, burying her face in my side at the rash of grunts that came out of the usually sweet Ivy.

It seemed like it took forever, but then everything became hushed as Ivy slumped back.

"Okay. That was awesome. You're doing amazing. This little girl? It's a girl, right?"

"That's what we overheard at the doctor's." Ivy's voice was weak.

"Well, this little girl is going to come out in no time. I just need you to hang in there with me, okay?"

Ivy nodded.

August seemed at a loss and he kept trying to reach over the couch.

"Just rip off the back if that's what you want to do." I absently stroked Dani's hair.

August looked up. "Really?"

"Go for it. That's going directly into the scrapyard after this little incident."

August squatted down and his big hand slid down the side of the back of the couch. He pulled something off his belt and after a little work—far less than I thought should hold a damn couch together—the backing came loose. He jerked it up and threw it onto the floor so he could kneel on it "Better. Hey, sis."

"Well, that's one way to do it." The paramedic shook her head then gripped Ivy's knee gently. "We're going to push again in a minute, okay?" When Ivy didn't answer, she repeated herself.

"Yes."

August slid his arm behind his sister to support her. Kinleigh did the same so they were practically hugging Ivy. Their other hands were clasping each of Ivy's as she slowly tensed again.

"Here we go."

August looked over his sister to Kinleigh and the air seemed to charge. Hmm. Well, that was interesting.

Then it was all about the baby. Gideon came to meet me and Dani, standing behind us. Rylee sidled up to the other side of me and grabbed my hand.

I didn't even bother trying to step away from any of them. It was as if one unit was banding together in each camp. I wasn't even sure how much time had passed. The paramedic's soothing voice never changed. Even when I was pretty sure Ivy was going to tear her head off.

August and Kinleigh were a combined unit in this weird little bubble around her. I couldn't take watching Ivy crying about how tired she was. I tried to break away, but instead of letting me walk off, Gideon turned me around and held on.

When the baby's crying filled the room, I sagged against him.

Thank God.

"Big bad boss lady afraid of a little blood?" Rylee asked. "You were good when I was giving birth."

"Yeah, well, there were doctors and I didn't have to see… everything." I waved my hand behind me.

Dani looked up at me. "Is the baby okay?"

"Hear all that crying going on? That's a good sign."

She glanced to her father. "That true?"

"The pros tell me so." He smiled down at Dani, then hugged me closer, brushing his lips along my temple. "I think I better get her home."

I nodded and stepped away from him. "It's late."

"I want to see the baby." Dani folded her arms.

"Give Ivy a minute with her family over there and we'll see what's what." His pocket started buzzing and he took out his phone. His face went stony and he shoved it back into his jeans.

"Everything okay?"

He glanced at Dani then back at me meaningfully. It took me a second, but I caught on quick. The ex. Nothing like the blond bombshell of his past to throw some cold water on everything.

Kinleigh had gone around what was left of my couch to hug August as Ivy took a minute to show Rory his new baby. From all the squeaking and crying both from baby and mom, I was pretty sure everything was good.

Ivy was wrapped up in blankets and the hot water came in handy to get the baby cleaned up enough to take a ride in the ambulance. She waved us over.

"Meet Rhiannon Grace Ferguson." She cradled her close but turned her out so everyone could see.

Dani stood on her tiptoes and leaned in to get closer to the baby.

"Dani..." Gideon started.

Ivy shook her head. "It's okay. Isn't she beautiful?"

"She's all squishy," Dani replied.

Gideon hung his head and we all laughed.

"Well, she's been through quite a bit tonight."

Dani touched her little pink hand. "Wow."

"Yeah, pretty much all I can say too," Ivy whispered. She looked up at me. "Sorry I kind of put on a show."

"At least it wasn't in the middle of lunch." I placed my hands on Dani's shoulders to gently pull her back.

Ivy laughed and kissed the top of her daughter's head. "No. Small favors there." She craned her neck to smile up at August. "And I had my backup coaches here."

"She's beautiful, Ive." August's voice was deep with emotion. "Mom and Dad will meet us at the hospital." He finally released Kinleigh. "Why don't you go with her on the ambulance and I'll follow in the truck."

Kinleigh nodded. "Yeah, definitely."

Rylee came forward to say hi to the baby. "Vee is going to be pissed she missed it."

"At least there would have been cookies. I'm famished." Ivy laughed and kissed the baby again. The baby's hair was so fine, but it seemed to have a bit of a red tinge to it.

"Hey, Ash, you want to go get a few cookies from the bakery cabinet for our new mama?"

"Yeah." She ran without a limp. Guess that sore ankle was miraculously feeling better now that she didn't have time to think about it. "Can I have one too?"

I caught Gideon's gaze, but he was obviously somewhere else. His furrowed brow was back, and he was on his phone again. I was pissed enough to make the executive decision that he deserved to have to deal with his daughter and double chocolate cookies at eleven at night.

"Sure can. Two for you too."

"Excellent."

The paramedics were quick to pack Ivy up onto the stretcher and start for the door.

Dani raced back in with a little white bag. "Here you go."

Ivy took the bag with a little wave.

Kinleigh was hot on their heels and August stood behind the wreckage of my former couch. I could tell he was torn between racing after them and helping us.

I nudged Rylee. "Come on, Mocha. It's time to get our muscle on." I crossed to the couch and pushed August aside. "Go. You should be with family."

"But I can help first."

"Go. We're not helpless. I can make Gideon help if need be."

Even if he was busy texting like a madman. Dani was happily stuffing chunky chocolate chip cookies into her face.

I gathered all the towels and threw them on the couch, then got out the trash bags I kept tucked behind the cans in the garbage stations.

"Why do we always get cleanup duty?" Rylee muttered.

I handed her a bag. "That's a very good question."

Gideon finally seemed to notice we were cleaning up and came over to help. Between the three of us, we managed to get the couch out back. I was pretty sure my customers didn't need to see the crime scene the next morning.

Gideon was quiet and I didn't know what the hell to say, so I opted for nothing.

"I'm going to go give all the things a quick mop." Rylee looked between us and gave me a *yikes* look. "I'll check on Dani."

"Thanks." Gideon raked his hands through his hair.

"I'm assuming that phone deal wasn't awesome?"

"Not really."

Since he didn't elaborate, I sure as hell wasn't going to beg for information. "Right." I stalked to the back door of Brewed Awakening.

Gideon caught my arm. "Macy, wait."

"It's not my business."

"Of course it is."

"No, it really isn't. Just because we got naked doesn't mean I'm privy to all the details of your life."

"What if I want to tell you?"

"Then tell me." I put my hands on my hips.

"Jessica is coming back to town."

"When?"

"I don't know, she left a vague message and won't reply to my texts. Typical shit she always pulls when I don't jump and do whatever she wants when she wants me to."

I fisted my hands in my jeans pockets. "She must have been a spectacular bang for you to put up with that."

His eyes narrowed. "I'm definitely not wading into those crocodile-infested waters."

"Look, it's fine. We're fine. We got that itch scratched."

He took two long strides and caught me before I could back up again. He curled his arm through my stiffened arms to drag me into him. "That itch isn't going to be scratched from one fuck. I didn't get to take my time with you."

I flattened my hands against his broad chest. My heart slammed against my ribs and I had the strongest urge to run and to drag him up to my apartment at the same time.

He lowered his mouth to mine. The kiss was scorching and thorough. By the time he was done with me, he was lightly tugging on my lower lip with his teeth. Kind of the same way I'd done to start the night.

"Just because I have a crappy ex to deal with doesn't mean I want what's happening between us to stop." He rested his forehead against mine. "I don't want to lose this."

I slid my hand up to tease the long ends of his hair he tried to tame. "Someone to scratch an itch with?"

"You know it's more than a fucking itch. And can we stop saying itch? I want to touch you because I like it. If I just wanted to get my wick wet, I could do that easy enough."

I stiffened. "Asshole."

He lowered his hand to cup my ass, dragging me against him to show me just how hard he was. "I'm not that guy. No matter how much you want to slot me in there as a quick fuck and chuck, it isn't going to happen."

I rose onto my toes. My brain kept telling me to back it up, but my body leaned in. My instincts really wanted to embrace everything he was saying. "We aren't supposed to get complicated."

"Too late, Mace." He kissed me again, then turned me toward the back door. "Now let's get this place cleaned up."

By the time we got the café back to rights, I was so exhausted I didn't have to fight insomnia for once in my damn life.

Wasn't that a bitch?

THIRTEEN

Gideon

It had been a week since Ivy gave birth. I'd managed to get some time in with Macy once, but that had been more of a chilly makeout session. Literally chilly—in her freezer when I'd gone on the hunt for coffee.

That thing with cold and dicks shriveling wasn't really a thing when you had a gorgeous Amazon crawling all over you. Jesus, she was going to kill me.

However, all the lingering good parts of the week were now absolute shit. Jessica was coming back to town on her way to New York City. She wanted time with me, and time with our daughter.

So much for believing the relative silence from her since she'd gone back home—after a quick visit with Dani, where she'd clucked over her sprained ankle and asked who had been watching her when she'd gotten hurt—indicated maybe she'd changed her mind.

Not so much.

It was important, she'd said. Would we be able to spend an evening with her later in the month?

Which meant she hadn't changed her mind after talking to her lawyer and her handlers and the legions of other people who seemingly helped her to run her life.

I hated what she was doing. Hated that she was building in false hope that maybe she would back off. That she was confusing Dani. And I didn't want that woman fucking with my head again. I'd made peace with the fact that she was the mother of my child and would never truly be cut out of my life.

But she was persisting with this bullshit reason to take my daughter from me. Even if she was asking for more visitation—even if she was entitled to it as her mother—I couldn't shake the pervasive feeling that this meant I'd failed. Despite busting my ass to take care of Dani and to keep her life stable, if the judge awarded Jessica more visitation, that would mean that I hadn't done my job as well as I could have. Whether or not that was the reality didn't mean jack.

Hell, it could be true. Otherwise Dani wouldn't have thought she needed to get her poor old man a date, which had helped to lead to the whole situation with Macy.

Not including that kiss she'd planted on me the night Dani hurt her ankle. No wonder I'd looked for any way to lock her down. We'd already danced around each other for years. If I hadn't grabbed her in front of the television crew, she probably would still be dancing away from me.

It was one of her best skills.

As amazing as we were right now, I was a realist. It wouldn't last forever. As soon as Macy's escape hatch opened up—one I had willingly given her—she'd be gone. I couldn't even blame her. I had no desire to walk away from the good thing we had going, but I also wasn't going to beg her to stay in a situation that obviously would never be truly what she wanted. She didn't like kids. That she seemed to be meshing so well with Dani was just a bit of blind luck. It wasn't a permanent situation, and it might not even make one bit of difference with the judge. But it had given me some moments I would never forget.

I was already pissed at Macy, and she hadn't even left yet.

It didn't make sense, but it did leave me short-tempered with everyone around me. My father had hung up on me twice this week.

One day soon she'd end this, despite offering her a no strings situation. At the moment, we were in a holding pattern due to this visitation thing, but soon enough, she'd snip them and be gone.

And I had no say there either. I'd already had my say when I'd told her we could end things without a ripple.

Except now? There were ripples all over the fucking place.

"Hey, dude, I think it's in."

When I didn't look up from hammering, Luc tapped me on the shoulder. I'd heard him speaking to me, but the words had been nearly unintelligible over the Foo Fighters song blaring in my headphones. I'd turned the music up to the loudest decibel possible to drown out the construction noises surrounding me. Normally, those sounds were almost soothing to me.

Today, I was afraid any noise would set me off.

I reared back with an elbow to get some space, but Luc had already moved back. He cocked a brow at me and motioned for me to take off my ancient headset.

"What?" I demanded, yanking off my safety glasses.

"You're mangling the shit out of that fascia." He nodded at the piece of wood I'd been unintentionally tormenting. "Unless you're going for a different look for Macy's shelving than we discussed."

I looked closer at the wood and noticed the nail was crooked and I'd chipped off a corner of the decorative engraving.

"Fuck." I tossed the board on the scrap pile. "Obviously, today isn't the day for me to do anything requiring precision."

"Think Robert needs some help in back."

"You mean tiling the wall above the sink?"

Luc shrugged. "Hey, it's something even you can you do."

"Thanks." I usually wasn't the lame duck of the crew. Far from it. But today, I didn't trust myself to do much.

Right now, my team would probably do better without me.

I turned off the music app on my phone and set down my hammer. It was probably better that I quit while I was ahead.

"You guys good here?" I called up to Moose once Luc had ambled off to heckle Pamela, the newest member of the crew. He'd probably have asked her out by dinner.

Moose pulled off his protective ear gear and backed down the ladder he'd been stationed on to work on the top of one of the built-ins. "Looks good here. You taking off for lunch?"

"Yeah." And maybe more than that if Macy could take a break.

"That's good. You've been here long hours and no matter the job, it can make you cross-eyed after awhile."

"You too."

"Just trying to log as many hours as possible before the twins come. I really appreciate you being so generous with the time off afterward."

"Well, first off, it's the law, and secondly, it's not every day a man has twins."

"That's a true statement, although thank fuck I'm not the one actually having them." Moose swiped a hand over his dusty forehead. "Women are amazing, man. Once you see your wife give birth to your child, you never forget they're basically like Wonder Woman. And two? Vee's so small." He shook his head. "I keep worrying they'll get stuck."

I smiled as I clapped Moose on the back. "It helps they don't actually come out at once. She'll do just fine. She's a warrior."

"Yeah, she is." He wiped off his hands on the bandana hanging out of his jeans pocket. "You ever think about doing it again?"

"Having more kids?"

"Yeah. You know, the family deal." Moose's ears tinged pink. "Not that you and Dani aren't a family."

"No, I know what you mean. I haven't really considered it."

But now that he'd mentioned it, I was back on that track of being annoyed at the world again, specifically Macy. She hadn't done a damn thing to me, and that was the problem.

Things were going too fucking well. We just worked. She made me laugh and got me out of my head and I liked to think I did the same for her. Being with her just felt easy and natural—with the added layer of snark and sexual tension that seemed to flow between us like oxygen. The only sticking point I'd anticipated involved her being with Dani, and those concerns had turned out to be unfounded.

They'd been spending a ton of time together since Karen had been out of commission, with Dani coming by the café after school most days while I worked.

Every time, I went next door to make sure she wasn't driving Macy too crazy, I found her being put to work either decorating something or helping clean up or even to shepherd the little kids in the reading nook. And Dani talked about Macy and the coffee shop constantly, so she was clearly enjoying herself.

Which only pissed me off more.

Everything with Jessica just reaffirmed the ticking clock with Macy. If somehow the visitation problem went away, would Macy vanish too?

She agreed to date you before Jessica showed up. You don't know she wouldn't keep it going even after the whole Jessica thing goes away.

If it did.

Fuck.

Why didn't Macy know we were so fucking good together? We could be even more so if we didn't have these supposedly reasonable dating parameters boxing us in.

No strings, my ass.

"Look, man, I didn't mean to bring up a sore subject."

"It's not sore. Who says it's sore?"

"Well, just was figuring with you dating Macy, but Macy being Macy, we all know that's not really her bag. So, I have to figure more isn't your bag either. Or you're not thinking about that. Christ, can I step in it any more?" Moose let out a laugh. "Sorry. It's just been long enough I've been married that I forgot being single is a different thing. And also, that all guys aren't like me."

"No, not every guy wants to get married on the first date if he could." I regretted the sharp tone I'd used as soon as the words were out, but Moose simply nodded.

"I knew she was the one before the first date actually. She was it for me from the first moment."

"Oh, Christ on bikes. Is it time for tiny harps and hearts shooting out of asses again?" Luc swung by to borrow Moose's ladder.

Moose put his bandana away. "You're just jealous."

I nearly laughed out loud at that until Luc grabbed the ladder and took off.

He couldn't be, could he? A guy like Luc who seemed to absolutely love the single life and going after every woman he wanted?

"Hmm, speaking of sore spots." Moose raised a brow. "I guess no one likes being alone. Even Luc. No matter how many nights you're with someone, there's always one where you gotta face yourself."

"Psychoanalyze someone else, would you?" Luc called from the back, slamming around tools for emphasis.

Moose shot me a look.

I said nothing. I had to agree on the being alone part. It fucking sucked.

I was tired of it. I didn't want any more of it, not when I was realizing exactly how much better it was to have the right person in your life.

Macy and I were still so new. I didn't know for sure she was the right person. But I was beginning to think so more and more with each passing moment.

I grabbed my plaid flannel and shrugged it on. "I'm going next door." Saying it aloud felt like a declaration.

Fuck time limits. Fuck safety. Fuck artificial dating arrangements that felt more real than anything else ever had in my life. And if Macy needed a reminder of that, I'd be happy to provide one.

As many times as it took.

"Good idea. Fucking the boss will make her feel more charitable about you screwing up her fascia." Luc gave me a thumbs up as I passed, and I flipped him a middle finger.

"Hey, while you're over there, can you pick up our lunch—"

I went out the back door, letting it swing shut behind me. Nope, I wasn't picking up any orders. I didn't know when I'd be back.

Hopefully, not until lunch was long over with.

The two buildings were joined by a parking lot and separate loading docks behind each building. I didn't really want to go around the front of the café to find her. Somehow she was always busy.

Then I spotted cardboard flying. What the hell?

I jumped off the loading dock to cross the parking lot. Another huge piece of cardboard shot up into the air. Guess someone was recycling. Maybe I'd be in luck after all. At least I could sneak in the back door to Brewed Awakening and maybe convince Macy to take a long lunch with me.

The clunk of a pile of cardboard hitting the recycle bins was followed by a very familiar grumble. I leaned against the pole on the edge of the dumpster gate.

"Whatcha doin'?"

She jumped and whirled with her box cutter out.

"Easy, Killer." I held up my hands.

Macy sagged. "You do not sneak up on a woman."

"This is Crescent Cove, Mace." I moved into her space.

She wiggled back. "I'm a hot mess."

I buried my face into her neck where loose pieces from her ponytail slid along the neck of her light denim jacket. "You smell delicious."

"Yeah well, my newest employee—former—just spilled a new order of coffee beans everywhere. I've been cleaning it up for an hour."

I straightened, digging my fingers into her tight and grip-worthy ass. "No second chances?"

"Not when you look at me and say, 'My bad' after spilling four hundred dollars worth of coffee beans."

I pressed my lips together. "Guess I should have fired Lucky awhile ago."

"That's a true statement if I've ever heard one." She tried to twist away.

I held her still. "What's up?"

"Nothing, just feel gross." She looked down at her hands. "Pretty sure I'm going to be scrubbing coffee out of my nails for days."

"Thinking that's not all."

She narrowed her eyes. "Did I mention the triple digits loss?"

"Come on, spill it." She crossed her arms in between us. Damn, she was stubborn. "You can vent to me."

"I'm freaking out, all right? It's middle of September and I'm so behind on everything."

"No, you're not. We're right on time based on the schedule we put together last year."

"Yeah, well, I just lost my freaking chef. Do you know how many I interviewed for that freaking spot?" Her dark blue eyes flashed. "Six months I spent on interviews. And I have to find one in less than six weeks? How?"

I rubbed her arms. "Did you have any backups? You always have backups."

"Yes. Of course I did, but they already took jobs. I'm so freaking screwed."

I knew it couldn't just be the coffee. That was shitty, but when it came to restaurants, random accidents or crappy shipments happened with the product all the time. I'd been renovating enough of them to know.

I kissed her forehead. Looked like my afternoon bang was probably going to be put on hold. "I can put some feelers out for people looking for a job. I kinda know…everyone from doing the renos I do."

"Yeah. Thanks." She unwound her tight arms and played with the tails of the plaid shirt I'd pulled on. "What are you doing over here anyway?"

"Came to bug you."

"Yeah?" She hooked her fingers into one of my belt loops. "Or came to try and get laid?"

I shrugged. "The two are not mutually exclusive."

She snorted.

"It's been a shitty morning for me too." I widened my stance, so we lined up a little more. I loved how tall she was. I didn't have to crick my neck to get a taste of her.

That and I never knew when she was going to climb me like a cat. It had happened a time or two already, but I hadn't gotten more than a taste of her in days.

I was already addicted. And I was was in fucking withdrawal.

Her fingers slipped under my T-shirt to scratch through the hair along my belly. "Is that so?"

"What?"

She grinned up at me. "Shitty day."

"Right. Sorry, distracted."

She swayed against me. "So I feel."

"You drive me crazy some days."

"Ditto." She went onto her toes and bit my lower lip. "Shall we distract one another?"

"God, yes." I lowered my mouth to hers and there was no sweetness. Thank God for her. I didn't have to worry I'd break her or hurt her. At least not physically.

I fisted her ponytail and bent her back with the force of my kiss. Instead of shrinking away from me, she gave back just as aggressively. The kiss was hot and messy and more of a fight than romance.

My blood fired. Just what I needed to diffuse this frustration clawing at my damn bones. Wanting her and being pissed at another woman at the same time was exhausting and confusing.

I broke our mouths apart. Hers was bright red from my teeth and beard. Swollen with how harsh I'd been. I lifted my thumb to smooth across her lower lip, but she didn't seem to want the sweetness.

She nipped my finger. "Upstairs?"

I didn't want to go inside and get distracted. Because no matter how capable her team of people was, she couldn't help but get involved in her business.

She was too Macy.

I tugged her forward. "Go for a drive?"

Her eyebrows rose. "What are we, teenagers?"

"I've been sporting a hard-on half the day like one. Might as well see how far I can get in my truck."

Her lips spread into a rare wide smile. "All right. I'll remind you how bad an idea it was when we can't get it right."

"My truck is much roomier these days."

"You saying you need room for us?" She slid her fingers into my back pockets and squeezed none-too-gently.

"I'm saying I need room to get you on top of me, Mace." I gripped her ponytail to match her hold on me. "I need inside you. And not the easy, sweet kind of way."

"Well then." She dug out her phone from her jacket pocket and flashed off a text, then grabbed my hand.

Both of us had a long stride, and we got to my truck in record time. I went around to open the door for her. Again, her eyebrows shot up. "Boy Scout," she said against my mouth.

Because my truck was parked off to the side under a huge oak, I didn't have to worry about prying eyes. I dipped my fingers into the front of the stretchy pants she wore all the damn time. I went straight under her panties and slipped two fingers inside of her.

She hissed out a breath and braced herself on the open door.

I dug deep inside of her, groaning at the building heat waiting for me. Was she just as wound up all the damn time as I was? I ground the palm of my hand along the top of her slit where her clit was already begging for a touch.

She growled against my neck and held on as I finger-fucked her like there was no one around. Like it was just us and no one could interrupt. Instead of feigning that she didn't want this, she opened for me. She lifted her hips up to meet each of my grinding strokes.

I nudged her jacket and shirt aside enough to get to her neck and sucked hard along the sensitive skin between her shoulder and neck as I drowned in her. As I pushed her up and through two orgasms before she could take a breath.

When I pulled back enough to look into her eyes, I drowned in the dark blue depths. I let her see me and know it was me who was giving this to her. Demanding it from her.

She tried to tip her head back to break the connection, but I slammed my mouth against hers, both of our eyes open as she cried out in my mouth. I swallowed each of her cries and groaned as her sweet pussy clenched around my damn fingers instead of my cock.

But it was enough.

For right now, it was enough.

I slid my fingers out of her as she sagged against the seat. I looked down at how soaked my fingers were and watched her as I licked every bit of her off me. I didn't say a damn word as I hiked her up into the truck.

She wouldn't look at me when I closed the door.

Pissed or shocked, I wasn't quite sure.

I walked around the back of the truck and gave myself a quick moment before I opened my door. I was as hard as a fucking beam, but I was strangely even, knowing I could have her like that.

That she'd allow me in like that had quieted the rage brewing inside me.

The ride out of town was quiet. The days were getting shorter, but we still had a good bit of the afternoon to ourselves. I should probably take her back to my place to give her an actual bed.

She deserved so much more than these quick, stolen moments.

"Pull off here," she said quietly.

I glanced over at her. The flush had left her cheeks, but now there was a little something else there.

"You know where we are?"

"Lookout lane?"

I laughed. "No, that's the other side of the lake."

She unhooked her belt as we came up over the rise. It was a less-traveled road, but at least it wasn't dirt. The view of the lake was stunning. The sun was near blinding off the cool, calm water.

"Rylee and Gage have a house over this way. I got lost while I was going there the first time and I found this." She gripped the dashboard as she went onto her knees. "See that house?"

I followed her eyeline to the rambling Cape Cod with the burnt orange shingle siding and white trim. It had a large wraparound porch and was quite overgrown.

Obviously, the old girl had been on the market for a good long time.

"I don't need a house that size, but I just couldn't stop looking at it." She flushed. "Anyway, sorry. But that's a killer view." It seemed like she was upset that she'd shared with me.

She crawled over the bench-style seat of my truck. The intent in her eyes made me want to push back. To see if I could get her to talk to me a little more. I had so few pieces of Macy to work with.

But she was determined, and I was fucking weak.

"Is there a way to get this…ahh, there we go." She flipped up my steering column so she could shimmy onto my hips. She lowered her mouth to my belly as she pushed up my shirt to get to skin.

The little medallion I wore slipped across my skin as she scored her short nails up my chest. She leaned to the side and hit the lever to recline my seat the last few inches available. I was a tall guy and took up most of the room in the truck already.

"Know your way around a truck."

She shrugged. "I know a little about a lot of things." She pushed at my shirt again and we both wrestled with it and my flannel until she got me just how she wanted me. Her gaze was hot and calculating as she stripped off her jacket and tossed her shirt onto the passenger side of the seat. She wore a midnight blue lace bra that made her golden skin glow.

I held her off from undoing the clasp and plucked lightly at her nipple straining against the lace. With the other, I tugged at the black band that forever kept her hair back away from her face. "Goddamn, you are beautiful."

She shook her hair back self-consciously. "You don't need to flatter me." She rolled her hips to ride the hard-on I was still sporting. She looked down between us to work at my belt.

I gripped her hair to raise her eyes to mine. "I don't need to, no. But I want to." I lowered my mouth to hers, lightly licking her lower lip. "I like to."

She let out a little sigh that was part growl and part breathy release.

My girl was not into compliments for sure, but this felt like more than that. I dragged her head back more to get to her neck and lower to her breasts. She was draped over my steering wheel, her back arched so goddamn beautifully that I couldn't stop myself from flipping the little cups up to get to her skin.

She as salty and soft. The pervasive scent of coffee filled my truck as condensation started to form. Already we were generating enough heat to fog the windows.

I found I liked it that way. As if it was locking out the world while we got skin to skin.

I reached around to drag down her stretchy pants, careful not to rip them in my haste to get to her.

Again, I didn't really have the space and the time to give her the attention she deserved, but at least I could give her this.

Her shoes fell to the floorboard as she struggled out of her pants. I lifted my hips enough to get my jeans unzipped. Christ, I needed my damn wallet.

I lifted higher and the tip of my dick dug into her thigh.

"Hello." She laughed as she reached between us to palm me. "God, so well-fucking-hung. I do love when a man is proportionate."

"Thanks, I think."

She fisted my cock and grinned that devilish smile that always got me revved. It was a rare one. She was a smirking type, thanks to her sly comments, but this was dangerous and playful.

She swiped her thumb over the head of my cock and caught a drop of pre-cum. She brought it to her mouth. "Hurry."

Finally, I unseated my wallet and dug into it. For the first time in years, I'd actually had to buy a box of condoms. And damn right I'd refilled my wallet.

She spotted the trifold of rubbers and laughed. "Sure of your trip to the café today, huh?"

"Hopeful." I ripped one off and suited up. "Always goddamn hopeful." I dragged her back down over me and groaned as I stretched her open.

She tipped her head back. "I do love a good Boy Scout."

I gripped her hair again and bowed her back. "You keep calling me a Boy Scout, and you're going to make me mad."

Her teeth clicked together audibly as I thrusted up into her. "My plan is working." Her laugh was evil and drove me crazy.

I gripped her hip and sweat poured between us as I angled up to find...there. She cried out, her pussy fisting around me. I hammered into her again and again once I knew where she needed me. Where I knew I could make her fucking fly.

Her nails raced over my chest and up to my shoulders. She left claw marks while her shouts reverberated around the cab of my truck.

"Don't you stop," she shouted.

"Damn, I love when you order me around." I reached down to whatever reserves I had and ignored all the straining, burning muscles in my thighs and core as I drilled into her with everything.

I gave her all I had.

Frustration seemed to dent the pleasure that vibrated through her. She dropped down on top of me, her eyes crazed. She held onto me like I was the last thing on earth. She rode me, searching for something that seemed just out of reach.

I banded my arms around her back until we were skin to skin in every goddamn way. The friction between us and the absolute lack of space made her go a little mad. Her hands clawed my shoulders, and I wasn't sure if she wanted to get away.

For a moment, I wondered if I'd gone too far. Then her hands opened, and she wound herself around me. The wild thrusts went slow and deep.

Her huge, dark blue eyes went blind as a sob broke free. She clenched me so tight in every way, I could do nothing but finally let go. Maybe she'd needed that surrender first.

Maybe I needed it.

I came hard and let out a matching shout to hers. She shuddered over me and I covered her mouth, swallowing her cries until they were soft sighs. Until she laid her cheek against my shoulder and relaxed. Until she was finally mine.

I slid my hand up into her hair. Christ, I wanted her to be mine. Maybe forever.

I was so fucked.

FOURTEEN

MACY

I didn't really have words for what that had been.

It had started off like any other wild and fun bit of sex. Then again, nothing had truly been just a bit of anything when it came to me and Gideon. I couldn't even pinpoint when it had actually turned into more.

And I wanted to push him out of the damn truck and drive away. Or better yet, run and dunk my stupid head in the lake.

His large hand stroked up and down my back, easy and sweet. I wanted to bristle against it. To laugh it off. Anything but sink into him like I was.

It was as if my body instinctively knew this is where I should be. And I wasn't sure if that instinct was lust-drunk or…worse.

I was truly afraid *worse* was the culprit.

I slipped away from Gideon. He took care of the condom and we rearranged our clothing once more. Instead of starting the truck, he hauled me back across the bench seat and slung his arm around my shoulders.

"Is this the cuddle portion of the day?"

"Stop being a smart ass."

I buried my smile into his chest. "Not sure I can do that. Kinda comes with the coffee. Two-for-one deal. Extra cinnamon so to speak."

He kissed the top of my head. "I'm not really interested in going back to the real world quite yet."

I peered up at him. "How come?"

"I can't just like spending time with you?"

I shrugged. "I'm cool with chilling out for a little while." I tapped my finger on his thigh.

"Do you even know how to chill out?"

"Nakedness usually helps. Ramen noodles and Oreos also are good alternatives. Give me a horror movie and a hot chocolate, I might even cuddle."

"You seem to be cuddling pretty well right now, Killer."

"Post-coital glow."

"Oh, is that what it is?" He lowered his mouth to mine. The kiss wasn't consuming like the last few had been. And maybe that was why it was even more disarming.

Most guys weren't into kissing. It was usually just the conduit to getting naked. Gideon liked kissing. Long, slow kisses that reminded me of how he worked. Methodical and very detail-oriented.

I lifted a hand to cup his cheek. I loved his beard. It tickled and buzzed against my mouth. It was a whole different level of attraction. Especially when he went for my neck. Good God, I couldn't remember a time that I'd been so wound up about a guy.

I wanted to climb into him.

Christ, that was terrifying.

His kiss gentled even further. It was like his damn superpower. And I was all limber and loose, thanks to all the orgasms. I really wasn't used to having so many in a row. Even when I took care of myself, it was a one and done and roll over kind of deal.

"What made you move to the Cove?"

"Well, it wasn't the New York taxes, that was for sure."

He laughed against my neck, then twisted in his seat. He lifted me as he swung his long legs along the bench seat then settled me along his body.

"Huh."

"What?"

"I didn't think you could fit in here like that."

"It was actually one of my prerequisites. I've taken many a nap in the cab of this truck. My old man taught me to be an expert napper."

"Oh, is that so?"

He eased me up closer until my cheek was resting on his chest. It was surprisingly comfortable. He flicked a button and the cool September air off the water flowed in through his open window.

"Yeah, he's a long haul trucker. Not sure I mentioned it. We don't really talk family."

I played with the little medallion he wore. I traced my nail around the tiny footprint. "Now this makes sense."

He cupped his hand around mine. "Yeah. I got the birth certificate in the mail with her footprint and had this made. Maybe a little bit of personal penance for not being with Jessica when I should have been."

"It wasn't your fault."

"No, but it didn't stop the guilt. She actually went out and found a part in a movie where her pregnancy was a way to get the role. Her career was always the most important thing."

"Nothing wrong with that." I tucked the chain back into his shirt. "My career is really important to me too. Especially The Haunt."

"Not saying it isn't." He was quiet for a while. My hair was still down, and he kept stroking his fingers through it. Lulling me into a soft, dreamy place.

"Is that why you're so against kids?"

My eyes popped open. I instantly stiffened and he kept up with the smooth strokes.

"It's okay if you don't want to tell me. I'm not going to say it's none of my business."

"Who says it is?"

"I do. I'll wait you out though. I've been waiting you out for a damn long time."

"You're iceberg level, buddy. You know you could have made a move."

"Every time I thought about it, you were so quick to split the damn area. It's like you didn't want me to ask."

"Maybe. Then again, I still didn't know about Dani."

He tugged my hair lightly. "And look at that, you like her."

"You still didn't mention her."

He sighed. "I didn't want to know what you'd say, I guess. Everyone knew you didn't like kids."

I rubbed my cheek against his hard chest. "That's not entirely true. I had one once. Kind of."

His fingers paused and I could hear his heart thundering under my ear, but then it evened out and he resumed the steady strokes.

"I fell in love with one of my brother's friends. He was always around my house. I kinda always had a thing for Lou, but I figured he wouldn't want to have anything to do with me."

"You have a brother?"

I lifted my head to rest my chin on my hand so I could look up at him. "Yeah."

"You never mention him." He tucked my hair around my ear.

"My family is kind of a mess. Some my fault, some not."

His gaze was brutally kind. "You can tell me however much you want to. Or none at all if you're not ready."

My eyes burned and I took the easy way out. It was so much easier to tell the story without looking at him. Besides, if I saw pity in his gaze, it would kill me. I laid my cheek back on his chest, this time without the buffer of my hand.

His steady heartbeat leveled me out.

"My dad died a few years ago. It was a long, drawn out process that put a lot of stress on the whole family. Nolan—my brother—got out as soon as humanly possible. He hated my dad. Most of us did, to be truthful. But not my mom. She loved him so hard, even at his worst."

Gideon's arms tightened around me.

"It wasn't like he was abusive or anything like that. Unless you count abusing himself. Which he did spectacularly. Drugs, alcohol, you name it, he tried it. But all that junk wasn't what killed him, at least not directly."

"What it did to his actual body."

"Guessed it in one. Namely, his heart. Medical bills and medications just put everyone through the wringer. My mom worked three different jobs to keep a roof over our heads. When he died, I mostly just felt relief." I slipped my hand under Gideon's shirt. I needed more than just the grounding of his heartbeat. I needed his warm skin.

He cupped the back of my head, massaging lightly.

"Nolan couldn't stand to be in the apartment. He took off before our dad died. He took whatever jobs he could. Sometimes he sent some back to help us, but mostly, it was to pay for his real love. He was—is still—an amazing artist. That crazy espresso machine I have? He built that out of an old machine. Boosted it and improved it to handle my style of espresso beans. Then made it badass. It was the hub of my coffee truck in Chicago. Only thing I kept when I sold it."

The memory of all that cigarette smoke in my folks' old apartment made my eyes sting. I turned my face into the center of his chest and drew in his clean scent. Bringing myself back to the truck and the Cove.

"Anyway, after my dad died, my mom didn't last too much longer. She'd always been chasing him to the grave. First with work, then with a broken heart. I was lost after that. My whole life had been taking care of them. So, when Lou came around with a little boy in tow, I just naturally gravitated to him."

He made a low sigh that was half groan and half mumble.

"Yeah. It was great at first, but Lou definitely had me pegged. Malcolm—his little boy—was almost four and dying for a mom. I just wanted to stop feeling so damn lonely. I should have driven my truck out of Chicago and started over, but that sweet little boy became my everything. And I was already enamored with Lou. He was funny and a little dangerous."

Dangerous with my heart was more like it. Now I could see it, but back then, it had felt like I had a ready-made family all my own.

"I missed the signs at first. I was too happy to set up his house. Painting the rooms and raising Mal. He was the sweetest little boy.

Loved everything *Ghostbusters* and *Teenage Mutant Ninja Turtles*." I laughed harshly. "Lou had the perfect setup. I wanted to take care of his kid and treated him just like he was mine. Only he wasn't mine."

"Fucking piece of shit."

I finally looked up at Gideon again. "Can see where this is going, huh?"

"He fucking cheated."

"Oh, so much worse."

He sat up and cupped my face in his huge hands. "How can that be worse?"

"Cheated with Malcolm's mother. The woman who flaked out on him and left her little boy alone."

"Jesus."

"Yeah. I didn't quite fit into that happy little setup. So, now here I am."

"That's a big fucking leap forward."

I sniffled and hated myself. I didn't even realize I was crying. There was only so much I was willing to lay bare for him. He didn't need to know the true colors of the old Macy who almost took Lou back so she wouldn't lose the little boy. That Macy who didn't care as much about Lou as she did about his child. "So, yeah. I had a kid for almost a year. Then I didn't."

"And you moved to Babytown, USA."

"Yeah. That's a story in itself."

"I still think there's something missing in there. Why didn't you go to your brother?"

"My brother didn't choose me."

"Maybe he had a good reas—"

I scrambled back and sat on my feet on the far side of the truck. "To choose a friend over his own sister?"

"I don't mean it like that."

I held up my hand, my gut churning with all the old feelings. "Look, I get it. You weren't in the middle of all of that. But would you choose anyone over Dani?"

"No."

His answer was so quick that my belly calmed down. When he reached for me, I braced at his touch.

"It shouldn't have happened that way." His voice was almost a rasp. "You should have been able to rely on your family."

"I couldn't stand being in Chicago after that. I literally threw a dart at the map in Malcolm's room. And I started over."

I had literally walked away and built a new life. One that I loved so much. And Gideon was already a huge cornerstone of it.

"That's not going to happen with me." He wrapped his arms around me.

"You can't know that."

"I do."

I slowly melted into him. I didn't know if it made me an idiot or a fool, but I wanted to believe him. I climbed on top of him again and lost myself in him. In the almost promises that might be blooming between us.

For the first time in a damn long time, I stepped into the unknown.

The sun was lower in the sky, burnishing his dark hair with chestnut streaks from the summer sun. September had arrived and with it, the shorter days.

Soon, it would be time for us to go back to our jobs and responsibilities. His included the child I was growing to love so very quickly. This time with an equal, if not more overwhelming, attachment to the father.

That was what terrified me the most.

This time, it might actually break me in two.

His mouth found mine without the brain-melting passion that usually flared between us. The way he branded me with beard and teeth left me breathless and spinning.

This time, it was slow. It was thorough and soft. A seduction instead of a campaign to show me how hot we could be. He slid to the center of the seat and widened his legs to be on either side of the console that took up space in the center of the bench seat. And because I was so tall, I had room to straddle him without being hampered by the steering wheel.

We took our time. Soft sighs and a touch of laughter as we shifted more clothing out of the way. It wasn't a race. Exactly what I needed after spilling all my ghosts into the small space we shared.

We put them in the past where they belonged.

There was only now.

Only him.

Only this connection I would hold onto.

When he slid into me this time, it was just us. When I tried to hide my face in his neck, he held me fast. Our eyes locked as the intensity hit.

"Gideon."

He gripped my hips, dragging me tighter to him. The friction and the emotions slammed together like a seawall. And Gideon held. He was that stone wall that would take anything.

I curled my arms around his neck until we were chest to chest, mouth to mouth, and the reassuring thunder of his heart synced up to mine.

My thighs shook and the vibrations snaked up my body until there was nothing but his name shuddering through my lips. He held me. Split me open and put me back together.

His eyes went blind with pleasure and I caught the groan with my mouth and swallowed it whole. Took it inside for the dark nights when there wasn't a sun outlining him.

When he wasn't in my arms.

Just for in case.

Just for me.

FIFTEEN

Gideon

THE WEEKS HAD BEEN A FLURRY OF COMPLICATIONS AND FINALIZATIONS for The Haunt. We'd managed to get the kitchen ready ahead of schedule, but Macy was still on the hunt for a new chef.

She'd been stressed with the interview process. Both in hunting them down and taking applications. Three of her more promising people had fallen through. Each time it happened, I'd get dragged away for a rage fuck.

I wasn't quite sure how to react to her need to get distracted with orgasms. I'd tried to talk to her about it, but I'd only gotten a growl in response. One time had ended in a blow job behind my truck just to shut me up.

Her words.

Other times, it was perfect. Dinners in the café after hours. She practiced endless forms of hot chocolate on Dani. She even encouraged my daughter to name them.

Dani had been delighted to see her concoctions make the menu board more often than not. She was getting closer to Macy every day while her mother was even more distant.

The anvil of her custody demands was forever hovering over our heads. Again and again, Jessica had been blowing me off in favor of meetings with her agent or auditions for some new project she was after.

Talks about taking Dani for more visitation had all but stopped, but she wouldn't give me a straight answer about any of it.

Luckily, the restaurant was almost done. Most of my crew had moved onto other projects. The late fall season was full of wrapping up outdoor projects. Some of my older clients needed winterization before the brutal cold came through.

Central New York was no joke when it came to snow and blustering winds off the lake. The lake effect alone ground a lot of my jobs to a halt. It was just too hard to get supplies in and out when a foot of snow could come out of nowhere.

Frankie jogged into the main dining room with a stack of papers that instantly gave me an eye twitch. "Hey, boss."

"Don't tell me Spinelli screwed up another order."

Frankie rubbed the back of his neck. "Wish I could. Two dozen bat candle holders that are supposed to go along the vestibule are wrong."

I sighed. "Macy will be thrilled. What did we get instead?"

He handed me the top form.

I skimmed the order and groaned. "Flower mason jars? What the fu—"

"Did you say mason jars?"

I looked up at the voice. "What the hell are you doing here?" I handed the papers back to Frankie and crossed to the prodigal son who had returned to Crescent Cove a few months ago. We shook hands and did a half hug. "Where you been, man?"

Mason Brooks flipped the brim of his baseball hat around and gave me a dimpled grin. "Been here and there. Couch surfing at Jared's house was getting old. Besides, he's all rules and regulations these days."

"Comes with the badge."

"Tell me about it. My brother, the sheriff. Not quite sure how that happened. And if those nosy busybodies in the town council knew the shit he got into when we were younger, they would've never voted him in."

"Yeah, well, Jared was always a wily one. You were the one who kept getting caught." I wasn't from Crescent Cove, but I'd played baseball and ran in the same circles as the Brooks brothers.

"Guilty." He gave me a sheepish grin. "I blame Charlotte Burke and her perfect breasts."

"Well, they were pretty spectacular. Still are, to be truthful."

"Very distracting."

"You just here to shoot the shit? I have to deal with this order, but we can grab something in the café if you want." I could use the distraction and maybe I'd get a bonus round with Macy.

"Actually, I'm here to talk business. And I'll take a look at those mason jars."

I nodded to Frankie. "I'll take care of the delivery."

Frankie gave me a grateful smile. "Thanks. I'll go work on the chair railings."

"Great." I gestured for Mason to walk ahead. "What's up? Did you finally buy a house?"

"Not exactly." He glanced around at the web of twinkle lights along the ceiling rafters. They were on super thin wires to give off a spooky almost-lit vibe that highlighted the wild carvings on each end. Bats, ravens, skeletal hands—they all caught the eye and made you do a doubletake.

The few people that had been in here already were always aiming their gazes skyward. Mason was no different.

"This place is insane."

I grinned. "I hope you mean that in a good way."

"Definitely. This is my third walk-through and each time, I see different stuff. That animatronic zombie caught me off guard both times I was here at night."

"I haven't seen you once."

Mason shrugged. "Lucky loves showing it off. We head to the Spinning Wheel whenever I'm in town. You're always too busy with your pretty new girl."

"Macy would lop off your head and add it to one of her decorations for calling her a pretty girl."

"How about hot?"

I laughed. "That might work. She'd respect you more if you talked about her coffee though."

"Her coffee is a religious experience."

"See, now that's how you talk to Macy." And yeah, she was definitely my girl. I couldn't help wanting to spend every available moment with her.

Spinelli was sitting on the edge of the dock, thumbing along the screen of his phone. His perpetually scraggly hair stuck out from under his dirty baseball cap. When he spotted me, he popped up to his feet. "Hey, Gideon. I thought Frankie would come back."

"You screwed up another order."

He looked down at the boxes of mason jars with the top one opened. "What do you mean? Every restaurant needs a mason jar."

"I'll have to agree with him," Mason said good-naturedly.

I rolled my eyes. "By chance, did you notice what the name of this place is?"

Spinelli looked down at his clipboard. "The Haunt."

"And would floral mason jars go with that aesthetic?"

"Aestheta-what?"

I bowed my head and prayed for patience.

Mason stepped forward and dug out one of them. "A little pretty for my taste, but I've been collecting these things for my own place."

My eyebrows shot up. "Your what?"

"So, do you want this order or not?"

"Call your boss, Spinelli. I need those bat candles here by the end of the day."

"What? I have to drive all the way back out there—"

"Yeah, you do. We need this order to finish up the front of the restaurant for the soft opening this Friday."

"Man..." Spinelli's already stooped shoulders sagged. "I'll be right back." He dug his phone out on his way back to his truck.

Mason whistled. "Such a taskmaster."

"Dude, I'm not messing with Macy's plans."

"That bodes well for me then."

I folded my arms. "You starting a business, MB?"

He grinned. "I am. I bought the old Nelson farmhouse on the lake."

"Man. Hope you got a good deal."

He laughed. "I did. I've been talking to Lucky about the build you guys have been doing. This place is freaking incredible."

"Thanks. It's been a bitch, but it came together."

"That's for sure. I'd like you to do my place. I'm calling it The Mason Jar." He picked up one of the pink-hued glasses in the box. "I've been collecting them from all over on my travels. It's kind of been my dream ever since I started culinary school."

"I had no idea."

He shrugged. "I'm tired of working for other people. My last head chef used my head for target practice one too many times."

"Jesus."

"Yeah, Colorado is kinda crazy."

Chef. Huh. "So, you saved up for this place?"

"Yeah, I've been stashing money away, and I have a business plan in place with the local bank to renovate. The historic people in town were thrilled that I wanted to keep the integrity of the old place. It's over a hundred years old."

"That's quite the undertaking. I'm not really—"

"Gideon, this place is phenomenal. You and your guys can totally make my place come together. If we can get a decent quote put together."

I laughed. "Well, we can certainly discuss it. It's going to be a long project. I don't remember you being exactly handy."

"Oh, hell no. I want to pay people to take care of that stuff. I'll help with some demo if you let me."

"Everyone wants to do demo." I shook my head. "But you were pretty good with a bat, so maybe you can do a few swings with the sledgehammer."

He flipped me off. I laughed. Mason Brooks had gone to college on a baseball scholarship. His parents hadn't been exactly thrilled when he picked cooking over going pro.

"So, what are you going to do in the meantime?"

He shrugged. "Jackson over at the Grille has been bugging me to work there, but I'm not really looking to get back into another second-in-command situation. Especially when I'm focused on getting my own place moving."

"How would you feel about working here?"

Mason's eyes bulged. "Here? Doesn't she have a chef?"

"Macy's been looking for a replacement. Her guy flaked on her and took a job in Brazil, I think." I pulled out my phone and shot a text off to Macy. "At least maybe talk to her?" I grinned down at my cell. "She says if you move, she'll hunt you down."

Mason laughed. "Guess I've got an interview." He tucked the glass jar back into the slot in the box. "Hell of a day."

"Where is he? Who is he?" Macy's voice carried before she reached the loading dock.

Spinelli was getting out of his truck, then changed his mind and shut the door. I didn't really blame him. Another fucked-up order would send Macy into a rant that even I didn't want to listen to. Instead, I'd just fix it and she'd be none the wiser.

Hopefully.

"Wait, Mason?" She climbed the steps to the platform. "What are you doing here?"

He held out his hand. "Looks like I'm interviewing for a job. At least temporarily."

She narrowed her gaze at me. "Are you messing with me?"

I slapped Mason on the back. "Mason is sticking around in town. Wants to build his own restaurant. However, it's going to be quite the project."

Macy folded her arms and zeroed her focus on Mason. "Let's talk."

I shuffled them toward the door. "I'll deal with the delivery while you guys discuss things."

Mason laughed and nodded toward me. "Is he like this all the time?"

She shrugged. "You get used to him being bossy. I'm worse though. Think you can handle it?"

"Are you going to throw things at my head?"

"Depends on if you piss me off or not."

"Good to know." Mason glanced over his shoulder at me. "We'll talk soon?"

"Definitely."

Mason ducked inside while Macy stood at the threshold of the back door. "You wouldn't be trying to handle me again, would you?"

"Me? Never." I walked over to her and snuck a kiss. When she didn't kiss me back, I tried a little harder. "It's pretty perfect."

She twisted her fingers into my T-shirt. "You're trying to get rid of me." She went on her toes. "I see Spinelli over there trying to hide from me."

"I got it handled, Killer." I kissed her again.

"Hmm."

"Go talk to MB. Things are looking up. We should celebrate. Come to dinner at my house tonight." I brushed my nose along hers. "Stay over."

"Like a sleepover?"

"Yeah. A sleepover."

"All right. We can do that. I'll make sure I have coverage for the early shift."

I lifted her onto her toes again. "Perfect. I might even make you my famous pancakes."

Her lips twitched, but she cupped my face, brushing her thumbs over my beard. My damn heart turned over. "Looking forward to it." She kissed me, then stepped back. "I'll bring the coffee though."

I laughed. Damn right she would.

SIXTEEN

MACY

Gideon's hand slipped up my inner thigh. "When I said sleepover, I didn't mean work all night."

I tried to ignore his hand for my search history on my laptop screen. "Almost done. When we were decorating the hutch, I saw your Halloween candy. I'm impressed with your selection by the way."

He flicked my hair back over my shoulder to get to skin. "I have a pair of Halloween-crazy girls in my life. You think I'm going to skimp on it?"

"You are a smart guy." I glanced over to where he was pulling my sweater down for more access. When his clever hand snuck into the opening, I hissed out a breath as he ran the back of his knuckles over my nipple. "Distracting as well."

"Then I'm doing my job."

I tried to focus on Trick or Treat. Finding the paperwork for that business on the edge of town was becoming an obsession. Something about it kept niggling at me. "I just want to know who freaking owns it. And this stupid site gives me no freaking details. Isn't it supposed to be public record?"

He sighed and peered at my screen. "Well, that's because he used a registered agent." He went for my neck and did that bite-nibble thing that made the hair on the back of my neck stand on end.

"What the heck does that mean?" My limited scope on business terms sometimes bit me in the ass. I researched what I needed to know when I needed to know it. Otherwise, it was boring as fuck.

He closed the laptop. "It means the owner doesn't have to use his real name." He set the computer on his side table. "And it's time for work to be over." He rolled me under him and peeled open my slouchy cardigan. "I do love finding your version of lingerie, Killer."

"Shut up." I pulled him down. "You like my pussy tank tops."

He laughed into my mouth. "The first part is right."

I sifted my fingers through his hair. "We don't get to do this in a bed very often."

"I know. Why I wanted you to sleep over." He inched over until he was seated between my thighs. "I like it. And I have a very nice bed."

I snuggled down in the crisp navy sheets. "Gotta agree. I was expecting white hotel sheets, to be honest."

His cheeks grew ruddy. "I bought these last week."

I laughed and curled my arms around his neck. "Now that's my Gideon."

"Shut up. White goes with everything."

I buried my face in his neck and drew in his fresh from the shower scent. It had been the perfect evening. Dinner had been meatloaf and mashed potatoes that Karen and Dani had proudly made for us. Now that the soft opening for The Haunt was practically on top of us, it was harder to keep track of Dani in the café.

Luckily, Karen, Dani's usual babysitter, was finally strong enough to take over when we needed her to.

We. God, I was already thinking in *we.*

We'd been stealing moments in between working, setting up, and my training sessions with my new employees. A few people like Rylee and Clara were pulling double duty at both places. Clara wanted full-time hours, and she'd become a solid employee at Brewed Awakening.

If I was lucky, I could possibly train her to be the head waitress.

She was quickly growing a spine, but still had a healthy respect for my wrath. As one should.

"Hey," Gideon lifted his mouth from his very active exploration of my chest. "Where did you go?"

"Right here."

"No." He dragged my tank down enough to suck my nipple hard. "You are definitely somewhere else."

I combed my fingers through his hair. "And why would you say that?"

"Because you're not making that little purring hum you make when I...there it is."

I sighed and let Gideon's very talented mouth drag me out of my head. "Sorry, my brain is like that stupid dog in *Up*."

"Man, she made you watch that?"

I shrugged. "It was a good movie. A little sad, but really good." Damn Pixar movies.

He inched down and dragged his chin over my belly. "Let's see if I can distract you."

I tried to grab his ears, but he wiggled further down and nipped my inner thigh. All thoughts of work and the scary *we* word dissolved. "Do you really want me to scream my head off while your kid is sleeping across the hall?"

"Lucky for you, she sleeps hard." He grinned up from between my legs. "Lift."

I gnawed on my lower lip, but I lifted my hips for him to rid me of my panties. And then there was blissful mindlessness.

The soft heat of his tongue and the tickle of his beard had me arching under his touch. I tried to reach toward him, but he stretched my legs out so he could wedge his massive shoulders between them to keep me in place. I cupped my breasts and tugged at my nipples to release some of the crazy ache.

He watched me, his eyes blazing with that dominant streak that came out every once in a while. This was the Gideon who'd fucked me to within an inch of my life in his truck, then held me while I cried.

I rolled my hips against his mouth, searching for that combination that would let me freaking come, but Gideon had other plans. He kept backing off and letting me coast on the frustrating edge before driving me back up again with his long, thick fingers and perfectly rough tongue.

"Jesus." I arched and grabbed for anything above my head. I found the heavy headboard with sturdy slats for me to hang onto. He moved to his knees and held me splayed open as he filled me with his fingers and lapped at me. I was beyond blind and incapable of watching at this point.

I was in survival mode as I thrashed under his touch.

"Fucking come, dammit," he said before he sucked on my clit hard enough that I saw all the damn angels and stars in the freaking sky. I hoped to freaking hell I wasn't really screaming because in my head I certainly was.

"Yes."

I wasn't sure if he said it or me, but it was a *fuck, yes.* I came so hard my breath stopped, and the world went black and silent.

Then he was over me. Inside me. The part of him I needed most finally filling me up.

I wrapped my legs around his hips as he drove into me, bracing one arm on the headboard to create even more of an angle. I tore at his back, bit his shoulder and neck. I tasted myself on his beard as our kisses became erratic and wild.

He wrapped one big arm under me and held me close as he battered me into the mattress with every ounce of the passion that always seemed to sneak up on us. And for the first time, I wished there was no condom. Nothing between us.

I held on as I broke again, but this time, he was with me.

He threw back his head and the cords in his neck stood out in stark relief before those crazy green eyes that I loved so damn much zeroed in on me. He touched his forehead to mine as he gathered me in close and collapsed on me for a moment.

I laughed and let out a strangled, "oof."

He grunted and rolled us over until I sprawled across him. "I might need another shower after that one."

"Showoff."

He laughed and slipped out from under me to take care of the condom. When he came back from the bathroom, he grinned down at me. "I like you in my bed, Mace."

"If those are the perks, I'm liking it quite a bit myself."

"Shove over. I'm not one of your cats who's happy with a slice of the bed."

"Ah, you've never slept with a cat before. It's the human that gets a slice, not the cat." But I moved over and we settled in. Surprisingly, a heavy male arm around me worked as the cure for insomnia.

Or maybe it was the orgasms because the next thing I knew, the alarm next to his bed was blaring. I peeled one eye open and then sat up like a shot before I remembered I didn't have to be at the café. I hadn't slept until six-thirty in the morning in…

I couldn't even remember.

I was then ceremoniously body-slammed into the mattress again.

"It's not time yet," Gideon grumbled into my neck as he spooned around me.

"Then why did you set your alarm?"

"Because if I don't set my alarm, I'll sleep until nine."

"Yeah, well, I don't usually sleep."

"You were out." He wound his arms around my waist and cupped my breast. "So, my orgasms are a sleeping pill?"

"Not sure there's anything to preen about with that statement, pal."

"Fucked you into a coma? Yeah, I'm good with that."

I elbowed him and squeaked when he bit the back of my neck.

A knock came at the door. "Dad! Dad! Wake up."

I stilled and hiked the sheet up to my chin. "Oh my God."

"She doesn't—"

The door flew open and Dani held out her arms. "You guys are still in bed?"

"Is she like this all the time?" I asked out of the side of my mouth.

"Nope. Special case, evidently."

"Go start the batter. It's a pancake morning."

"Yes!" Dani turned on her heel before her stomping footsteps receded down the hall.

Gideon's hand firmed on my breast. I elbowed him. "Are you kidding?"

He laughed. "What? You haven't heard of a quickie?"

"Not that quick, buddy." I slipped out of bed and grabbed my bag before bolting for the bathroom.

"Damn, you've got a nice ass," he yelled after me.

I was smiling as I dug my way through my overnight bag.

"I'll go down and start breakfast. You gonna take a shower?"

"Yes." I opened the door to peek out. He was wearing ancient sweatpants and a wrinkly white shirt. His hair was sticking up and he was stupidly attractive. Me? I was afraid to look in the mirror. I knew what I looked like in the morning.

It wasn't hot.

"Give me fifteen."

His eyebrow went up. "Really?"

"I mean, I can probably do ten."

He laughed. "You do know who I used to live with. I was expecting an hour."

"What part of me seems like it would take an hour? I'm nothing like that—"

He reached in and pulled me through the small space. "Nothing about you is like my ex. That's why I... like how we are so much."

I narrowed my eyes at him. "Like how we are, huh?"

"You really want me to go there this morning, Macy?"

That was a no times three thousand. I wiggled out of his arms and closed the door in his face. "I'll be downstairs in fifteen."

I actually made it in ten. My wet hair was pulled back in a tail, and I hadn't bothered with makeup. I followed the scent of bacon and paused at the kitchen doorway. Gideon had a towel tucked into the front of his sweats, and the radio was playing.

Dani was conducting with a spatula as One Direction sang, "Olivia". She was singing at top volume and Gideon was laughing at her.

It was so obvious that he loved her. It was always obvious, but he knew the words to the song too.

Dani spotted me and jumped off her stool. "Macy, you took forever."

I tugged on her ponytail. "I barely had time to put my jeans on since you interrupted."

"There's no sleeping on sleepovers, didn't you know?"

I laughed and caught Gideon's gaze across the room. Definitely wasn't touching that one. "Smells amazing in here."

"Dad's making his pancakes. Do you like bacon?"

"I love bacon and all forms of meat."

Gideon's lips twitched. "Well, you're in luck. I also put the electric kettle on so you could make coffee in the French Press."

"Look at you all fancy."

He shrugged. "Only way I've figured out to make my coffee taste remotely like yours."

"I'm sure you still fail spectacularly."

"You're a hard woman, Macy."

But there was nothing but humor in his voice, so I didn't bristle up. Instead, I crossed to the man holding out a piece of perfectly crispy bacon for me. Perfect enough for me to eat it even before coffee was saying something.

He stole a kiss before I got the bacon and I wasn't mad about it.

Dani happily chirped about school and buying more decorations for the house. I'd helped attack the dining room with decorations Dani had dragged out from the attic last night, but she wanted more that were like mine at the store.

"It's a little late in the season, but that usually means we can get a good deal." I took a healthy sip of my coffee. "We'll go this week."

"Awesome." Dani stabbed her fork through a heart-shaped mini pancake.

Gideon's phone started buzzing halfway through the meal. He tried to ignore it, but it kept going off. He looked down at it finally when it turned into a phone call instead of his text message tone. "I should take this."

"About The Haunt?"

He shook his head. "For once, no."

Unlike him to not give specifics. The back of my neck buzzed, but I forced myself to ignore the sensation.

He looked at his watch and swore. "I've got to take her to school."

"I'll take her on my way."

"Really?"

I shrugged. No big. "Yeah, sure."

He growled at his phone ringing in his hand again. "That would help me a ton." He gave me a distracted kiss on the cheek and stalked out of the room.

I gathered the dirty dishes on my way to the dishwasher. "Guess it's you and me, kiddo."

"Can we listen to One Direction in the car?"

I laughed. "Only if you clear the table."

She raced around the table and collected cups and dishes at a truly impressive rate of speed.

"And if you know all the words."

Dani grinned. "Alexa play 'Drag Me Down'."

And look at that, she knew all the words.

SEVENTEEN

Gideon

I FLIPPED MY KEYS BACK AND FORTH AROUND MY FINGER AS I PACED outside the front of the Rusty Spoon. As usual, Jessica was late. Fucking hell.

My gut churned. Again, she hadn't given me anything to go on. In fact, she'd deliberately left the entire meeting vague. I'd been so pissed off that she had intruded on what had been a perfect morning, I'd made her meet me at the diner. In hindsight, that probably wasn't my finest moment.

Especially since Macy was right across the damn street and I hadn't told her about seeing Jessica.

Hell, I should have told Macy right when I got the call. Instead, I'd run into the other room. Hiding it like some dirty secret.

And it wasn't. I didn't care about Jessica in the least, but I cared that she'd try to take Dani from me. That was the only thing I could focus on right now. I'd do whatever it took to change her mind about adjusting custody.

She'd left us high and dry for weeks after her little bombshell.

And now she thought she could snap her fingers and make me come to heel? Yeah, that wasn't happening. My keys snapped together louder as I kicked a leaf out of my path.

Finally, a black Escalade pulled up. At least it wasn't a freaking limo this time.

I shoved my hands into my Carhartt jacket pockets as she waited for the driver to walk around the SUV to open the door. I sure as hell wasn't going to be her lackey again. Once upon a time, I'd done everything I could to please that woman.

Now all I could think about was what was the quickest and least traumatic way to get her out of my life again. I hated thinking that way about my child's mother, but every time she came back into Dani's life, things went very sideways.

Dani loved her mother—of course she did, and she should. However, Jessica looked at motherhood more like a weekend at a spa with a little girl to play dress up with. She didn't do discipline. It was far easier for her to shower Dani with gifts than to find a way to be a true mother.

I wasn't even sure Jessica knew what reality was any longer. She certainly didn't fit the part of the up and coming actress I'd met all those years ago. That Jessica had been more down to earth. More accessible and less plastic.

My eyebrows rose as she stepped onto the sidewalk with a little sneer at the gazebo swathed in orange and purple lights for Halloween. She handed the driver her bag then swiped her...was that a cape?

Jesus.

She swung some extra long part of it over her shoulder and it draped over her lush body as if she'd just stepped off the runway. Add in the slouchy hat that seemed improbably placed on her head and the yard of blond hair, and I didn't recognize any part of this woman.

She took her bag back and flitted her fingers at the driver. The guy nodded at her and returned to the driver's side, got in, then pulled away from the curb.

Well, shit. That didn't bode well for a quick conversation.

I sighed and opened the door to the diner. "Nice of you to make it."

"Don't give me that snide tone, John." She swept by me on a cloud of expensive perfume.

I sighed and followed her inside. She paused in the vestibule for a moment before stalking down between the row of tables to a booth in the back.

"Hey, Gideon." Gina Ramos came through the swinging doors. "I didn't know you were coming in today. Thought you only came in when we had the roast beef special."

"Macy keeps me fed with trying out her new menu items for The Haunt's opening."

"I'm so excited to go this weekend. I was thrilled to get an invitation to the friends and family opening."

"So, you're going to be there?"

"I wouldn't miss it." She flipped her raven dark curls over her shoulder. "I'm trying to figure out a way to get Jared to take me. He seems to think things are going to get out of hand."

"Sheriff Brooks likes to pretend Macy's horror restaurant is going to change the town into some crazy stop for freaks."

Gina laughed. "Jared said the same thing when Tish came to town too. Talk about worst case scenario thinking. Sometimes he acts more like he's fifty-five than thirty-five."

"Why the town council loves him."

"You got that right. Go on and sit down with your fancy friend. Coffee or a soda?"

"I'll grab a Coke."

"For her?"

"Got any fizzy water or something? With a lime, if you've got it."

"Sounds like you know her well."

I glanced over at Jessica, who was waiting to sit down. Maybe her pants were too tight. Probably more like she didn't want to put her couture fabric-wrapped ass on the vinyl. "I used to. Thanks, Gina."

When I reached my ex, I resisted the urge to sigh. "It's not going to bite, Jess."

She looked over her shoulder at me and let her wrap-thing fall off her shoulder. She handed it to me. "Why did you pick this place? Rusty Spoon, was it? Aptly named."

I rolled my eyes and shoved her version of a coat into the booth next to me.

"That's cashmere, John."

"I'm sure the sheep didn't wrinkle. It'll be fine."

She sighed. "This is one of the million reasons we didn't work."

I rubbed my cold hands together, then laced them together in front of me. I forced myself to look her right in the eye. "Glad we're in agreement there. Maybe you can come to the same conclusion about our daughter. She should be with me just like we agreed upon years ago."

"John—"

"No, let me finish." Nerves tried to claw their way out of my gut. "I'm not sure what possessed you to actually ask for additional visitation rights. And I'd one-hundred percent support you if I thought you actually wanted to change your lifestyle and make room for her, but all of this," I waved my hand at her cashmere coat and the head-to-toe cream-colored outfit she had on, "is not what your daughter is about. She's all about Halloween and adventure books. She wants to play softball with her friends and sing boy band songs at the top of her lungs. She's happy here. We're making an amazing life with Macy—"

"Okay, stop right there."

I shut my mouth with a snap of my molars. *Shit. Shit. Shit.* I hadn't meant to drag Macy's name into the conversation. Jessica didn't exactly like Macy for a number of reasons. And that probably wouldn't help my cause.

Funny that Macy had seemed like the clear choice to show what a stable influence I was, and now just mentioning her could ruin my chance of keeping this out of the courts. That couldn't be how this went.

"Macy is amazing with Dani. She's the last woman I'd ever have pictured as the perfect stepmom, but she stepped up the very first day she met Dani. After that insanity with the women who descended on the town—"

Jessica sat back and crossed her arms. "I guess our little matchmaker of a daughter got exactly what she wanted all along."

I gripped my hands tighter. "What does that mean?"

"Did you know that it was Dani who introduced me to Steven?"

"Who is Steven?"

Jessica sighed. "You really don't look at the news at all, do you?"

"Not your kind of news."

She gave me a bland look. "When Dani and I were in Maui this summer, she made friends with another little girl at the pool. She's Steven Dahl's niece."

"You say the name like it means something to me."

"He's on *Whiskey Tango Foxtrot*."

I frowned at her. "Wasn't that a movie with Tina Fey?"

"You know who Tina Fey is, but not Steven Dahl?"

I hunched my shoulders as I leaned forward. "Can we get to the point soon? I have to pick up Dani from school."

She held her hand up. "Regardless, Steven and I began dating. And it was wonderful for a while. He is very interested in starting a family."

My gut started churning again. "You wanted to increase visitation because of a guy?"

"He made me wonder if I was missing something more."

Of course she was missing something. The fact that Jessica treated Dani like a pretty doll she could take down when she was in the mood to play with her had always frustrated me. But she had never seen motherhood the way she should have.

Some of it might have stemmed from how her own mother had treated her. Jessica had been a pageant kid and had graduated to television as a teen. Pretty, shiny things had always been her main focus. Not to say she wasn't a decent person under the gloss, just a very self-involved one as of late.

I swallowed. "And are you?"

"I'm not built to play house, John. You know that more than anyone."

"No, staying at home always made you crazy." I lifted my chin. I wouldn't sugarcoat it. Not now. Now it was about what was best for our daughter. That was me.

And Macy.

Jessica laughed, but it sounded a little sad. "Sometimes I wish I was built for that. That it could be enough for me. Because I see the way Danielle talks about you. There's a light there that I wish was there for me." She folded her hands together to mirror mine. "But there's not."

"She loves spending time with you."

"Yes, I know. I make sure of that, don't I?"

I looked down at the chipped Formica tabletop.

"I'm well aware I'm more the fun aunt than her mom in her eyes."

I opened my mouth to refute it, but the truth was so stark and cutting, I couldn't.

She reached across the table to cover my hands. "I'm not taking her away from you, John. The more time I spent with Steven and the way he talked about us becoming a family, the more I railed against it. I barely knew him, and he had this crazy fantasy about who he thought I should be."

"Macy loves her so much. I didn't mean for it to happen, but I'm not sorry. Watching them together makes me—" I cut myself off. I didn't need to be cruel.

"Wish I'd been the same?"

I lifted my gaze to her. "No."

She slipped her hand away and slid it back to her side of the table.

"I'm sorry, Jess. We barely worked for the short time we were together. Macy's the woman I've been looking for all my life."

Her eyes shimmered and she gave a half laugh. "Well, that's that, isn't it?"

"I'm sorry."

She shook her head. "The best part of you was always your clear and linear thinking. I used to envy it because I'm so not that woman. The only clear path I've ever had was to a soundstage. For Jessica Kyle to be a household name. And I might have the chance to do that."

I leaned back in my seat. "And what does that mean for me and Dani?"

She lifted one long, ringed finger with a dagger of a nail. Jesus, that was a weapon. "I don't like this Macy person."

I had to look down and press my lips together. "That could be a problem. I'm going to marry her."

Date her.

Date her.

Holy shit.

I lifted my head to find Jessica's eyes comically wide. "What?"

"I mean—"

"No, you didn't. You meant that. You're going to marry this woman?"

"I..." My heartbeat thundered in my brain and all the spit dried up in my mouth, but then a breath tumbled out. "I love her."

"Well, obviously. You wouldn't marry a woman if you didn't love her. Or knock her up." Her gaze narrowed. "Did you knock her up?"

"God, no. Macy's not the kind of woman who takes motherhood lightly. If at all. But she loves Dani. I have no doubts there. She just has some baggage. But we all do."

"You have an irreplaceable ex-wife."

"Sure. We'll go with that."

She raised one golden eyebrow. "Regardless, this woman is going to be in my daughter's life. I need to know she's good enough." She lifted her chin. "For you too, John. We may not have worked together, but I still love you."

At my started look, she laughed.

"Not that way, darling. More like as a mostly wonderful memory, and of course you did give me Danielle. I'll never regret that, no matter what you may think of me."

"I know you love Dani." As much as she could love someone.

"I do want to see more of her. A daughter should know more than vacation destinations with her mother. That much I do want to change. But that's more like maybe part of winter break. Next year. This year, I have a new film, possibly the start of a series if things work like we think. It's a Netflix series, which seems to be the way things are heading." She reached for my hand again, excitement filling her eyes. "I may be on the cusp of getting everything I've ever wanted."

Relief flooded my system.

I ached a little for my baby girl. No matter what Jessica said about changing her ways, I knew that her career would always be more important than Dani.

Macy was just as driven, but she'd never once made Dani feel like she was a burden or had to be shoehorned into her schedule. And even if Macy never wanted to have a child with me, how much she cared for my little girl would always be more than enough.

Hesitantly, Gina came over to our table. "I didn't want to interrupt."

Jessica accepted the water with lime gratefully and took a sip. "Surprisingly delicious."

Gina gave me my Coke with a half smile. "Can I get you anything?"

Jessica leaned toward me. "I think I want gravy fries. This is exactly the place I should have them, is it not?"

"We make the best in the county," Gina chimed in.

"Perfect. My trainer will kill me, but I don't care. It's time to celebrate."

"Burger with the works for me."

"I'll go put that in." Gina winked at me and spun on her heel.

We hashed out a schedule around her new movie and over plates full of carbs. The noises she made over the gravy gave me a few flashbacks of our life before. When we were good. When our values hadn't clashed yet.

She used to tell me all about her dreams for the future. And I'd listened. I'd always listened. She'd never cared about mine.

Right now, I was sort of glad about that. Because then I'd never have met Macy.

It had taken me a damn long time to get moving when it came to her. But I never had any doubts she was for me.

My watch buzzed a reminder, and I quickly dropped the money for lunch on the table. "I've got to go get Dani. Do you want to come with me? I guarantee she has a Christmas list to show you. I've gotten three different versions of it. One text, one email, and one handwritten."

Jessica laughed. "She emailed me one too. Even posted it on her Instagram."

"I really wish you hadn't set that up for her."

"Really? Pretty sure you wouldn't be with that waspish woman otherwise."

I had to laugh. That was probably the most appropriate word to describe Macy I'd ever heard. She did have quite the sting. But she also loved fiercely and would defend her people until the end.

God, I loved her.

Jessica blotted her lips then pulled out a compact to fix her flawless face. "Besides, our daughter loves to play matchmaker. We're lucky she didn't go *Parent Trap* on us."

I choked on my fry. "Jesus, no."

She gave me that haughty look I would never miss in all my days on this earth. Then suddenly, there was a touch of worry. "Will Danielle be excited to see me?"

"Always." I slid out of the booth and held out her wrap for her. "Let's go get our daughter."

EIGHTEEN

MACY

My ordinary day ended with the café door opening and my boyfriend strolling in. Except he wasn't alone.

Somehow I'd just bought myself a one-way ticket straight into my past.

As my fingers clenched around the twenty in my hand, I kept breathing. What else could I do?

"Macy? My change?"

I barely heard Mrs. Coy. I certainly didn't react to her. How could I, when I couldn't look away from the sweet family scene happening right in front of me?

John and Jessica having an animated conversation. John shaking his head with a smile. Then Dani letting out a little squeal and rushing across the room to throw her arms around her mother. Jessica idly stroking Dani's braid—a braid I'd put in her hair after school—with glossy nails that had probably never had coffee grounds or anything untidy underneath them.

I lifted my hand and studied my own manicure. Oh, yeah, that's right. I didn't have one. Because I had my hands in soapy water half a dozen times a day, and I was brutal on any polish. But I still could braid Dani's hair just fine. I could still laugh with her and take her to school and field her embarrassing questions.

Like on the way home today, she'd asked if it felt good to tongue-kiss, because she was convinced tongues were slimy and she'd rather eat worms.

At the time, I'd evaded and tried to act like yeah, it felt good, but it only in a committed relationship. Then I'd backtracked and said it was okay to kiss someone even if you weren't committed, as long as you wanted to, and you liked them. That kissing could be fun, but it was important to set boundaries. Fumbling through every damn word but being so careful I didn't unintentionally fuck up Gideon's kid.

All the while, Dani had frowned at me as if I was making no sense. I probably hadn't. I wasn't a mom. Probably never would be.

Some people were cut out for it. In this town, it seemed as if everyone was.

For some reason, I kept falling for kids I could never have.

I didn't care about the man. He'd just helped me break my dry streak. It wasn't as if I had actual feelings for him—

A tear splashed on the back of the hand gripping the twenty and I stared at it in shock as it burned my skin. Like fire. Like if I watched, a hole would open up in my skin like the pit opening up inside my chest.

"Macy?" Mrs. Coy's voice gentled as she reached out to touch me and I jumped back as if she'd hit me with a bucket of blazing hot water.

I could feel more tears trying to gather, the process almost painful because I didn't usually fucking cry so easily, dammit. I wasn't that person. I handled my shit. It had been a long, tiring day and I was running on empty, but I didn't normally weep as if my heart was breaking.

What heart? No one in town thought I had one. I'd almost convinced myself.

Then John looked away from Dani and his gaze caught mine. For a second, just one, his smile softened. Something that sure as fuck seemed like genuine emotion shifted over his face and my pulse slowed, the panic receding, a calmness dropping over me.

There was an explanation. There had to be. He'd gotten that strange call that had niggled at me all day, and it had obviously been Jessica. There had to be a reason why it hadn't told me.

I'd spent too much time with them, gotten too close, for this to happen again.

Then Dani grabbed her mother's hand, tugging it toward her father's, and I couldn't watch anymore because I didn't care how this horror movie scene ended. I was done watching.

Done participating in my own eventual heartbreak. Because, surprise, that eventual day was here.

Right now.

"Here you go." I shoved the money back at Mrs. Coy without bothering to make change. "Your drink is on the house. Enjoy it. Have a lovely day."

"Macy, wait."

Before she could finish, I whipped off the apron I'd donned after dousing myself with part of a mug of coffee an hour earlier. My shirt and bra were still fucking damp, but I hadn't wanted to take time to run upstairs. I was watching Dani and—

I was the bloody fool who was taking a fifteen-minute break.

Without another glance back, I marched into the kitchen and dumped my apron on my desk chair. I jerked straighter when the door swung open behind me. Freaking Vee was so intuitive that if I so much as swallowed hard, she would rush over and try to mother me. Add in pregnancy hormones, and she was fifty times worse.

"Look, not sure what you think you saw, but I'm fine. Peachy keen." I turned around and took one look at Gideon, then aimed straight for the exit.

"Wait a second. Just you wait a fucking minute." He slammed a hand on the door as I started to open it, and I stomped on his instep without compunction.

He let out a startled *oof,* but I didn't use my opportunity to escape.

Fuck no. This was *my* kitchen. My coffee shop. My life I was fucking fighting for, in the realest sense.

"Let's get something straight, okay? I may have spent time with you. May have fucked you. May have even enjoyed it. But you do not get to come in my place of business and throw your weight around. You definitely do not get to attempt to prevent me from leaving. My life. My coffee shop." I jammed my thumb in my chest. *"My* rules. Got it?"

The door to the dining room opened and Vee stuck her head in, her eyes going wide as she glimpsed the two of us. But she didn't back down or step away. Instead, she clenched her jaw.

"Need backup, Mace?"

Gideon looked between us with a mixture of frustration and exasperation. I hated how well I could read him now. I didn't need his facial expressions or much else to gauge his emotions. It felt as if I was absorbing his irritation through my pores.

"Backup for what? I was trying to have a conversation with my girlfriend and she just went fucking mental on me."

"I'm not your girlfriend. That little 'fake date' thing we had going? Done. Finito. You're going to get back with Jessica, so you don't need me anymore. And I definitely don't need you."

He glared at me. "So, it was fucking fake when you were begging me not to stop last night?"

Vee cleared her throat. "Okay, I'm going to go. I'll be right out—"

"Right, because I was horny, and I liked your dick. Did you hear that past tense? Liked. As in over it now. Had fun though. It was a great way to pass some hours. Now let's not make it messy."

"Messy? Is that what this is?" He started to laugh a little too loudly and the first hint of concern flared in my belly. This flame of an argument was about to spill over into one helluva inferno.

And I was at work. Dani was just outside the door. My customers and friends were out there too. I couldn't do this. I'd worked too hard to build my little empire to burn it down with one heck of a lit cigarette.

But right now? I didn't give a flying fig.

"You better have your wife take your daughter outside. Because shit is about to get very real in here, and I don't want her to be hurt."

Unlike Gideon. I wanted to rain punches on him until I was numb. Until this void inside me was full of anything but confusion and pain.

Tears stung my eyes as I turned away to slam my palms on the counter by the sinks. What did I do wrong this time? Was it my fault? Could I just not have a healthy adult relationship without the guy running back to his ex, no matter how much of a witch she was?

"*Ex*-wife, as you damn well know. Dani and Jessica are gone. Dani wanted to come back here and say goodbye, but I told her she could talk to you later."

A single tear escaped, and I swiped it away with the side of my hand. There would be no later.

For a second out there, I'd almost let myself believe everything was fine.

Oh, you're being silly. Over the top. Seeing old ghosts that don't exist.

So what if an eight-year-old draws her parents' hands together when they're in the same space for a rare couple of moments? What else would you expect her to do other than to hope her parents would one day get back together?

And that wasn't even the crux of it. I was already jealous of Jessica. Not that I didn't have plenty going on myself—because thank you very much, I did—but I wasn't blind. She was beautiful and famous and beyond that, they'd made a child together. I had no clue what that bond must feel like. And now I never would.

There was no way I could deal with this kind of pain again.

I risked shifting to look at him. "You didn't tell me you were going to see her, and it didn't just slip your mind. You lied to me."

"Oh, for fuck's sake, it's not a lie when someone doesn't tell you something. It's like the night of our first kiss all over again. Maybe they really did forget."

"It's not a they, Gideon, it's *you*."

"Maybe *they* weren't thinking about how you'd see it for one fucking second because I was worried I was going to lose my daughter. Not forever, but more time with her, and that feels like forever."

I spun around and stared at nothing. I couldn't make out shapes or colors right now. It was all an indistinct blur.

"Mace." Gideon gripped my shoulder—not a soft touch, but a serious hold like he meant it. I flinched, but I didn't jerk away. "Look at me."

"Why?" I hated that my voice broke as I asked the question. Absolutely hated it.

"All of this is really because I didn't tell you I was meeting Jessica this afternoon?" The faint note of dubiousness in his tone had me digging my fingers into the unforgiving countertop. "I meant to, but I didn't because I was tied up in myself and my worry about Dani. I admit it. It was selfish and unfair to you and I'm sorry. But it wasn't the only reason."

I pivoted to face him, and the lines of worry bracketing his eyes—so many more than had seemed to be there just weeks ago—had me clamping down on my tongue. But those lines definitely didn't lessen the lump in my throat.

He looked absolutely exhausted. He was so terrified to lose more time with Dani. Why shouldn't he do whatever necessary to ensure his daughter had a stable home? She was his first responsibility, not some chick he'd been messing around with since the end of summer.

"If you take her back, you won't have to worry she'll take your kid away from you anymore." The words left me in a hot rush that hurt my throat.

Gideon stared at me as if I was speaking a language he'd never heard before. "I don't want Jessica back. I definitely didn't before, but how could I even think about her when I have you?"

The words carved away slices of me. Even if that were true, I couldn't face the bone-deep weariness in his eyes without accepting I had the power to end it.

Or at least to release him from whatever was tying him to me, whether it was misplaced guilt over my situation with Lou and

Malcolm or maybe because the sex was good. Even if he did have genuine feelings for me, they couldn't come above his concern for his daughter.

And they shouldn't.

I wasn't going to make him choose. I also wasn't going to hang around and wait until he got there himself. Our so-called dating arrangement had earned me some freaking intense feelings, and I had to think about self-preservation at this point.

"She's backing off." He took hold of my wrist and tugged me to him, but this time, his touch was a silken cord. Barely enough to keep me in place. "She's got a movie. She's going to leave us alone. You, me, and Dani."

I couldn't have missed the undercurrent in his voice. A thread of desperation that matched the band squeezing the air out of my chest.

"What about next time?" I couldn't speak above a whisper. "Anytime she changes her mind, you're just going to live at her mercy? And what, make up dating arrangements with whomever is around then, just so you can make sure you'll get to keep your own child? It doesn't have to be that way. You made a baby with her."

Some part of me wanted to throttle myself for saying this shit. For trying to pretend it was empowering for me to send him back to his ex. Like he was a gift I could give away.

Not because I had ownership—God, no—but because he was a fucking awesome guy who just wanted to be with his kid.

I couldn't blame him. If there was a way he could ensure he'd get to keep her, I wouldn't stand in the way.

Maybe in time, he'd see I was right. Smart. Practical. We both so loved being sensible.

"I honestly can't believe you think *this* is the answer." He closed his eyes, the deep furrows in his forehead standing out in sharp relief. "To avoid risk, I'm supposed to live a lie?"

He had been smiling when he walked into the café with Jessica, and now he was on the verge of losing it because of me. Didn't that just say everything?

"We agreed to no drama." I fought to keep my tone steady. "To just let this run its course and when it had, when the threat was gone, we would end it."

His eyes popped open and his grip tightened. "The threat isn't gone. You just said it. And if I have to play this fucking dating game to keep you in my life, fine, I'll do it. I vowed I'd never play games with anyone again, but you've put me back in that place, haven't you?"

I tried to yank my wrist free. It took a second, but he finally let me go and held up his hands. "You know what? You're right. We agreed not to do this. No big breakup."

Yeah, fine. Right. I bit my lip until I tasted blood, but I nodded.

"I just never guessed you'd take the coward's way out because you're too fucking scared to see I'm not Lou. Dani isn't Malcolm. If you want to rewrite this story and stick your own ending on it, go ahead. But don't tell yourself that you were magnanimous enough to push me toward a woman I don't love when I know who I do."

My head reared up, but it was too late. All I saw was the back of his jacket before he slammed out of the kitchen.

What the hell had he said? What did he mean? He couldn't—

God, could he?

I moved forward, already in a full-on run, and collided with Vee in the doorway. She toppled a tray, and I wasn't sure which one of us screeched louder. Immediately, I went into mom mode, patting her down, asking if she was okay, if anything hurt.

No need to ask me, since literally every part of me did. Body. Mind. Heart. And my freaking eyes were leaking like someone had left on the tap.

"Macy, stop. Mace." She dropped the stuff in her hands on the counter before cupping my face.

Just like that, a fissure opened up inside me. One that had been stitched closed with the thinnest of wires these past few years, and now they were giving way.

"Let's sit and talk, okay? We'll go upstairs." Vee rubbed her thumb over my cheeks. "I'll make tea—" Catching my expression, she laughed. "Sorry, mom instinct. Coffee. Of course coffee. You'll tell me what happened, and we'll figure it all out, all right?"

"I think it already is figured out, just figured out all wrong." I swallowed over the razor blades lining my throat. "I just told the guy I'm in love with, the father of the kid I love, to go back to his ex." I squeezed my eyes shut. "What the fuck have I done?"

NINETEEN

Gideon

I stormed into The Haunt. "Fuck."

My heart was thundering, and my brain was going to fucking explode. After all of the shit we'd been through, Macy actually thought I'd ever choose my ex-wife over her? No freaking way.

Had I really been so wrong about her?

August Beck peeked around the tall, skinny armoire I'd commissioned for Macy's soft opening. She didn't know about it. Hell, I'd barely been able to give her one small surprise in this entire endeavor. Damn woman was a control freak's control freak.

"Is that a 'fuck' because something broke? Or a 'fuck' because you're trying not to throttle a woman?" August went back to calmly stroking stain over the leg of the Ash wood.

I tipped my head back. I thought I'd be alone in here of all places. I sagged against the bar stool and propped my elbows on the ebony bar. The place was completely finished. The floors shone in the filtered sunlight through the walnut-stained slatted blinds. The booths were lined up perfectly. The bar was flawless behind me.

For a horror-based restaurant, at this moment it would stand up to the most stringent white glove test.

August was sitting cross-legged on a large drop-cloth—far larger than the piece required—and I probably could have kissed him for it.

"What are you doing in here, man?"

"Quiet. Well, it was." He moved his long, even strokes with the brush up the side of the unit. "Kinleigh has Aretha Franklin going at top volume next door. Not that I don't love the queen of soul or anything, but if she plays 'Respect' one more time today, I'll probably break her vintage gramophone she loves so goddamn much."

I pinched the bridge of my nose. "Women are the bane of my existence right now."

"So, door number two. Got it. Eh, not surprising when you have a woman as fiery in spirit as Macy Devereaux. Dude, French and slightly crazy. With those wild eyes, I wouldn't be shocked if there was some Irish in there too."

"Are you checking out my woman?"

"So caveman of you. Don't let Macy hear you say that."

I laughed, even though I didn't feel like laughing. August said whatever was on his mind. Most of the time, I wondered if there was much going on in there since he was often exceedingly quiet. But then he said stuff like that.

"Do you want to talk or some shit? Or just sit there and ruminate on it?" August asked after we didn't speak for a few minutes.

I so wasn't the guy who talked things out. I wanted to just *do* and not discuss. "I'm good with quiet."

"Works for me."

The whisper of his brush over wood was hypnotic. My mind evened out and the rage receded back into anger. "Macy thinks I should get back together with my ex for the sake of Dani."

"Did she hit her head recently?"

I bowed my head with a chuckle. "I'm beginning to wonder."

"Did you give her reason to think such an idiotic thing?"

That was where I was fucked.

"Silence says yes, sir."

"I may have had a slightly incognito meeting with Jessica today to talk about our custody issues."

August whistled. "Not good, man."

"I was freaking out, that's my only defense. Regardless of the meeting, Macy should know that I'd never go back to her. That we're solid."

Except we'd never said the big words.

I was willing to let Macy hide from putting a real title on what we were just so I wouldn't have to face her choosing to leave.

"Fuck."

"Did a lightbulb go on over there?"

"Man, you are a sarcastic son of a bitch today."

August got to his feet and stretched his back. "I'm always sarcastic. I just usually keep it to myself. You seem to need a little bit of truth sauce today."

"I didn't do anything wrong."

"You wouldn't be so quick to get angry if that was the truth."

"She overreacted. Yes, I didn't tell her about the meeting, but it was only because I was…"

"Worried about yourself? Your kid. Both?"

"Shit." I slumped back against the bar again. "Yes, mostly about myself. I've been so afraid of Jessica taking Dani from me, I haven't faced any of the shit between me and Macy."

"Understandable."

"She's so goddamn squirmy when it comes to actually admitting she wants to be in a relationship. Wants *me*, outside of a quick bang. Or a long one." I exhaled. "I didn't want to tell her the threat from Jessica was gone in case she decided her duty was done. Why stick around now when we've had our fun and I don't need her anymore? Except I do. So fucking much."

And I hadn't even fully realized how much that was holding me back until I'd said it out loud.

"Sounds like you just gotta do the big Hallmark kinda deal. So she can't say no."

I folded my arms over my chest. "Hallmark?"

"Dude, you met my sister. She watches those things day in and day out this time of year. If I want to see my niece, I get that as background noise. Always with the noise."

"Yeah, the noise thing never stops. Sorry, bud."

August sighed. "They're cheesy, but they do those endings better than any action movie. At least when it comes to the romance stuff. Macy probably needs over the top romance more than any other woman in town. I don't know her story, but if she's got that kind of shit in her head, she's probably been pretty hurt before."

"She has." I'd blundered my way right into hurting her because I was too afraid to face the truth. She had to pick me. And I really didn't trust that she would.

I'd fucked up just as badly as she had.

My phone buzzed in my pocket. I dug it out and swore. I was racking up the points for being an absolute dick, that was for sure. Lucky for me, Jessica had taken that one moment to be the responsible parent while I had a temper tantrum.

Jesus.

The text was from Jessica with a picture of Dani holding a huge pumpkin with misshapen eyes and a wide cut-out smile missing one front tooth, just like my daughter.

I have to catch a flight, or I'd take her for the night. Is everything okay with Macy?

It will be. Where are you? I'll come pick up Dani.

We're at the Hummingbird. They were having a pumpkin carving party.

I laughed. Guess that was my sign.

I'll be right there.

I grinned at August. "I think I just figured out my big reveal."

"Awesome. Pictures, or it didn't happen. At least that's what Ivy says."

"If she says yes, there will be all the pictures."

"Yes?"

"I'm going for the holy grail."

August's eyes went wide. "Dude, I said get your woman back, not propose."

"It's all or nothing at this point."

He whistled and held out a hand. "Good luck."

I hauled him in for a hard hug. "If you could put the finished armoire in Macy's office here, I'd appreciate it."

"You got it."

I strode out of The Haunt and to my truck in the back. I wasn't sure if this was smart, but I had a feeling August was right. Macy needed all the big gestures. I'd all but told her I loved her earlier today. And I'd seen the shock under the hurt.

The fact that she didn't know I loved her already was definitely on me.

Before I went to The Hummingbird's Nest, I called every damn pumpkin patch in the county. I'd need a damn lot of pumpkins for this plan to work.

There were a ton of cars parked near the bed and breakfast, and the squeal of children greeted me as soon as I opened the door to the dining room.

Sage Hamilton was in the middle of it all, clad in a crazy orange shirt with flashing lights set in the pumpkin face. She was directing parents and children in the fine art of using a template. Oliver, her husband, was off to the side with their daughter, cutting precise circles for the eyeholes of her jack-o-lantern.

I spotted my daughter and my ex with a clear poncho over her clothes. I was surprised to see as much pumpkin juice near her and on her makeshift smock. Dani spotted me and gave me a huge gap-toothed smile.

"Daddy! Mom has the best carving nails ever. I can't believe how cool she made our pumpkin!"

Jessica looked at her nails with a sigh. "Good thing I'm getting a manicure tomorrow."

I stood next to her and bumped her good-naturedly. "You took one for the team. I'm proud."

"Yes, well, I figured I owed you this much."

"Thanks for taking care of her. I'm sorry I disappeared."

"Love makes everyone crazy, John. Even you."

"That's the truth." I moved over to Dani's station and crouched in front of her. "Hey, sweetheart."

"Are you going to carve a pumpkin with me?"

"Actually, I think I might be."

"Yay." She gestured at the whole pumpkin next to her. "I hoped you would. I kept one of the good ones for you."

I kissed her forehead. "Thanks, kiddo."

She turned back to her pumpkin, her blunt-edged knife in hand. "We have a lot of pumpkin guts for roasting the seeds. Maybe we can even make a pie."

I laughed and took the knife out of her hand. "I have a question to ask you first."

She tipped her head. "What's wrong, Daddy? You look…sad."

"Not sad, kiddo. So glad. But I did make a mistake with Macy, and I really need your help to fix it because you're the best woman I know. And you'll make sure I don't screw this up."

She patted my cheek. "Of course. Is she mad at you?"

"Yes. But more importantly, I hurt her feelings and I really didn't mean to."

"Did you say you're sorry?"

"I need your help to do that. Think you can help me? I need to show her I love her in a big way."

"Oh, Daddy. She knows you love her. You show her all the time. Just like you show me."

My eyes burned. I pulled her in for a hug. "I hope you always know that about me, Dani."

She patted my arm. "I do."

I sniffed. "Okay, so one last question before we do this big plan."

She rubbed her hands together. "I love plans."

"Would you be all right with me asking Macy to marry me?"

Her green eyes, that matched mine so completely, widened. "Are you for real? That's sick!"

"Sick?" Not that again.

"Yes, so cool. Get with it, Dad."

"Sorry."

"Yes! Yes times a million." She clapped and hopped around in circles.

At least she was on board. Whew.

"Okay. Now I've got a plan. But I think I need help from everyone in here." I stood up and took her sticky hand. It was probably going to get a lot stickier. "Let's go talk to Miss Sage."

I crossed the room to where Sage was counting pumpkins. "Oliver, did you pick out a pumpkin to carve stars into for our little girl?"

Oliver had their curly-haired daughter on his hip. "We've carved three pumpkins already."

"Our little Star deserves all the pumpkins." She turned around and gave me a wide smile. "Why, John Gideon, I'm so glad you made it. Your little girl is a master pumpkin carver."

I shook her hand and smiled down at her. "Good thing. I'm going to need some assistance. I've got three different farms delivering pumpkins."

She looked down at the pallet of pumpkins. "I think we have enough."

"Not for what I have in mind. I'm going to need a lot of help." I turned to Oliver. "And a big favor, which may turn into a sale if I'm lucky."

"Sale? Those are magic words for a realtor." Oliver brushed a kiss along his daughter's temple. "I'm intrigued. Guess we have some things to discuss."

"It's going to take a lot of pumpkins and a lot of help from my friends." Plus, a metric ton of luck.

And love, but hopefully we had that part squared away.

Sage grinned. "Is there romance in this little favor?"

"Of course there is."

Sage clapped just like Dani had a moment ago. "I'm so in."

TWENTY

MACY

"You can do this. You can do this." I stared at myself in the mirror in my bathroom. I'd been hiding in my freaking apartment for the last thirty minutes. I couldn't face watching the door to see if people would actually arrive.

"Of course you can do this, you're a badass."

I whirled at the sound of Rylee's voice, my heart racing. "You're like one of my damn cats."

Ry grinned, propping her hand on her scarlet red-clad hip. She wore a form-fitting wrap dress that belied the fact that she'd been pregnant recently. "My child is a ninja. I had to adapt."

"More like you're a Houdini."

She flipped me off. "It's not breaking in if you gave me a key."

"Obviously, I had a moment of insanity." I stepped out of my bathroom to find we weren't alone.

Dahlia was using my full-length mirror to fluff out her midnight skirt. Little crystal chips sparkled like stars as the hem of the skirt floated around her knees. "Did I just hear you being a bitch ass in there?"

"Sue me, I'm a little nervous."

"You're the most capable woman I know. You're going to rock this shit tonight." She narrowed her eyes at me. "I'm wearing a dress. You should be too."

I smoothed my hands over my hips. I was wearing a short skirt with matching black tights. "I'm not a dress girl. But hey, you got me in a skirt." I actually had a dress for the Halloween grand opening for the public. This was just a dry run for friends and family to show off my place.

I squashed down the quick pang that none of my family would be there. My mom and dad hadn't been a big part of my life for years, but I hated that I'd lost touch with my brother. I hated that he hadn't believed in me. And the man who should be my family wasn't here either.

Gideon.

Oh, he might be at the party because his company had worked on The Haunt, but he wouldn't be there for *me*.

Your own fault.

"You're dressed like the waitstaff."

I shoved all those stupid thoughts aside. I would not be a hot mess until after the party. I could fall apart and then figure out a way to make Gideon see I'd been an idiot. "No, I'm wearing all black."

"Yes, like the waitstaff."

"Actually, my employees wear black and red." Which Dahlia knew very well, since she'd gone with me to pick out fabric.

"Semantics."

Rylee dropped onto my bed and gave Isis a long stroke. She suddenly laughed. "Are those jack-o-lantern faces on your knees?"

I looked down at them. "Yes. Did you think I wasn't going to put on something Halloween-ish tonight?"

"No, I was expecting a full ensemble from a movie, to be truthful."

"That's at the grand opening."

"There's my Macy."

I gave her a half smirk and turned to pick up my black clutch with sparkly blood drips at the zipper. You could really buy anything on Etsy these days. I'd left my hair down and added dangly silver bats for jewelry both at my ears and throat.

I'd been going through the motions for the last three days. Rylee and Vee were taking point at the café while I made sure all my staff were ready for The Haunt's debut. Mason had been a surprisingly perfect addition to the project. He was a damn good cook and could pretty much bring everything I thought of to life in food form. I let him create too, which served me quite well. The menu for the actual opening was even more perfect than I'd come up with alone.

eVe had handled the pastry items, and Rylee had been training two of my bartenders to become mixologists for some of the crazier drinks coming out of the big cities. Ry had a lot of crazy knowledge from her years of bumping around from job to job. She'd become an invaluable partner through all of this.

So much so that I would be talking to her about expanding upon that movie idea for the back patio at Brewed Awakening.

Assuming I didn't lose my damn mind over the restaurant first. Or because I ached for a man I'd shoved out of my life like a fool. Take your pick.

Rylee stood. "Come on, let's do this thing."

I nodded, then stopped. "Wait. I just wanted to say thanks. I don't do so well with the emotional shit, but you guys really helped make this dream come true."

"Aww, look at our Macy getting all sweet." Rylee fanned her hands in front of her eyes. "Don't make me screw up my makeup."

I rolled my eyes. "You're such an ass. I'm trying to have a moment here."

Dahlia came over and gave me a hard hug. "Horror girls unite."

I hugged her back. "Damn right." I stepped back and gave Isis a quick scratch under her chin then picked up Trick who had wound her way around my ankles. "Be good tonight." I set her next to Iris, then grinned when they rolled into a play fight before settling together in the middle of my bed in a fur pile.

The bed I hadn't slept in since my fight with Gideon.

I really hadn't missed the insomnia that seemed to have magically disappeared after I'd gotten together with him, but my apartment was spotless.

I followed the girls out of the room and downstairs.

"I'm going to check in with the café and be right over." Rylee took the hallway down to the side door to Brewed Awakening while Dahlia and I headed for The Haunt.

Voices were already coming from the main dining room. My extra backup waitstaff were winding around patrons with trays full of Halloween-inspired finger food. I tried to navigate my way toward the kitchen to make sure everything was okay.

Instead, I ended up shaking hands and hugging a dozen people before I got through the side door. So many townspeople had come to see my little place. Even people I'd assumed would politely decline had showed up to see my horror-themed restaurant.

Irene Whitaker from the town council was standing right next to my life-size Michael Myers and sipping from a smoking green punch. That was definitely something I hadn't expected to see tonight.

Lucky was hitting on some blond from the wine bar down the street. I'd advised against children coming since there were so much monster-type memorabilia and lots of special effects, but it hurt to acknowledge Dani was nowhere in sight.

I wasn't surprised that her father wasn't here, even though all of his crew had shown up. I didn't quite know what I was going to say to Gideon, but I desperately wanted to at least *see* him.

Even if killed me.

I tried to duck into the kitchen, but a voice behind me killed that dream.

"Macy, this place is amazing."

I turned to smile at Seth and Ally Hamilton. "Hey. I'm so glad you guys could come."

Ally waved me off. "You can stop with the hostess smile."

I gave my aching face a break. I wasn't sure I had ever smiled this much before. "It's been nuts. I still haven't made it into the kitchen to check on Mason."

"The food is awesome. Be careful or Sage will try to steal him for the B&B."

"Actually, Mason is making plans for his own place, so I only get to keep him for a little while anyway. At least it gives me some time to find another decent chef."

"Well, I'll be going to his place for sure."

I laughed. "Thanks."

Ally's cheeks pinkened. "You know what I mean." She glanced up at Seth. "Care to take a whirl through the Freddy section over there? There are even dioramas. It looks freaking cool."

"That's one of my favorite corners. I hope you like it."

Ally waved as she slid her arm through Seth's to lean into him.

I tried not to let my heart shred itself. It wasn't even like Gideon and I were super PDA-types—well, except when it came to kisses, which we tended to steal often—but I did miss his strong arms around me. Especially in the dead of the night.

Especially every frigging moment.

I didn't make it back to the kitchen for the next hour, but I'd already been around so many people that my head was throbbing double-time. Instead, I escaped to my office. I went right to my desk and found my bottle of Advil, then looked up and dropped the cap.

I hadn't allocated much space for my office. It never seemed important for me to have a space to do paperwork. It was just a necessary evil. But tucked in the corner, there was a tall armoire with an intricate design of bats and jack-o-lanterns and skulls along the front. It was obviously August's handiwork for the furniture portion.

But the middle panels were pure Gideon.

The bats along the top matched the little carvings in my bar. I came closer to smooth my fingers over the relief pattern he'd designed, and my eyes swam at the three pumpkins in the bottom half. They had such character. So much life in their little faces. They were me, Gideon, and Dani.

A knock on my door had me dashing away tears. "Just a second," I called out. Probably some freaking emergency.

I cleared my throat and opened the door.

Dani stood there swaying back and forth in a swishy little A-line dress with pumpkins all along the bottom of the skirt. She gave a delighted laugh and pointed at my jack-o-lantern tights. "We match."

"We sure do." I crouched down in front of her. "What are you doing here?"

"It's your party, duh. Of course I'm going to be here."

I pulled her in for a hug. "I'm so glad. Where's your dad?"

"He's here."

My belly flipped. "Where is he?"

"It's a surprise."

I let her go and stood up. "Is that so?"

She held out her hand. "Can you come outside with me?"

I took it and followed her out into the main dining room. Where there had been only spooky decorations and flickering glass before, now there were a few dozen lit jack-o-lanterns crammed on every available space. People had glasses of punch and were still talking among themselves as if they hadn't just rearranged my entire place.

"What's going on?"

"You'll see." She kept pulling me through the restaurant to the front door.

"I can't leave my own party, kiddo."

"Sure you can. Don't worry, Rylee and Dahlia said they'd take care of it." She walked faster, and I hurried to keep up.

There were more pumpkins with crazy faces set around the front entryway. Some obviously had been done by children, but others were crazy impressive. I spotted some of Dahlia's handiwork as well.

We took a left onto the sidewalk and Gideon's big steel gray truck was parked at the curb with him leaning against the side panel. There was another cluster of lit pumpkins around the tree right beside his truck. When he spotted us, he straightened.

"Hey, Mace."

"Hi."

Dani pulled me over to him and did a literal handoff. Gideon took my hand.

"What's going on?"

Gideon laced our fingers. "You need to come with me."

"I don't need to do anything."

His jaw tightened. "No, you don't. But I'm asking you to come with me." He ruffled Dani's bangs. "You going to be all right with Rylee for a little bit?"

She nodded and turned to wave at Rylee in the doorway of The Haunt.

Rylee waved back.

"So, she's in on this?"

Gideon shrugged. "Maybe."

Dani wrapped her arms around my waist and held on tight for a moment, then ran back to Rylee. "Say yes!" She called out and waved.

I looked back at Gideon. He'd bowed his head and his shoulders were shaking with repressed laughter. "That kid."

"She's a pretty great kid."

"I know it." He opened the car door but didn't release my hand. Instead, he helped me climb in.

"What the heck is going on?"

He finally let my hand go. "We're going to take a little ride, and we're going to have a talk."

"Sounds ominous."

He shook his head. "Only you would say that." He closed the door and went around to the driver's side.

We didn't say anything for the first few minutes. When he started driving out by the lake, I gave him a sideways glance. "Are we going to talk?" I frowned as more jack-o-lanterns seemed to dot every corner we passed.

"I love you, Macy. I'm not sure you actually understand that, but I do."

"Holy crap." I swallowed down the lump in my throat. I didn't know what to say. I mean, he'd kind of said it to me after that awful scene over Jessica, but he'd never actually said the words. It had been so long since anyone had said those words to me, period.

"Yeah. Kinda what I said when I figured it out."

I turned toward him in the seat then grabbed his hand. "I'm so sorry, Gideon. I don't know what came over me the other day. I just saw you and Jessica and all I could think was that it was happening again. He's going to choose her. He's *not* going to choose me." My throat was on fire, and I cursed the flowing tears. But I wasn't going to run this time. I was going to fight. "I was wrong. So wrong."

"Yes, you were, but I didn't help matters by being secretive and I'm sorry for that. I was afraid too, but for a far different reason."

"I know. It's about your kid. That great kid back there who I love with all my heart."

He pulled the truck over on the dirt road that was far too familiar. "Dammit, Macy."

Dusk had set and there wasn't much light near the lake over here. But there was enough for me to see him. To make sure he knew how important he was to me. I undid my belt and slid over to him. "I love you too. When it was me and Lou, it was all about his child. It's not that way now. It's so different between us. I know you're a good man. A good man who would never hurt me. I just messed up for a minute."

He undid his own seatbelt and grabbed me, dragging me in for a hot, desperate kiss. I held onto him, my fingers crawling up his shoulders so I could wrap myself around him.

I wasn't ever going to let him go again.

"*Shh*, baby. Don't cry. God, don't cry. You'll kill me."

I sniffled. "Yeah, well, I don't like doing it, pal. And I'm not pretty when I do it."

"You're beautiful, and you're mine. I love you, Macy Devereaux. So fucking much."

"I love you too."

"Thank God. Because there's a little more we need to discuss." He opened the door and pulled me out.

"Gideon." I was wearing heeled boots, and they were *not* made for walking on a dark path.

"I should have thought of all this when I came up with this plan. I'm not used to you pulling all this girl stuff on me."

I punched him in the arm. "Excuse you."

He laughed and dragged me into his chest. "I mean, the skirt and heels. Fucking hot, by the way."

"I wore heels on our first date." Somewhat mollified, I only pinched him lightly.

"Ow."

Not that lightly.

He dragged me up the dirt lane and I laughed. "What the hell is going on?"

"Figured I was going to screw this up."

"Screw what up?"

I cursed his name when he didn't say anything more. "Would you stop manhandling me?"

"You're the one who wore heels, dammit. I'm trying to make sure you don't end up like Dani."

Finally, we ended up where we'd been that day in the truck. The place I'd taken him to. The moon was rising, shimmering on the lake.

"Okay, there."

"I appreciate the trip down memory lane, but you should have driven the truck up here if you wanted to make out again."

"We did way more than make out in that truck, woman."

I laughed. "True."

"No, take a look that way." He angled me to the left. In the distance was my house—well, not my house exactly, but the one I allowed myself to dream about—and it was freaking glowing. Hundreds of pumpkins were flickering with flames.

"Marry me. Make a home with me. Make a life with me."

I turned to him, and he was down on his knee with a ring. "Oh my God."

"That's not an answer."

I leaped into his arms, knocking him on his ass. "Yes. Yes! This is crazy." I looked at him, then at the house with its wraparound porch and land. With the space for a family.

"I know it. But I didn't want to wait anymore. I'm all in, Mace. No matter what."

"I want babies with you," I blurted out. I straddled him and gripped his shirt. "Your babies."

"What?" He fell back in the leaves.

I caged him in. "Yes, I'm willing to, you know, go for it. A Halloween baby seems my kinda thing, don't you think?"

"I didn't ask for that. I wouldn't." He cupped my face, the ring stuck on the first knuckle of his forefinger.

"I know you wouldn't. But I want your kid. If you want one. I mean, you need to be a willing—"

He covered my mouth with his, the kiss wild and passionate and so very us. Then he sat up and pulled me tighter into him. "I do." He kissed me again before pressing his forehead to mine. "I want a family with you so badly, but I swear it would be enough to have a life with just you and Dani."

That was why I wanted it most of all. Because he'd never ask it of me. I could give it to him freely.

I held out my hand and when he slid the ring down, it fit perfectly. It was too dark to see exactly what he'd gotten me, but I already knew I would love it. I brushed my thumbs through his beard along the hollows of his cheeks. In the limited light, I was pretty sure Gideon's eyes were shining just like mine.

He hugged me close. "Can we go look at the house now? My ass is frozen."

"I can't believe you got me a freaking house."

"Well, I don't have it yet. But I'm working on it. I wouldn't make such a large decision without you." He dragged me up with him.

"Good answer, but it was probably just in case I said no."

"I knew you'd say yes."

I poked him in the ribs.

He hooked his arm around my shoulders. "Eventually."

I peered up at him in the low light. "Since you're gonna be my husband, does this mean I get a reduction on my bill? Maybe a deal on future renovations?"

"Macy Devereaux, do you think I'm that cheap?"

"How about bat carvings for blowjobs?"

He scooped me up and tossed me over his shoulder. I hung down and slapped his ass. "Upgrade on siding for butt stuff?"

"I think we can figure something out."

EPILOGUE

Macy

A couple weeks before Christmas

WHOMEVER HAD DECIDED PREGNANCY WAS BEAUTIFUL DESERVED A KICK in the rear with steel-toed boots.

Actually, no. They would get the second kick. The sperminator in question should get the first one. A man got to enjoy making the baby and then just sat back and waited for the cigars. While the woman gained weight from looking at a cookie and then tossed them up whether or not she'd even eaten any.

"Goddamn you, John Gideon, I hate you." I gripped the edge of the toilet bowl in our new house. We'd just moved into it, for pity's sake, and I hadn't even made it two weeks without indoctrinating it in an unexpected way.

Not wholly unexpected. I'd opened these floodgates the night of Gideon's proposal. But I'd been thinking the baby would come, you know, sometime in the future.

I definitely hadn't meant to get pregnant near *this* Halloween.

Hello. The kid would be born in July most likely, and my cats hated fireworks.

They probably hated babies too.

Which was one more irony, since Trick, that hussy, had gotten herself knocked up, a fact I'd only discovered this morning during a routine vet appointment. She'd escaped a couple of weeks ago through an open door, and since she was an indoor-only cat, I'd never gotten around to getting her spayed.

My lesson was a litter of kittens that would be born…soon. She'd damn well be getting spayed after that.

Dani would dance on the ceiling. Gideon? Not so sure. He was still adapting to having two cats, never mind half a dozen. But since he was the one who'd left the door open while reinforcing the jamb or some such, this was basically his fault.

He was to blame for lots of pregnancies around these parts lately.

That horrible mouth-watering feeling came up again, and I swore as I rapped my engagement ring against the porcelain bowl. My perfectly gorgeous solitaire ring had gotten an upgrade with an honest to God black diamond bat ring wrap from my husband-to-be.

Unfortunately, I wasn't used to the extra heft and banged it on every-freaking-thing.

It dug into my finger as I heaved again and prayed for the agony to subside. My Google-Fu had shown me not all women got morning sickness. Or afternoon sickness, or whatever the heck this was at just past noon. I'd always loved being the exceptional one.

Closing my eyes, I wiped my mouth with a wad of toilet paper and rolled on my side on the nice, fluffy bathroom rug. As places to die went, there were probably worse.

The next time I opened my eyes, it was past two and I was almost late to pick up Dani at school. Holy fuck. I'd actually passed out on the rug like a hungover socialite with an angry minion in her belly.

My only day off this week from my *very* successful businesses was not going as planned so far.

I thought longingly about a shower and decided I'd take one before bed. Or maybe I'd take a bath. With bubbles. Which usually was not my idea of a good time, because who wanted to sit in their dirty body water? But I was now operating as if every potential self-care item was a must do, on account of the fact I had actually let Gideon knock me up *on purpose.*

No accidental sip of the Crescent Cove water here. We'd tossed out the condoms and he had lied in my face that it usually "took awhile" so "no rush."

I stared down at my flat-ish belly. "Tell your kid that, pal. Seems like he or she disagrees."

After changing my shirt, I grabbed my jacket and my keys and hurried out to my car. I wouldn't say I speeded to pick up Dani, but let's say that when a cop came up behind me, I started readying the waterworks to pretend to be a scared new mom with diarrhea or whatever would get me out of a speeding ticket.

So, I needed to Google more. So, sue me.

But Sheriff Brooks turned on his siren to get me to move over and waved as he passed, so I dodged that bullet.

I slid into the carpool line at Dani's school and had to grin when she came bounding out a few minutes later with some crazy art project that looked like a reindeer had chugged too much eggnog.

"What is that?" I asked with a laugh as she slid into the backseat.

"Hello, it's Rudolph. It's for the mantle. See, his legs dangle." She tugged on the spiral paper that served for legs and the whole thing nearly came apart, but I smiled and nodded as if it was entirely secure.

Besides, I had Super Glue and I knew how to use it.

"Did you get the bats?" she asked excitedly, snapping on her belt before I signaled back into traffic.

"Yes. But your father is going to flip. You have to pretend it was all your idea."

"It basically was. I was the one who suggested pastel bat Christmas."

"You were." I had to beam with pride. "We'll put them on the other tree I got, not the main one so your dad can pretend he still has a measure of control. I also got some hard hats to put on them. He's gotta like that, right?"

"Oh, that's sick." I looked in the rearview mirror as Dani gazed at me with wide eyes. "We don't have much time. We need to be done decorating before he gets home or else he'll wig out."

"Pretty sure wigging will be on the table tonight anyway." I took a deep breath and tapped my fingers on the wheel as instinct took over. "What do you know about babies?"

"You did not."

I slid a glance at the rearview mirror. "Excuse me?"

"Shut up."

Now my eyebrows lifted. "You know you're not supposed to say that, Danielle."

"Okay, hush up. Really?" She started bouncing up and down, straining against her seatbelt. "When? Soon? A boy? A girl? Oh, oh, oh! Both?"

I had to laugh, mainly so I didn't start sobbing. I hadn't even considered twins.

Dear God, I had to spend less time with Vee. What if that shit was contagious?

"I literally just found out. Like this morning. I mean, I suspected, but you know, PMS can be rough."

A glance back showed Dani was nodding sagely, although she had no clue. But she would.

"So, um, yeah, I took a test. And surprise! I mean, we aren't even married yet and it's nice to be before you start propagating the earth. But definitely not necessary, since this isn't the dark ages. But it's good," I added, remembering impressionable ears were listening to my panic babble. "Very good. Marriage is sacred."

"No one wants to be the size of a moose in a wedding gown. At least that's what Toby's mom said."

Toby's mom was either a genius or a jerk. I'd puzzle it out later.

"I'm supposed to be the flower girl," Dani reminded me. "Does this mean I have to wait forever?"

"No. I don't know. It's a lot." I gripped the wheel and focused on slow breaths, in and out. Practicing for when I would eject a small water buffalo from my private area.

Right, there was the thought to calm me down.

"But weddings are fun. You get to dance and get sick on cake. Plus, I'll have a pretty dress."

"You sure will, especially since I have an important question I've been wanting to ask you." She went still and quiet as I chanced a quick look at her in the back, still clutching Rudolph. "Will you be my maid of honor? I know you had your heart set on flower girl."

"No way. That's like the best job of them all, isn't it?"

"Pretty much, other than getting married to your dad. Which you can't do, because illegal."

She didn't laugh at my joke, just wrinkled her nose as if she was waiting for the punchline.

Me too, kid, me too.

She still hadn't answered when I pulled into the driveway a short time later. "So, what do you say? Don't leave me hanging here."

"I say yes, but does that mean the baby will be the flower girl or boy?"

"Maybe it'll be before the baby. I don't honestly know. Your dad doesn't even know yet."

Dani's eyes grew huge. "Uh oh."

"What uh oh?"

"You should let me tell him."

"I should? Why?"

"Because I know how to handle him. He's special."

While I couldn't fault that logic, I had to admit curiosity at what she was getting at. "Do you think he won't be happy about the news?"

"Oh, sure, he'll be happy, but if I tell him, he'll be even more happy because then he won't have to worry about, you know, sibling rivalry. Toby hates his brother. He tried to kill him with a plastic phone once."

"Um..." I hoped she was being metaphorical. "So, you're sure you're okay with this? I know we haven't had much time together just you and me and your dad, but the baby won't be here for ages."

"I thought it took nine months. Only elephants are longer."

There wasn't much chance of slipping anything past this child, that was for sure. "Yeah, but that's a while. We'll do lots together before then. And you'll have fun with him or her, I'm sure. I mean, I loved my brother to pieces until he betrayed me, but honestly, brothers and sisters are the best."

Pretty sure I wouldn't be winning any parenting awards this year. Or ever.

"I'm excited. I will teach her everything she needs to know about dealing with Dad. You, I'm still figuring out." With that, she exited the car.

So, according to Dani, we were having a girl. Or else she was decreeing it so since boys sucked. Right now, when I was hungry enough to salt my car bumper and eat it for an appetizer, I couldn't claim to disagree.

I followed her up on the porch and we went inside to go through the loot I'd gotten at the craft store. Thank God bats seemed to be popular for the spooky types all year now, since they were kind of out of season. It helped that the store was ginormous and stocked basically everything.

"I have an idea," Dani said a little while later, tilting her head. We were surrounded by bats and hard hats and garland and other Christmas doodads. "Let's spell out baby with the extra bats. Or…we could dress up Trick in a baby outfit?"

"Definitely the first." I cleared my throat. "Speaking of surprises, guess what? Trick is having kittens."

"Really?" Dani shot onto her knees and clasped her hands, her face glowing with utter delight. "Can we keep them? Please, please, pretty please?" She crawled over to me and hugged me, making me laugh as she rained sloppy kisses all over my face. "Please, please, pretty please. I'll clean their litter box and play with them and brush them, and I'll let them sleep in my bed and—"

The front door opened, and Gideon stepped in, smelling of sawdust and with white paint flecks dotting his dark hair. He stopped dead to take in the chaos we'd begun to unleash in the living room.

"What is this I just heard about cleaning litter boxes?" He narrowed his eyes at Dani. "You have two cats now. You don't get more."

Dani made a face. "You're not supposed to eavesdrop. It's rude."

"You were practically yelling. I'd need earplugs not to hear you." He gave me a hard stare, and it was probably because he'd injected me with baby serum, but holy crap, he looked hot today. "No more cats. Right?"

Dani crossed her arms. "If we can have more babies, we can have more cats."

So, yeah, guess that particular feline was out of the bag.

Coincidentally, Trick chose that moment to appear and rubbed against Dani. She gave a loud sniff and picked her up, pressing her face into the cat's dense black fur. "Let's go read, Trick."

"What about the bats?" I didn't look at Gideon. At least I hadn't heard his body hit the floor.

Then again, my heart was stampeding so loudly, I was fairly certain I wouldn't have heard an ax murderer yell, *yoohoo, honey, I'm home.*

"I'm sure he won't allow them. Because he's *mean*." Dani flounced past Gideon, and to add insult to injury, Trick swiped out at him with her paw as they passed.

He didn't seem to notice. I wasn't sure he was even still conscious. Could someone faint while standing up?

Well, if he wasn't going to say anything, neither was I. I was good at denial too.

"So, how was your day?"

He dragged a hand down his face. "I'm awake, right?"

"Far as I can tell. Though you do look like an extra from *The Walking Dead* at the moment." I rose to greet him the right way, because again, he was super hot.

Besides, he'd already knocked me up. The barn door was wide open, so I might as well explore the pregnancy benefits.

I'd no sooner laid a hand on him that he grabbed my cheeks and searched my eyes as if I was holding back state secrets. "You're not... she was kidding...you can't be...that soon?"

I cleared my throat. "So, what about those Yankees?"

"Outta season, Mace. You're serious right now?"

"As serious as the word *pregnant* on that little white stick." I had to admit to a little sick glee at the way his jaw sagged. I patted his chest. "Congratulations, Daddy."

I was prepared for him to reach for the nearest chair. Maybe even to flee from the room entirely while he processed the reality of having the fastest swimmers on the block.

So, maybe not the fastest on *this* block. This was Crescent Cove, after all. All sperm were in competition for the Olympics. But still, he'd done just fine.

However, I was not prepared for him to sweep me up into his arms and kiss me like he hadn't seen me in five years or had just come back from the war or—well, something way huger than just a day at work.

"I fucking love you." He tugged on my lower lip with his teeth. "You're incredible."

"I love you too. So are you, obviously. You clearly set some land and speed records, dude." Laughing, I wrapped my arms around his neck and kissed him back. Eagerly. Hungrily. I may have rubbed against him like a needy kitten.

Maybe if we were really quiet, Dani would be none the wiser.

Welcome to enjoying sex while parenting 101, Macy. Hope you enjoy your eighteen-year-plus stay.

But Gideon wasn't finished with his praise. "Your ovaries are like, commercial grade."

I had to pause mid-kiss for that one. "Thanks? I grew them myself."

He started to laugh as he tipped his forehead against mine. "Oh my God. It was supposed to take like a year so you didn't flip out."

"Surprise."

"Yeah, the best surprise. The best one I've ever gotten after Dani. And now I have two." His Adam's apple bobbed as he gazed at me, still holding me in his arms as if I was weightless. Not struggling at all. Just staring at me as if I'd created atoms with the power of my mind.

And I kind of had—although other parts of me had been involved, while my mind had definitely been absent—but he'd helped. This amazing thing was one we'd built together.

Kind of like The Haunt. And the renovations on this house. And even the café. He'd been there with me in one form or another since nearly the beginning of my journey here in Crescent Cove. All along the way, we'd been adding bricks and markers. Solidifying our foundation. Creating something real that would continue on beyond us.

A life. A legacy. A family.

"Now you've done it." I waved my hand at my face and started doing times tables backward in my head. I had been doing so well. I hadn't shed one tear so far today.

Other than when the vet had told me Trick was truly a trick, but c'mon, how many pregnancies could one woman hear about in a day and not go a little crazy?

"What? Oh, shit, did I hurt you? It's new. Did I do something? Here, let me set you down."

"I'm fine." I had to laugh through my misty moment as he carefully set me in the nearest armchair. "We're fine."

He crouched in front of me and gripped my hands, bringing them to his mouth. I wasn't one to get fanciful, but I'd never seen a more reverent look on someone's face in all my life.

"We're is such a good word."

Smiling, I brushed the hair off his forehead and decided I wouldn't kill him today. Maybe not even this week. Because right now? Being pregnant felt pretty damn good. "The best word."

Thanks for reading DADDY IN DISGUISE!
We appreciate our readers so much!
If you loved the book please let your friends know.
If you're so inclined, we'd love a review on your favorite book site.

Jump into more of Crescent Cove with our next release, MY EX's BABY.
All books are standalone romantic comedies with a happily ever after.

CRESCENT COVE CHARACTER CHART

BEWARE...SPOILERS APLENTY IN THIS CHARACTER CHART. READ AT YOUR OWN RISK!

Ally Lawrence:
Married to Seth Hamilton, mother to Alexander, stepmother to Laurie, best friends with Sage Evans

Andrea Maria Fortuna Dixon Newman:
Mother to Veronica 'Vee' Dixon

Asher Wainwright: CEO Wainwright Publishing
Involved with Hannah Jacobs, father to Lily and Rose

August Beck: Owns Beck Furniture
Brother to Caleb and Ivy, involved with Kinleigh Scott

Beckett Manning: Owns Happy Acres Orchard
Brother to Zoe, Hayes, and Justin

Bess Wainwright:
Grandmother to Asher Wainwright

Caleb Beck: Teaches second grade

CRESCENT COVE CHARACTER CHART

Brother to August and Ivy

(Charles) Dare Kramer: Mechanic, owns J & T Body Shop
Married to Kelsey Ford, son Weston (mother is Katherine), son Sean, brother Gage

Christian Masterson: Sheriff's Deputy
Brother to Murphy, Travis, and Penn, sister Madison 'Maddie'

Cindy Ford:
Married to Doug Ford, mother of Kelsey and Rylee

Dahlia McKenna: Designer/Decorator who works with Macy

Damien Ramos:
Sisters Erica, Francesca, Gabriela, Regina

Doug Ford:
Married to Cindy Ford, father of Kelsey and Rylee Ford

Gavin Forrester: Real estate owner

Gabriela 'Gabby' Ramos:
Brother Damien, sisters Erica, Francesca, Regina, best friend Hannah Jacobs

Greta: Manager of the Rusty Spoon

Hank Masterson:
Married to JoAnn Masterson, sons Murphy, Christian, Travis, Penn, and daughter Madison

Hannah Jacobs:
Involved with Asher Wainwright, mother to Lily and Rose, best friend Gabriela Ramos

CRESCENT COVE CHARACTER CHART

Hayes Manning: Owns Happy Acres Orchard
Brother to Zoe, Beckett, and Justin

Ian Kagan: Solo artist
Brother to Simon, engaged to Zoe Manning, son Elvis, best friend Rory Ferguson, friends with Flynn Sheppard and Kellan McGuire

Ivy Beck: Waitress at the Rusty Spoon and owns Rolling Cones ice cream truck
Sister to Caleb and August, engaged to Rory Ferguson, best friend Kinleigh Scott, friends with Maggie Kelly and Zoe Manning

James Hamilton: Owns Hamilton Realty
Father to Seth and Oliver Hamilton

Jared Brooks: Sheriff
Brother to Mason Brooks, best friend Gina Ramos

Jessica Gideon: Famous actress
Ex-wife to John Gideon, mother to Dani

JoAnn Masterson:
Married to Hank Masterson, sons Murphy, Christian, Travis, Penn, and daughter Madison

John Gideon: Owns Gideon Gets it Done Handyman Service
Daughter Dani, ex-wife Jessica Gideon

Justin Manning: Owns Happy Acres Orchard
Brother to Zoe, Beckett, and Hayes

Kellan McGuire: Lead singer Wilder Mind, solo artist
Brother to Bethany, married to Maggie Kelly, son Wolf, friends with Rory Ferguson, Ian Kagan, and Myles Vaughn

CRESCENT COVE CHARACTER CHART

Kelsey Ford: Elementary school teacher
Married to Dare Kramer, son Sean, stepson Weston, sister Rylee Ford

Kinleigh Scott: Owns Kinleigh's
Cousin Vincent Scott, best friend Ivy Beck, involved with August Beck

(Lucas) Gage Kramer: Owns J & T Body Shop, former race car driver
Married to Rylee Ford, daughter Hayley Kramer, brother Dare Kramer

Lucky Roberts: Works for Gideon Gets it Done Handyman Service

Macy Devereaux: Owns Brewed Awakening and The Haunt
Sister to Nolan, best friend Rylee Ford

Madison 'Maddie' Masterson:
Sister to Murphy, Christian, Travis, and Penn

Marjorie Hamilton:
Ex-wife of Seth Hamilton, birth mother of Laurie Hamilton

Mason Brooks: Owns Mason Jar restaurant
Brother Jared Brooks

Maggie Kelly:
Married to Kellan McGuire, son Wolf, best friend Kendra Russo, friends with Ivy Beck and Zoe Manning

Melissa Kramer: Owns Robbie's Pizza
Married to Robert Kramer, mother of Dare and Gage Kramer

Mike London: High school teacher

Mitch Cooper: Owns the Rusty Spoon

CRESCENT COVE CHARACTER CHART

Murphy 'Moose' Masterson: Game Designer/Construction Contractor and Owns Baby Daddy Wanted
Married to Vee Dixon, son Brayden, brother to Christian, Travis, Penn, and Maddie

Nolan Devereaux: Owns Tricks and Treats Candy Shop
Brother to Macy

Oliver Hamilton: Owns Hamilton Realty and the Hummingbird's Nest
Married to Sage Evans, daughter Star, twin brother Seth Hamilton

Penn Masterson: Graphic novelist
Brother to Murphy, Travis, Christian, and Maddie

Regina 'Gina' Ramos: Waitress at the Rusty Spoon
Brother Damien, sisters Erica, Francesca, Gabriela, best friend Sheriff Brooks

Robert Kramer: Owns Robbie's Pizza
Married to Melissa Kramer, father of Dare and Gage Kramer

Rory Ferguson: Record Producer/Rhythm Guitarist
Brother to Thomas and Maureen, engaged to Ivy Beck, best friend Ian Kagan, friends with Flynn Sheppard and Kellan McGuire

Rylee Ford: Barista at Brewed Awakening
Married to Gage Kramer, daughter Hayley, sister Kelsey Ford Kramer, best friend Macy Devereaux

Sage Evans: Owns the Hummingbird's Nest
Married to Oliver Hamilton, daughter Star, best friend Ally Lawrence

Seth Hamilton: Owns Hamilton Realty

CRESCENT COVE CHARACTER CHART

Married to Ally Lawrence, daughter Laurie, son Alexander, twin brother to Oliver Hamilton, ex-wife Marjorie

Tish Burns: Owns J & T Body Shop, custom fabricator
Friends with Gage Kramer

Travis Masterson:
Brothers Christian, Penn and Murphy, and Maddie, daughter Carrington

Veronica 'Vee' Dixon: Pastry Baker, owns Baby Daddy Wanted
Married to Murphy Masterson, son Brayden

Vincent Scott: partner in Wainwright Publishing Industries
Cousin Kinleigh Scott

Zoe Manning: Artist/photographer
Sister to Beckett, Hayes, and Justin, engaged to Ian Kagan, son Elvis, cousin Lila Ronson Shawcross Crandall, friends with Ivy Beck and Maggie Kelly

*as of 10/30/19

Crescent Cove

GET HOOKED!

Have My Baby

Claim My Baby

Who's The Daddy

Pit Stop: Baby

Baby Daddy Wanted

Rockstar Baby

Daddy in Disguise

COMING SOON

My Ex's Baby

Daddy Undercover

Crescent Cove Standalones

CEO Daddy

COMING SOON

Stand-In Daddy

ALSO BY TARYN QUINN

AFTERNOON DELIGHT

Dirty Distractions

Drawn Deep

DEUCES WILD

Protecting His Rockstar

Guarding His Best Friend's Sister

Shielding His Baby

WILDER ROCK

Rockstar Daddy

HOLIDAY BOOKS

Unwrapped

Holiday Sparks

Filthy Scrooge

Jingle Ball

Bad Kitty

For more information about our books visit

www.tarynquinn.com

ABOUT TARYN QUINN

USA Today bestselling author, *Taryn Quinn,* is the redheaded stepchild of bestselling authors Taryn Elliott & Cari Quinn. We've been writing together for a lifetime—wait, no it's really been only a handful of years, but we have a lot of fun. Sometimes we write stories that don't quite fit into our regular catalog.

* Ultra sexy—check.
* Quirky characters—check.
* Sweet–usually mixed in with the sexy...so, yeah—check.
* RomCom—check.
* Dark and twisted—check.

A little something for everyone.

So, c'mon in. Light some candles, pour a glass of wine...maybe even put on some sexy music.

For more information about us...
tarynquinn.com
tq@tarynquinn.com

QUINN AND ELLIOTT

We also write more serious, longer, and sexier books as Cari Quinn & Taryn Elliott. Our topics include mostly rockstars, but mobsters, MMA, and a little suspense gets tossed in there too.

Rockers' Series Reading Order

Lost in Oblivion

Winchester Falls

Found in Oblivion

Hammered

Rock Revenge

Brooklyn Dawn

OTHER SERIES

The Boss

Tapped Out

Love Required

Boys of Fall

If you'd like more information about us please visit
www.quinnandelliott.com

Made in the USA
Monee, IL
29 January 2020